CASSEY

THE DARKNESS IS COMING

Raymond M Hall

www.raymondmhall.com

This is a work of fiction. Names, characters, events, and incidents are the products of the author's imagination. Any resemblance to actual persons, living or dead, or actual events is purely coincidental.

By the same author:

THE HAUNTING

THE WATER MAIDEN

Harry Bridges Detective Series
Book 1
THOU SHALT NOT SUFFER A WITCH TO LIVE
Book 2
BACK TO THE END

The Roger Sidebottom Comedy Series
Book 1
THE IMPORTANCE OF BEING ROGER
Book 2
ROGER'S RISE TO INCREDIBLE FAILURE

The Digby Rolf mystery series:
Book 1
THE HANGED MAN
Book 2
IN THE SHADOW OF THE REAPER
Book 3
MURDER AT HIGH TOR MANOR

"Circumstances are beyond human control, but our conduct is in our own power."
Benjamin Disraeli

"BEWARE, THE DARKNESS IS COMING!"

The old priest nodded sagely at the poster. They were everywhere, and he idly wondered who or what group was responsible. He knew of the dire warnings for mankind predicted in the Old Testament and supposed that one day they would come true. But surely, not yet...........

CHAPTER 1

Whitechapel

London, 1962

Father Clough nodded his head sagely as Mr and Mrs Dennis left his office. They had arrived earlier, Mr Dennis, cap in hand, to ask for his help.

'Honestly, Father, I don't know what to do with our little Rose. She is a sweet girl, but she worships an old doll she found. She calls it Cassey; it's a disgusting thing to look at, most of the hair pulled out, one eye permanently closed, and the open eye seems to stare constantly at you,' said Arthur Dennis.

'Rose's personality has completely changed,' said his wife.

Father Clough smiled at the vision this conjured up.

'Most young children become attached to an object or toy. Sometimes it's a Teddy Bear or fluffy dog; your daughter has found a doll, probably thrown out by a family with no further use for it. But to Rose, it has become her friend, her confidant if you like. I bet she talks to it all the time.'

Sally Dennis nodded her head in agreement. 'She does, Father; but it's worse than just idle chatter. I get the impression that the doll is talking back to her.'

Father Clough raised an eyebrow quizzically,

'I hope you haven't heard the doll speaking to your daughter?'

Arthur Dennis smiled grimly.

'No, we have not, but I wouldn't be surprised; there's something not right about that darned doll.'

'Not, right?' asked the priest.

'Bloody thing is evil, pardon my language!' Arthur exclaimed.

'Well, maybe I had better call around and see for myself,' said the priest, making a note in his diary, 'will the day after tomorrow suit?'

The couple left his office and Father Clough settled back into his chair. Odd folks around here, he thought. A mixture of cultures. The Jewish fraternity had their own beliefs stretching back to the beginning of time. There were a few Catholics like Arthur and Sally, but most people in the East End were Church of England. All had one thing in common: an undying belief in the *old ways.* Superstition ran rife in the entire community; all religions appeared to have a common thread, that of the occult and witchcraft. The ability of some to cast spells to the detriment of others.

He would speak to the girl but had no doubt it would be, as he suspected, merely a child's preoccupation with a toy. However, deep down, the priest suspected the supernatural was very real. If one could believe that the Father, Son, and Holy Ghost were one unseen entity, then surely one must allow for other supernatural forces.

It would be interesting to talk to young Rose Dennis; she was only nine years old, but sometimes the young were wise beyond their years.

Rose sat on the front doorstep of her house. It was scrupulously clean, as were all the doorsteps in the street, a matter of pride for the women occupants. The condition of the doorstep said a lot about the inhabitants.

Cassey was in her arms as usual. Rose talking to her endlessly, as if they were in mutual conversation.

The boy from three doors down approached, a mischievous look in his eye.

'You should throw that old thing in the bin, it's probably full of germs,' he said, casually cuffing the nearly bald head with his hand.

'Go away, Michael. You are not to hurt her!' Rose exclaimed.

This drew a laugh from Michael. He was older than Rose by a year and at the ripe old age of ten thought himself vastly superior to the soppy girl sitting on the doorstep nursing a dirty old doll.

'Go on, throw it away. It's ugly,' he insisted.

Rose bridled at the insult.

'She is not ugly, you are, with your twisted legs.'

Michael saw red. He was very conscious of the condition of his legs, twisted from rickets, a common symptom of poor nourishment.

'Give me the doll, and I'll get rid of it for you,' he said, grabbing the doll from Rose's clutches.

Rose exploded to her feet.

'Give her back or I'll tell!' She yelled.

'Telltale, telltale,' jibed Michael, turning on his heel and running for the alley leading to the rear of their terraced houses.

Rose followed as fast as she could, pursuing Michael running on his thin misshapen limbs.

In the back lane, Rose caught up with him, grabbing Cassey by the legs and dislodging the doll from his grasp.

'Don't you dare touch her again,' yelled Rose, swinging Cassey by the legs, aiming at Michael's head.

There was a sickening thud as the doll's head made contact.

Rose stepped back, still holding the doll, amazed at the amount of blood pouring from Michael's shattered skull. She didn't know what to do, so simply walked away, without looking back.

Cassey lay in the kitchen sink surrounded by dishwashing bubbles, languishing in warm water, as Rose gently washed away Michael's blood.

'There, there,' cooed Rose softly, 'that nasty boy won't bother us again.'

Cassey's face looked up at her from the serenity of the warm water, both eyes open. The solid, featureless, porcelain face had somehow changed. She was smiling.

CHAPTER 2

Father Clough had been informed of Michael's accident and made his way to his parent's house to offer comfort.

'What happened?' He asked gently.

The bereaved couple sat on a small settee opposite.

'We don't know; the police said that on the face of it, Michael was the victim of a violent attack,' said Michael's father angrily, 'possibly gang-related they said.'

Michael's mother cried out.

'Gang-related! What the hell are you talking about? He was ten years old. How could it be gang-related?'

'It's what the police told me.' Her husband said, crushed by the force of her outburst.

Father Clough took her hand.

'Now, now, Mrs Blacksmith, try to calm down. Your husband is doing his best.'

'They said he must have been struck with a hammer,' she said, tears spilling down her face.

'One blow was all it took. According to the Inspector, his skull was smashed,' said the father, impervious to the effect his words were having on his wife.

Bill Blacksmith, Billy to his mates, turned to the priest,

'Father, we need help, not just prayers, but real help. We must find out who killed our boy.'

'I will do my utmost to assist the police to find the killer or killers,' he said, adding, 'I'm so very sorry for your loss. We can talk later about the arrangements for Michael's funeral.'

At the mention of the funeral, Mrs Blacksmith dissolved into tears, becoming incoherent. The priest left the pair in peace.

There was nothing he could say or do for them at present.

The Dennis family was only three doors down, so he brought his visit forward. No doubt they would be aware of the murder and may need some words of comfort themselves.

Arthur and Sally sat in the kitchen. He knocked, then made his way through the house. Doors were seldom locked in the street during daylight hours, and neighbours were at liberty to come and go as they pleased.

Father Clough explained why he was calling a day early and they merely nodded, indicating that he should take a seat at the table.

Rose was busy at the sink.

'Hello Rose,' said the priest, 'you look very busy.'

'I'm giving my baby a bath,' replied Rose, letting the water out with a gurgle. 'She's nice and clean now, aren't you Cassey?'

The old priest smiled.

'May I see your doll please?' He asked, putting out his hands.

Rose gently placed Cassey in the priest's arms, standing close by.

He saw an old doll with sparse strands of hair and one closed eye. Rose had put her clothes on and smoothed the creases from the still damp dress.

'There, you take her. She might be more comfortable in your arms,' he said. 'Are you her mummy?'

'No, I'm not,' said Rose indignantly, 'Cassey is my friend.'

'Sorry,' said the priest, taken aback by the girl's vehemence.

'Perhaps this is not a good time for a visit,' he said to Mr and Mrs Dennis. 'The entire street is in shock over the boy's death.'

Rose walked off with the doll, but Father Clough caught the disconcerting glimmer of a smile on the young girl's face.

'Terrible business,' said Arthur Dennis, 'I don't know what the world is coming to; there's a rumour that a gang may have been responsible.'

The priest shrugged his shoulders.

'Hard to believe that any gang would target a ten-year-old child.'

Sally Dennis looked past Father Clough to her daughter carrying the doll.

'Who knows these days, it seems that nobody is safe.'

He spent only a short time with the parents, more interested in speaking with little Rose. Making his excuses, he walked down the hallway to the front door.

Rose was sitting on the doorstep nursing her doll, and the priest gently lowered himself down to sit beside her.

'You're very fond of that doll, aren't you?' He ventured.

Rose flashed her eyes at him, 'She's not *that doll*, her name is Cassey.'

'Sorry,' said the priest, realising the little girl was deadly serious, 'where did you find her?'

'I didn't just find her. She was a gift,' said Rose.

Father Clough knew he was conversing with an intelligent child, but it seemed like she was a great deal older and wiser than the average nine-year-old.

'A gift from a neighbour?' He asked.

'No,' said Rose.

The priest paused for a moment, not wanting to rush the child with too many questions.

'Then, where did she come from?' He asked.

Rose narrowed her eyes and looked at him suspiciously.

'Why do you want to know?' She insisted.

Again, the priest was bemused. Was he really talking to a child?

'Oh, no reason, I'm just curious,' he answered. 'It's my job to get to know everyone in the area in case they need help.'

Rose stared at Father Clough with her dark eyes, but he could not hold her look, instead, turning away with the distinct feeling that he was no match for the girl. The pretty little nine-year-old possessed an inner power that challenged his idea of an adult-child relationship.

Deciding he wouldn't get any more information from her, he got to his feet.

'Bye Rose, we'll talk again,' he said.

9

As he walked away, he could feel her eyes on his back. Pivoting quickly, he caught Rose staring at him. But not only the little girl. The doll appeared to be standing up in her arms, both eyes open and staring. Father Clough gave an involuntary shudder as he walked away.

Rose sat down on the step once again, encircling Cassey with her arms.

'Don't worry, he won't bother us. Nobody will,' she said, laying the doll on the step next to her. The doll's eyes closed, assisted by the internal mechanism. When Rose lifted her again, one eye opened but the other remained shut.

'You're playing tricks again, Cassey,' laughed Rose.

She loved Cassey and had done so since the day they first met. A special bond existed between them.

CHAPTER 3

It had been an overcast day, the clouds heavy with latent rain, a portent of yet another miserable day in London. More especially in the East End, where drab buildings ingrained with years of smoking chimneys blended into the grey sky. For Rose, it appeared normal, having spent all her nine years living in the area. She had never been on holiday, never experienced the country or seaside; none of the neighbourhood children had travelled either, so no one knew any better. They were not aware that outside the sprawling metropolis lay green fields, and further afield the sparkling waters of limitless ocean.

Rose had wandered along the streets of her neighbourhood, past the empty sites where houses had been demolished in the quest for modernisation. Traditional long lines of two-up, two-down houses which had served so many generations of Londoners were slowly being pulled down to make way for modern blocks of flats. But people didn't want them, knowing that their communities would be destroyed forever. Neighbourly camaraderie would no longer exist with families living on top of one another in isolation.

Soon, Rose's house would join the boarded-up and deserted houses awaiting the bulldozers, but she had no opinion either way; she was only nine years old.

'Don't go out of this street,' her mother had so often lectured when Rose was outside playing. However, today, she was bored with the line of houses and narrow streets separating the identical ones on the other side, so she set out to explore as children do. Outsiders seldom used their streets, and mostly the tenants never had cars of their own. Public transport was handy and efficient, both bus and tube train, so why bother to go to the expense of owning a car?

Rose reached the end of her street; glancing back and seeing nobody to stop her, she carried on around the corner. Before her lay a whole unknown world to explore. There was a long line of boarded-up houses on one side and a cleared area opposite, awaiting the start of new construction. In the middle of this desolation, stood the remnants of a warehouse. It was two stories high and had a deserted, creepy feel to it. Doors had been boarded over and the ground-floor windows too, but Rose spotted one doorway where the wood had been partially removed.

As she approached the door, her heart raced at the prospect of a new adventure. She peered inside the gloomy interior, feeling no fear, only the compulsion to explore.

Squeezing through the narrow opening, Rose entered the old building, staring with wide eyes as she became accustomed to the feeble light. The silence was all-encompassing and eerie, but she went further in until presented with a set of wooden stairs leading up. Her footsteps reverberated on the bare treads as she climbed to the top floor, echoing in the emptiness.

Reaching the top of the stairs, she was confronted by a hallway of sorts leading further into the warehouse. She traced her fingers over the walls, grimy with years of wear and completely covered in writing. She couldn't make out what it said, the words made little sense; just endless lines of meaningless writing, not in straight lines but scrawled higgledy-piggledy on all the walls. Looking up, she saw that even the ceiling was covered.

Rose carried on and turned to her left, following the line of the hallway. She saw an open doorway with a dim light. Plucking up courage, she peered inside to see an old man sitting at a desk. He appeared oblivious to her presence, engrossed in writing.

There were piles of paper at his feet, covered in the same writing. The light came from a small oil lamp sitting on the desk, its glow barely illuminating the desktop.

Still, the old man didn't look up, so Rose continued along the dreary hallway until she reached a door to her left. She could hear a clicking noise and curiously poked her head around the doorway.

The room was small and square. In one corner sat an old woman. To Rose, she appeared to be older than time itself. She had never seen such an old person, except for the man in the other room, who appeared to be just as ancient.

The clicking noise was coming from the woman's knitting needles. Rose's eyes widened still further as she took in the contents of the room, dominated by a long, knitted scarf winding around the floor several times with different colours dictated by the wool closest to the woman's hand. There seemed to be a mountain of wool, wound in balls of different hues.

Beside the woman was an old gramophone, playing a scratchy rendition of some ancient orchestra. Beside her, a similar oil lamp to the old man's cast the same dim yellow light.

The scarf covered everything on the floor, nothing escaped it. Rose saw countless dolls lying this way, and that, immersed in its coils. They looked ancient, and some had broken limbs and cracked heads; all looked decidedly unloved. A cat lay on the floor, partially covered by the scarf, and appeared to be sound asleep. Rose stepped into the room. She was very fond of cats and reached down to stroke it. Her hand involuntarily sprang back from the cat as she realised it was not alive. There was no softness or warmth to the fur, and the body was unyielding to her touch. Looking at the cat's unblinking eyes, she glanced up at the woman, who, without meeting her look, spoke.

'Stuffed, it's stuffed, dearie. He won't mind you touching him.'

Rose jumped, startled. The old man hadn't spoken, but this woman had. Her voice was harsh, gravelly, and devoid of emotion.

Rose should have been terrified, should have bolted down the stairs and run back to her house in the next street, but she didn't. She felt no fear. Instead, a feeling of belonging enveloped her.

She stepped further into the room and knelt to stroke the stuffed cat again, whispering to it.

'Hello, Albert, you're looking well.'

The old woman let out a cackle.

'Albert's been dead for years now, but I'm sure he would be glad you remember him.'

Rose made no reply. Instead, she walked towards the woman.

'When will you finish the scarf?' she asked.

'Soon, dearie, *the darkness is coming.*'

'Darkness?' Rose asked.

'Yes, it's coming soon; my husband has written it all down and when he's finished, the darkness will descend.'

Rose didn't question any further, bending down to pick up one of the dolls. It was dressed in clothes thick with grime and had very little of its original hair. Rose cuddled the doll, holding it close to her body. At first, the coldness made her shiver, but quickly her own heat entered the doll, and they became as one. The doll seemed to look at her; the eyes staring at her own. The connection had been made.

A mirthless laugh disturbed the scene, and Rose looked up at its source. The old woman nodded her head, the incessant clicking of her knitting needles never ceasing.

'Take her with you, dearie. She will look after you until the darkness comes. Her name is Cassey, but of course, you already know that.'

Ignoring the old woman's statement, Rose turned and walked from the room, calmer now than she had ever been, clutching the doll to her and talking to it in a low voice. She remembered the doll; it had been hers once before.

Sarah stopped her knitting as she heard Rose descend the stairs, calling out to her husband in the other room.

'The girl has a doll.'

Lionel Plunkett paused in his writing long enough to murmur a barely audible reply.

'The darkness is coming.'

He returned to his writing with increased vigour.

Time was running out!

CHAPTER 4

F ather Clough stood before his tiny church, smiling at the incongruity. The house of God was jammed in between two old tenement blocks of flats. He occupied a ground floor unit in one of the tenements, one of the two bedrooms serving as his office. The entire street had been given over to similar buildings. Well, not similar, rather they were identical in every way. Colours of bricks and paintwork were identical, although after many years of low maintenance, they had all adopted the dreary look of the downtrodden.

The flats were occupied by the same tenant families who had been there for years. They could be handed down to other family members on the death of the lessee. In that way, the buildings were constantly occupied, and rents were paid regularly.

The priest turned the key in the lock and walked into his humble accommodation. The first thing he noticed was the overpowering smell of urine; he had been burgled again.

He had lost count of the number of break-ins; they stole nothing of great value because as a lowly priest; he had very little worth stealing. It was more the inconvenience of having to clean the place after every such raid. His unwelcome visitors invariably urinated everywhere, whether from nervousness or some other peculiarity.

The collection box once again lay on its side beside his desk, the tiny padlock broken. Father Clough shrugged his shoulders; it would have contained only a few copper coins and maybe the odd shilling or sixpenny piece; hardly worth risking a jail sentence.

It was the same person each time, of that he was sure because of the urine; the local police had explained to him that many offenders repeated their little idiosyncrasies at each of their targets. Police referred to it as a *trademark,* which simplified the task of searching for a suspect.

Father Clough set to and began locating the various sources of the foul smell armed with a bowl of warm water, soap, and scrubbing brush.

Fortunately, there were no broken windows to contend with. Whoever was breaking in either had a key or was adept at picking locks.

He scrubbed the distinctly affected areas. The priest assumed there were either three burglars or one with a suspect bladder who suffered from a nervous disorder. He favoured the latter theory, supposing that if others were involved, there would undoubtedly be more damage.

This had to stop.

Father clough decided the time had come to address this issue and when better than the following Sunday service. He would use a scare tactic and relate to the congregation a description describing the ancient punishment of *flaying alive* for stealing from the church. Although an unthinkable act in the present day, it would give food for thought and might filter through the community and end this thieving once and for all.

He smiled as he considered the fact that the least favourite member of his congregation, Rose, might give his words some consideration.

She was, he believed, possessed by some incarnation of pure evil, and the subject of *flaying* would certainly be of interest to her.

As he continued to work on the unpleasant cleaning task, his mind drifted back to the Blacksmith family and the brutal bashing of little Michael. He wondered who could have done such a thing to an innocent child, and what could they hope to gain from it?

Rose, meanwhile, hugged Cassey as her parents engaged in yet another argument. It was not an uncommon event. The sounds of countless fights between couples were often to be heard up and down the street.

Her father had returned from the local pub, staggering as usual. He was full of bonhomie until Mrs Dennis made the usual allegation that he probably spent a sizeable portion of his weekly income on beer and cigarettes.

His good mood evaporated under the stern look from his wife.

'What a miserable cow you are; here I am in a cheerful mood, and you just have to pour cold water on it, don't you?'

'Cheerful mood, is it? Well, what about me having to eke out what's left of your wages for food in the coming week?' Sally replied, winding up to a full-blown argument.

'How about you go out to work?' Arthur said, rekindling an old theme.

'I can't go out to work, can I? Who's going to look after Rose?' Sally shouted.

'Oh, that's good, that is. The usual excuse, but she's your bloody daughter!'

'Don't swear, Rose might hear, and you know I'm trying to keep her nice.'

'Trying to keep her nice? What for? She's an East-Ender, for God's sake!' Exclaimed Arthur.

Sally began to sob.

'My parents warned me about marrying you. I could have been living in Hornchurch if I had said yes to Sidney Goldstein.'

Rose leaned against the wall outside the room. It was the same old argument. Sidney Goldstein, her mother's first boyfriend. She knew what was coming. Nothing was more likely to anger her father than Sidney Goldstein. Her father continued to deliver his usual statement on the matter.

'He would never have married you, you stupid cow. You aren't Jewish. His mother would never have allowed it. It would have stopped the family line dead in its tracks. A Jewish man must marry a Jewish woman. The family line can only continue through the woman.'

Rose pulled herself upright.

'My Sidney didn't care; he would have married me despite his mother.'

'Rubbish,' said Arthur, 'your precious Sidney married that fat ugly cow, Rachael Greenbaum. Her with the buck teeth and a face like a hatful of broken arseholes.'

Arthur was so engrossed in his lurid and unfair description of Rachael that he failed to see the dinner plate heading in his direction at high speed. It hit him squarely in the face, knocking him to the floor.

Sally rushed to his side, wailing that she hadn't meant it. She cradled Arthur's bleeding face in her arms, bemoaning the demon drink. It was the pub's fault.

Rose sensed that the argument had reached its climax and that peace would once again reign in her dysfunctional household.

Cassey languished in her arms, both eyes wide open.

'They are no better than the others, are they?' Rose said, making her way up to bed.

CHAPTER 5

Sophia

Christmas Eve, 1910.

Sophia sat wide-eyed, looking up at the biggest Christmas tree she had ever seen. The top was bent over slightly as it met the high ceiling of their sumptuous drawing-room. Millie, one of the many serving girls her parents employed, laughed gaily as she put the last layer of silver tinsel over the lower branches.

'I do not pay you to play the fool, girl.' Sophia's mother had entered the room unseen and stood now with hands on hips, frowning at Millie. The girl was no more than thirteen years old, and Sophia thought of her as more of a sister than a servant. Her mother smoothed the black crinoline of her dress and Sophia recognised the mannerism. It foretold of a coming outburst, and this time the target was Millie.

The girl faced her employer bravely, curtsying and averting her eyes as they had taught her when faced with her betters.

Charlotte Downes, Sophia's mother, walked purposely across the deep carpet towards the servant girl, now studiously looking down, awaiting her punishment, which she knew would surely come.

Sophia, although terrified of her mother, stepped in front of Millie as her mother approached.

'We were having fun, Mummy,' she whispered fearfully.

'I do not pay servants to have fun,' spat her mother, 'I pay them to work, nothing more.'

Sophia was standing against Millie, her head level with the

girl's chest, but it did nothing to stop the blow her mother delivered to the girl with the flat of her hand.

Millie screamed in both fright and pain as the hand connected with the side of her face. The slap had been delivered with frightening speed and accuracy, knocking her to the floor. Sophia was left standing as her mother once again smoothed the folds of her dress.

'Go below stairs, girl. Find some work to do,' said Charlotte.

Sophia looked up at her mother, wondering why the usual tears had not erupted from her eyes in the face of her mother's anger. She should have by now been lying on the floor sobbing uncontrollably, but this time was different. Her tears would not come. Instead, she stared defiantly up at her mother.

'You should not have slapped Millie; she was helping with the tree. Do you intend hitting me as well?'

Charlotte looked down at her daughter. Where had the fire come from? What had got into the girl?

'You see that wrapped parcel under the tree, the largest of them all?' Charlotte said, ignoring her daughter's tirade.

Sophia didn't take her eyes off her mother's face.

'Well, it is your present and if you want to open it tomorrow morning, I suggest you mend your ways, young lady.'

Turning abruptly, Charlotte swept out of the room, leaving Sophia staring after her.

'Evil bitch!'

Sophia looked around the room, searching for the owner of the voice, but she was alone.

The next morning was Christmas Day 1910. The new King was on his throne, and all appeared to be well. It had been the first year of George V's reign and heralded the end of the Edwardian era. During the preceding years of Edward VII's brief reign, the population had been released from the oppressive rule of the late Queen Victoria. People were stepping out in less sombre clothes. The rich, that is- the poor, continued in their drab clothes as before, nothing changed for them.

Sophia stood before the massive, decorated Christmas tree

eagerly awaiting the distribution of gifts. The servants were lined up as well. The one day of the year when the rigid rules of the household were relaxed.

Sophia's father, Victor Downes, stood beaming in front of the tree. He loved Christmas with all the spiritual goodwill it offered.

Charlotte Downes was less than enthusiastic. To her, the mere idea of sharing anything with the lower classes was highly undesirable. Her new fashionable gown did nothing to soften her attitude. Victor had spent a small fortune on his wife, insisting that she have a completely new wardrobe. The Victorian attire, which she had previously still insisted on wearing, had been meted out to the charity organisations that dotted the poorer areas.

Charlotte preferred the old ways. Severe black crinoline had suited her character admirably. Her husband had thought a new frivolous theme might have softened her attitude, but he had been sadly disappointed. Her bedroom door had remained locked as he retired to his own. The years of disappointment set to continue.

They had been happy, or at least what passed for happiness in their class, when first married. Charlotte dutifully left her bedroom open so that her husband could claim his conjugal rights at least once a week. After a silent, unemotional coupling, he returned to his room. She turned over and slept, pleased it was over.

One year later, Charlotte gave birth to Sophia. Her labour was long and hard, surrounded by servants and a midwife. Secretly, the servants enjoyed her pain. They hated her because of her constant complaining. She had struck one or two of them in the past, but they were about to receive an unpleasant surprise. Her arrogance only increased after Sophia's birth.

Victor was thrilled with the arrival of his daughter.

'A son next, my dear,' he asserted.

'Never again!' She exclaimed.

Victor noticed her bedroom door seemed always to be

closed to him. She banned him from entering at any time, not just at night. That was the end of the marriage. Divorce was out of the question as they were both Catholic, so like many others in the same position, they carried on with their lives. Outwardly, they appeared to be the ideal couple, but in reality, once behind closed doors, they were anything but.

'Merry Christmas,' said Victor, handing the wrapped oblong box to Sophia, who clutched at it, desperately wanting to unwrap the mystery gift.

She tore at the paper with eager fingers, shredding it mercilessly, leaving a trail of destruction on the floor. The servants laughed good-naturedly. Without exception, they all loved little Sophia. She possessed the opposite nature to her harridan of a mother, treating them as friends rather than servants.

'Just look at the mess you are making, child!' Charlotte exclaimed.

'Hush now, my dear, it is Christmas after all. A time for goodwill to all,' said Victor.

Charlotte stamped her foot angrily,

'Well, what about my present?' She insisted.

Victor handed his wife an oblong box. It was small and wrapped in the brightest Christmas wrapping paper.

She tore savagely at the delicate tissue, adding to the mess on the carpet made by Sophia.

They arrived at the contents of both boxes at the same time.

Sophia's eyes widened as she picked up a doll. Cuddling it to her body, she went to her father and thanked him, her eyes bright with unshed tears of joy.

Charlotte dropped her box to the floor, leaving in her hands the most beautiful necklace. A fine gold chain held a cluster of diamonds surrounding a magnificent sapphire, set in the finest gold setting.

Victor stepped behind to receive the necklace from her hands and drape it around her neck, fastening the almost invisible clasp.

'There, my dear, what do you think of that?'

Charlotte, for once, was lost for words, merely smiling at her husband. That was quite sufficient for him, who had not been granted any such smile for years.

'I will unlock my door this evening,' she murmured.

Victor smiled in return,

'Enchanté, ma cherie. Vous ête très gentil.'

Charlotte smiled her understanding; the upper classes were invariably fluent in French.

'I love my doll,' said Sophia, breaking the spell.

Victor laughed gently,

'It looks new, but it is actually very old. I purchased it from a well-known doll-maker on my last trip to Germany. He had this one high on a shelf and it caught my eye. Goodness knows why, but I just had to have it. The gentleman in the shop assured me it had been totally rebuilt. Apparently, and I cannot attest to the truth of it, they found the doll on one of the major battlefields of the Franko-Prussian war. One of the commanding officers was seen to be carrying the doll which led to many unkind comments by his men. However, it would be a very brave man or a fool that would laugh openly at a Prussian officer.'

'How did it get into the shop?' Asked Charlotte, intrigued by the story.

'I don't know, my dear. Maybe it found its own way there,' laughed Victor.

Charlotte, as always, poured water on the entire event. 'You could have at least chosen a pretty one.'

Sophia's face changed from smiles to anger at this vicious comment from her mother, but she knew it best to hold her tongue.

A movement in her arms startled her and glancing down, she saw the doll's eyes open wide, which was contrary to their design. When the doll was upright, the eyes opened automatically and when horizontal, the eyes closed by the same means. The doll lay in Sophia's arms, almost horizontal, but its eyes were wide open. As Sophia looked on, they seemed to harden, and the girl could have sworn the hard porcelain face twisted as if in anger.

She brought the doll up to her face and cuddled it even tighter, the lips of the doll close to her ear.

'Evil bitch.'

Those words again. Sophia looked down at her new doll and caught the glimmer of a smile in the porcelain features. How could that be?

The servants returned downstairs, each clutching their Christmas present, a shiny gold sovereign. It was the best possible present to receive. Money was always better than some useless, insignificant item they would never use.

Sophia thought that Christmas Day would never end. There seemed to be a constant stream of visitors, mostly family, coming and going, full of Christmas cheer.

At last, it was time for her evening bath and bedtime. The nanny escorted her, still holding her doll.

'Have you named it yet?' Asked Nanny.

Sophia's own words surprised her, 'It's not *it*. Her name is Cassey,' she replied gruffly.

Nanny, slightly taken aback by the child's tone, commented, 'And where did you find that name?'

'Cassey told me. She knows her own name, silly,' retorted Sophia, gruffly.

'Why don't we leave her in the bedroom while you have your bath?' Nanny suggested.

'No, Cassey stays with me,' insisted Sophia.

She sat Cassey on a chair in the bathroom while Nanny undressed her. Nanny tested the water and helped her over the lip of the bath. Sophia relaxed in the soothing warm water as Nanny stepped back.

She let out a whoosh! Nanny had fallen flat on her back. A cake of soap had somehow found its way onto the bathroom floor.

'Are you all right, Nanny?' Sophia said, concerned.

Nanny sat up and replied that she thought she was still in one piece. As she struggled to her feet, Sophia looked across at

Cassey. Her eyes were bright with laughter, and Sophia couldn't help but join in.

'It was not funny,' chided Nanny, 'I could have been seriously injured.'

'Sorry, Nanny,' said Sophia, glancing at Cassey. The doll looked back, and the girl could have sworn it winked at her.

The following morning at breakfast, Sophia's father was in an excellent mood. His eyes sparkled as he welcomed his daughter to the table. She had accepted he was still full of Christmas spirit and asked to sit on his lap. He laughingly hoisted her up, complete with Cassey firmly tucked under her arm.

What she could not know was that her father had let himself into Charlotte's bedchamber the previous evening, where he had satisfied many years of unfulfillment.

The mood at the table transformed as his wife entered.

'Sophia, get down from your father's lap, it's indecent.' Charlotte hissed, 'what will the servants think?'

Sophia dutifully clambered down and sat at the table, still clutching Cassey.

'Millie, take that doll and put it in the nursery where it belongs,' insisted Charlotte.

'But Mummy, Cassey will be lonely without me,' Sophia wailed as the servant made to take away her doll.

'Do as I say, girl, immediately,' said Charlotte, the anger in her voice undisguised.

Millie knew what would happen if she disobeyed and roughly snatched the doll from Sophia's grasp and made to walk from the room.

As she passed Charlotte sitting at the table, one of the doll's arms somehow slipped from her grasp and stuck straight out, neatly catching Charlotte across one cheek.

'How dare you? Striking your employer is an unforgivable offence!' Charlotte screamed.

'Now, now, my dear, I'm sure it was merely an accident,' soothed Victor.

'Accident my foot, the girl deliberately caught me with that blasted doll's arm. Is there a mark?'

Sophia looked across the table at her mother's face and was surprised at the size of the injury Cassey's outstretched arm had inflicted. Charlotte's cheek bore the marks that would be expected of a much more violent attack. As Sophia watched, her mother's cheek appeared to open in a wide cut and blood ran slowly down her cheek.

Millie couldn't move. it horrified her. How could such a gentle tap result in what she now witnessed?

Charlotte put her hand to her cheek and brought it away, covered in blood. Her anger knew no bounds now, and she sprung to her feet, grabbed the doll and hurled it across the room, where it struck the wall violently.

Sophia screamed, tears streaming.

'How could you hurt Cassey? I hate you!' she shouted.

General pandemonium ensued as other servants rushed into the room. The butler led Millie away, her face wet with tears.

Victor issued instructions that the doctor be called to attend to Charlotte's injury. Her face had now turned black with bruising and blood still oozed from the wound.

Another servant collected the doll where it lay on the floor, arms, and legs akimbo. She dropped it in shock as she witnessed the look on the doll's face. It no longer bore a bland ceramic visage but had taken on the appearance of an enraged person. Twisted features surrounding not crystal-clear hazel eyes, but black, staring, dilated pupils.

As the servant looked on, the doll resumed its previous looks. An inanimate object; Sophia's doll.

CHAPTER 6

Charlotte looked in the mirror in her bedroom. Staring back at her was the scar left by the doll. The doctor had been obliged to stitch the cut closed because it would not stop bleeding, and he worried it might become infected.

1910 had slid into 1911 with little fanfare from Sophia's household. Her mother walked around the house with black ugly stitches marking her normal peaches and cream complexion. The bruising had gone down, leaving the stitched cut emphasised even more.

Sophia kept Cassey away from her mother, spending hours in her bedroom talking. Any observer would have heard only the girl's voice, but she heard every word Cassey said.

'*The darkness is coming,*' the doll repeated endlessly. Sophia did not know what it meant, and Cassey refused to explain further.

The Downes' household enjoyed the fruits of Victor's labours. He was one of a new breed of successful entrepreneurs. Held in awe by the working class but hated by the aristocracy. They regarded them as nouveau riche and openly referred to them as *trade* at their exclusive parties where only the *best* were invited.

Victor considered it great fun to parade his wealth in front of the traditional upper class, whereas Charlotte seethed that she was never invited to parties reserved for *old money*. They may have sported minor titles, but in truth, the aristocracy was fast becoming the poor cousin to the newly established industrialists.

The only way Charlotte could compensate for her lack of

breeding was to flaunt her husband's wealth. They employed a tutor for Sophia and even more servants to run the household.

Once the stitches had been removed, Charlotte employed a beautician to teach her maid how to cover the blemish on her cheek. The task would take up to an hour, but she was not content until the scar was virtually undetectable.

Sophia spent most of the time upstairs in a room in the attic, which had been specially prepared as a schoolroom for her. Mr Thomas, her teacher, sat at his desk looking down on her as they went through the rigours of learning English literature, French, and simple arithmetic. Young ladies needed nothing more other than to learn the piano, for which she attended the rooms of a music teacher twice a week.

Cassey attended school with her and was never far away, sharing the small bench seat that was attached to her desk.

Piano lessons were different. Charlotte knew nothing of what transpired in the attic. She had no interest in her child other than that she should be educated as a young lady of quality so that a suitable husband might take her off their hands at the earliest opportunity.

She insisted Sophia attend her music lessons without the doll. In Charlotte's eyes, the beastly thing was a nuisance, and it was time their daughter consigned it to the toy box, permanently. As she gave strict instructions to this effect, she carelessly ran a finger over the scar that the wretched doll had caused. Sophia stared at her mother in defiance.

'Cassey goes with me, or I won't go,' she said, eyes blazing.

Charlotte almost slapped her face for the insolence but instead, wagged a finger in the girl's face,

'Either you go to your lessons alone or I shall instruct the footman to smash the ugly thing with a hammer.'

'You wouldn't dare!' screamed Sophia, tears streaming down her cheeks.

'Try me,' invited her mother, 'your precious father is abroad again so he cannot protect you.'

Sophia had lost, and she knew it. Throwing herself at her

mother's feet, she begged her not to hurt Cassey.

Charlotte was enjoying this victory over her daughter. She possessed a cruel streak and, never one to let an opportunity pass, called for the footman, Ham. His actual name was Fotheringham, but Charlotte thought it far too good for a mere servant, so had given him the shortened name, Ham.

'Fetch a hammer and bring it here,' ordered Charlotte, flashing a rarely seen smile.

'At once, Marm,' replied Ham.

'No,' cried Sophia, 'please, Mummy, I promise I shall not take Cassey with me; please don't hurt her.'

She was still crying when Ham reappeared holding a large ball peen hammer.

Sophia clutched Cassey to her side and wept.

'Please, Mummy, I beg you,' she said between sobs.

Ham laughed,

'Shall I smash that ugly doll to smithereens for you, Marm?'

Charlotte paused for what seemed to Sophia an agonisingly long time.

'No, not on this occasion, but keep the hammer in your room. Any more nonsense from this little madam and the doll goes into the bin, in pieces,' said Charlotte, sweeping out of the room, closely followed by Ham.

Sophia clung to Cassey so tightly that she heard the doll complaining,

'You are squeezing the life out of me.'

Out of sight of her daughter, Charlotte halted in the hallway. Ham careened into her as she turned into another small room in the attic. She laughed as the door closed behind them.

'Do it to me, Ham, like before. Victor was never like you, so strong and virile. I never knew it could be like this.'

The bare boards under her back appeared not to affect her as the footman did as ordered.

In the schoolroom, Sophia's composure was returning. Cassey's head twisted of its own accord, and she appeared to be listening to sounds that were not audible to the girl.

'What's the matter?' Sophia asked.

Cassey didn't reply, but both eyes were open and glowing.

It had been four weeks since the threat against Sophia's doll, and Victor had returned from his business trip.

Charlotte had welcomed him coldly, and he noted grimly that her bedroom door was still locked every night. However, it had not been locked when her husband was away. Ham had become something of an obsession, and he visited nightly. Charlotte was not the woman of Ham's choosing. She was considerably older than him, but in service, one had to comply with the demands of one's superiors, however distasteful they may be.

Life continued as normal after Victor's return until one morning a loud scream awoke the quiet household. It was very early and only the servants were about. Millie, who had a certain fondness for Ham, was taking him a cup of tea, hoping to catch him in his night attire.

As she opened his door, a gruesome sight met her eyes. Ham was lying in bed, the pillow under his head soaked with blood.

She dropped the tea and screamed at the top of her voice, rousing everyone instantly.

The police were called and clumped noisily upstairs on the uncarpeted stairs used by the servants, the racket reverberating throughout the house.

They examined the deceased footman who had been struck a severe blow on the forehead with a hammer that still lay on the floor beside the bed. It was obvious by the shape of the wound that the ball end of the hammer had been used, punching a neat hole through his skull. Ham would have died instantly, and in all probability would have been in a deep sleep, so would have known nothing.

Both Millie and Charlotte were near hysterical with shock and grief. Charlotte for the loss of her lover and Millie for the lost chance of perhaps making him hers.

A search of the household found no evidence of a break-in, and it left the police scratching their heads. Charlotte confirmed

Ham had the hammer in his room at her insistence. When pressed to explain the reason, she told them about the conflict between herself and her daughter over the doll. The police officers shrugged their collective shoulders at this strange statement. *Posh families*, they thought. Bloody mad, all of them.

The police had taken away the hammer. They insisted it remain with them; evidence, they said.

Later, in Sophia's bed, Cassey at her side, the girl whispered.

'The hammer has gone; you are safe now.'

The doll gently closed her eyes, and Sophia clearly heard the sigh of relief.

CHAPTER 7

February 1912

Two years passed and the family's financial position improved to where Charlotte was at last accepted into the *better* soirées. Sophia was becoming accomplished in both English and French; even her piano playing received compliments.

Much to the annoyance of her mother, the child still insisted on taking her doll everywhere. Charlotte was of the opinion that it was time for her to grow up and the doll was becoming an embarrassment, particularly when Sophia insisted on introducing her doll to visitors by name. The ladies politely asked after the doll to which Sophia replied Cassey was well and would they like to hold her, just for a moment.

Charlotte, blushing, would insist that Cassey should go down for her daily nap and shush Sophia and doll out of the room.

By this time the new footman, Simon, personally chosen by Charlotte, was well entrenched within the family. His closeness to his mistress had not gone unnoticed by her many lady friends, and behind her back they made observations that perhaps *mistress amour* might be more appropriate.

Most of the ladies had lovers of their own. It had been fashionable for years that both husbands and wives took partners outside the marriage, as long as they were discreet. Marriages among the upper classes were almost always arranged, and they expected the compromise. However, that Charlotte was so obviously romantically involved with one of her servants was considered *gauche*.

It was on a windy and cold February morning in 1912 that Victor made his announcement at breakfast.

'I have a wonderful surprise for you both,' he said.

Silence reigned as Charlotte and Sophia waited in anticipation. Sophia thought it might be a pleasant surprise, but Charlotte wondered if her husband had discovered her dalliance with the footman.

Simon stood to attention at the door, wondering if this was to be his last day in the employ of the Downes family.

'There is a magnificent new ocean liner about to make her maiden voyage to New York and we, as a family, are to join her, travelling first-class naturally. It will be the trip of a lifetime.'

Charlotte, rather relieved, asked the name of this new ship.

'The *Titanic,*' replied Victor, 'and well-named she is, too. She is huge, fitted out to the highest standards, and the agent assures me is unsinkable.'

'That is a relief,' said Charlotte, 'you know how I hate boats; I inevitably suffer seasickness.'

'Not on this one, my dear. You will hardly realise we are at sea. She is smooth and very fast.' Victor assured her.

Sophia entered the conversation. 'Can Cassey come too?'

'Certainly not!' Charlotte exclaimed. 'What will other passengers say when they see a girl of your age promenading with a doll?'

Victor could see the beginnings of the old argument about that blasted doll and moved quickly to end it.

'Yes, Sophia, you may take the doll, but only on the understanding that it remains in the cabin at all times.'

Charlotte was about to rise and continue the argument when Sophia spoke.

'I agree, just so long as I have Cassey with me at night.'

'That is agreed then,' said Victor with a glance at his wife that brooked no argument, adding, 'We shall all have to shop for new clothes and luggage.'

This announcement mollified Charlotte. She had become used to spending vast amounts of money on herself and was already planning a completely new wardrobe in her head.

'When do we sail?' She asked. They needed time for dressmakers to call, measure, and make.

'We sail from Southampton on April 10th,' said Victor. 'I have business in New York, so it is most convenient.'

The following weeks were a blur to Sophia. Her mother concentrated on acquiring the very latest in fashionable clothes for both herself and Sophia. Mother and daughter must be perfectly turned out for first-class travel.

Victor smiled good-naturedly at his wife as she spent money with wild abandon. He was looking forward to spending time alone with her. At least he wouldn't have to compete with the handsome footman. Victor knew well that what he himself was denied was readily available to the younger man. He had not become wealthy by being a fool and knew that Charlotte was entertaining a lover in his own household. Maybe the voyage would rekindle their marriage.

They decided to take Millie along to see to their needs during the voyage. First-class passengers always carried at least one maid.

Millie was thrilled and Sophia ecstatic. She would have at least one friend on board. Apart from Cassey, of course. Millie knew nothing about ships or how they were separated by class. The family would travel first-class. Victor had arranged for Sophia to have her own cabin next door to theirs, which she would share with the maid. He wanted his wife to himself. That she was sleeping with another man did nothing to dampen his ardour. He had plenty of opportunities to take another woman himself, but business was his only mistress. No, he wanted his wife, and the fact that she was being satisfied by another only sharpened his interest, bringing his competitive spirit to the fore.

April was fast approaching, and the household was abuzz with excitement. The family would be away for weeks, which meant the staff would have the house to themselves. The new footman was very pleased. He had been engaged by the family shortly after the unfortunate death of Ham. This time, Victor had chosen him, not for his references but for his lack of good looks. Charlotte found it hard to disguise her lack of enthusiasm for the new man when first introduced. Victor left the room with a smug grin spreading across his features.

April 9th found the family settling into a first-class carriage of a Southampton bound early morning train. They would spend the night before sailing at the best hotel the town could provide.

That evening, Victor and Charlotte dined together in the hotel's restaurant while Millie cared for Sophia in the room Victor had booked for them next to his sumptuous suite.

Both Millie and her charge were finding it difficult to sleep. They had already seen the enormous ocean liner they were about to embark on. It towered over the dock and every other ship in sight.

They were still awake when Victor and Charlotte returned from dinner. Millie was sharing a bed with Sophia and Cassey at the girl's insistence,

'I don't want to sleep alone. It's strange here,' said Sophia.

Millie had crawled in beside her but found Cassey barring the way. She had to be content to sleep beside the doll. Sophia had her arm firmly around it, and Millie could feel the unforgiving porcelain body cold against her own.

Muffled voices could be heard from the next room, and Sophia giggled quietly.

'Mummy and Daddy are back,' she said.

Billing and cooing noises coming through the wall told Millie that the couple were about to engage in a rare act of lovemaking. She smiled to herself as she wondered if the master could make his wife moan and groan as the footman, Ham, used to. She had listened to them with a glass held against the wall, the breathy noises of the adulterous couple raising her own emotions to the point where jealousy almost consumed her.

Millie made a wager with herself as to just how long the master could interest his wife. They would stay some weeks in New York after the voyage across the Atlantic, and she doubted he would last long in their hotel suite before he was obliged to ask for another room for himself, citing as the reason his wife's *delicate* constitution.

The following morning, the hotel dining room resembled Charing Cross Railway Station. People were milling about, chatting, and smiling. The majority of the guests were due to board the *Titanic* that morning for the great liner's maiden voyage to New York. Only the very wealthy could afford the ridiculously expensive prices of a first-class berth. Such was the demand that the shipping company had inflated the fares, but there was still a long waiting list for any cancellations that might occur prior to the ship's departure. The steerage area was full of hopeful migrants fostering the dream of a life in the New World. Even the fares for this class had been raised slightly. The company saw no reason to waste such a splendid opportunity to cash in on the hype of the *Titanic's* maiden voyage. All who came into contact with her held the *unsinkable ship* in awe.

At the docks, all was prepared to welcome the passengers. In one section, the steerage class passengers were herded like cattle up ramps to the main deck and then down to take their place below decks. These passengers would have a roped off area where they would be allowed to take the air during the voyage. However, at a predetermined time, all would be dismissed below to spend the night crammed together in rude bunks, placed as close together as possible so they might accommodate the maximum number of steerage class passengers.

For Victor, his family, and the maid, it was a different story. They were led to their cabins by well-dressed stewards and on entering were told of the many delights they might expect during the voyage. Nothing was too good for those fortunate enough to be in first-class.

Victor and Charlotte settled into their cabin while Sophia,

Millie and Cassey marvelled at the luxurious fittings in their own.

The family, with Millie in tow, climbed the stairs to the main deck, meaning to explore. The ship was so vast the corridors seemed endless. As they emerged from a finely constructed timber door onto the deck, the ship's siren let off one long blast. Sophia and Millie covered their ears. It was a deafening sound, signalling that the ship was about to leave the dock to embark on her maiden voyage. Cheering passengers lined the ship's rail, waving at the crowded shoreline. Ribbons were flying and a brass band played onshore as the *Titanic* slipped her moorings and crept away from the wharf, pushed and pulled by little tugboats.

As the ship moved into the estuary, it was finally under its own power. Her massive screws pushed the ship forward to meet the slight swell. Those on board had no sense of motion. The *Titanic* was like a huge floating city.

Inside the first-class lounge, a band was playing. The musicians were top class and had been specially hired to serenade guests. Victor and Charlotte were handed glasses of French champagne and encouraged to toast the grand occasion. A plentiful supply of cordial satisfied Sophia and Millie.

As the excitement gradually toned down, Sophia begged to be allowed back to her cabin. She was concerned for Cassey; her doll was not used to being alone.

Charlotte frowned as her daughter voiced her concern.

'Sophia, Cassey is merely a doll. It is not as though it has feelings; it is an inanimate object.'

Sophia rounded on her mother.

'She does so have feelings; more than most people I know,' she said angrily.

Charlotte dismissed her with a wave of her hand, at the same time taking another glass of champagne from a silver salver held by a steward.

As she did so, the steward bowed, and catching the glint in his eye, she smiled back. It was as if they had a secret code, but of course, it was the code common to all would-be paramours. Victor did not fail to notice either, but merely shrugged. Millie also saw the exchange and, not for the first time, wondered at the lack of morals in the upper classes. They preached about the higher order of things and how people must obey the good words of the scriptures, a leftover from the stern Victorian era. In Millie's view, this section of the ship was nothing more than a high-class brothel. As she looked around, she could see couples gradually separating, talking, and laughing gaily with people they had not known just an hour ago.

Sophia dragged Millie away by the hand, making her way back to the cabin and Cassey.

Lying on her bed was the doll where she had left it. In the twin berth room, Millie had the bed adjacent where she sat down and, turning, lay flat on her back contemplating the fancily adorned ceiling.

Sophia looked lovingly at her doll. Cassey looked back, but it was not a loving look, more of a snarl. Sophia wondered how her doll, made from unyielding porcelain, could bend its features to suit the mood. Subconsciously, she heard Cassey's voice,

'I don't like it when you leave me alone.'

The morning saw the ship well out to sea. While her parents mixed with the other first-class passengers, Millie walked down to the steerage section. Sophia followed, clutching Cassey tightly, not wanting to leave her alone after the stern rebuke she had received the last time. Her parents wouldn't know she had taken her out of the cabin. As they approached that part of the deck where the lowest class of passengers were allowed in the daytime, they could hear music. It wasn't the stuffy, boring music of first-class, more like Irish fiddle music.

The two girls stood at a rail looking down on a group of dancers, whirling around to the sounds of a boisterous fiddle and drum. It was intoxicating, and both girls began tapping their toes in time to the music.

One dancer looked up and waved.

'Come down and join in, there is plenty of room.'

Millie looked at Sophia and by mutual unspoken agreement, they ran lightly down the steps to join the throng below.

A strong-looking young man with a bright red neckerchief whisked Millie away. Sophia thought him to be very dashing, and the older Millie was in full agreement.

Sophia walked beside the rail, keeping out of the way of the dancers. She saw a doorway and curiosity getting the better of her stepped through.

Stairs were leading down, and she could hear the hubbub of voices drifting up together with the unpleasant odour of unwashed clothing.

She started as a hand reached out and grabbed her ankle. Looking down, she saw a middle-aged man sitting on the floor, leaning against a bulkhead. His voice was slurred,

'And what are you doing down here, my pretty one? You belong with the posh folks, I'll be bound.'

Sophia, although frightened, replied in her haughtiest manner,

'Let go of me or I will report you to my father.'

The man laughed gruffly, coughing at the same time.

'Come to see how the poor live, have you?'

'No, Millie and I heard the music and came down to investigate. Now, let me go!'

The man did nothing of the sort, instead, shifting his grip beneath her dress to her leg above the knee.

The next few moments were a confusing explosion of events which later, Sophia could not recall. She thought she may have fainted.

In her desperation to escape the man's clutches, she swung the doll at him. Cassey's little porcelain hand caught him neatly on the forehead.

In normal circumstances, the blow would have merely glanced off the man's head with very little impression. However, in this case, a hole appeared in his forehead, and he slumped to the ground in silence.

Sophia recovered her senses sufficiently to run out of the

doorway. The man's hand had lost its grip on her leg and all she could think of was escaping his clutches.

She spied Millie with her young man and, going over to her, insisted they both leave immediately for their section of the ship.

Millie could only but obey her young mistress and reluctantly left the embrace of her newfound beau to join her.

Of the man who had attempted to detain Sophia, nothing was heard of again. First-class passengers were insulated from the squalid squabbles of steerage. No doubt the man had been involved in a fight, and even though he had been killed, they were in international waters, so there could be no police involvement. A senior officer questioned a few of the victim's fellow travellers, but all were reluctant to comment. They transferred him to the on-board morgue where he was promptly forgotten. He had been a lone migrant heading for the promised land and would now reach his destination in a casket. At least part of his dream survived. He would have his own small allotment in America for all time.

Sophia woke the next morning to a patch of dried blood on her bedding. Examining herself, she could find not even a scratch. She noticed Cassy had a smear of blood on her hand and wondered how it had got there. Sighing as a mother would to a naughty child, she washed Cassey's hand in the basin provided in her room and drying it, tut-tutted.

'Where on earth did that come from?'

Cassey looked at Sophia blankly, one eye closed.

CHAPTER 8

The maiden voyage of the *Titanic* was progressing smoothly. Maintaining top speed, she would certainly break the trans-Atlantic record for a passenger vessel. Those on board were not aware of the ship's speedy passage. Her sheer size shielded them from the effects of her massive bows slicing through the Atlantic Ocean.

Passengers in first-class were treated to the best in dining, accompanied by the small orchestra, and Victor was dining without Charlotte.

'I simply cannot stand the noise in the dining room, not tonight. I have such a headache,' said Charlotte. 'I'll stay here in the cabin with the lights dimmed.'

Victor made his way to the dining room alone; nothing was going to stop him enjoying the delights of first-class travel on the most luxurious ship afloat.

There were several other passengers already seated at his table. Glancing around, Victor saw that most were couples. The chair beside him was vacant. The dining plan had allowed for his wife, but now it left a gap in the seating arrangements. The head waiter approached and deferentially asked whether Victor's wife would be joining them.

'No, my wife has one of her headaches,' said Victor blandly.

'In that case, might I seat another guest to make up the numbers?' Asked the waiter.

Victor turned as a wave of expensive perfume accosted his senses. The new guest had arrived.

'Good evening, my name is Esme, thank you for allowing me to join you.'

Victor stammered a reply,

'Delighted, I'm sure.'

In turning to greet this vision of beauty, he swept the cutlery from the table, causing an abrupt end to conversation. While waiters scurried to pick up the offending articles and relay his setting, Victor, red in the face, smiled an apology.

'So sorry, my fault entirely.'

Esme smiled back at him, murmuring,

'Perhaps not entirely.'

As the meal progressed with accompanying wine, conversation became easier.

'May I enquire why you are travelling alone?' Victor asked.

'I'm going over to New York to meet my husband,' said Esme, 'and you?'

Victor cursed his bad luck. If only Charlotte had stayed behind. Here was a conquest with no strings attached. In the past, he had not considered another woman, business first. But here, out of sight of land, he was looking at life with a different perspective and the idea of a brief affair d'amour appealed to him.

'My wife is indisposed with one of her headaches and will not be joining us this evening. I very much doubt whether she will surface at all,' he replied easily.

'What a pity,' murmured Esme, smiling sweetly, 'we shall just have to entertain ourselves.'

Victor ordered more champagne, and the couple edged their chairs a little closer. This could be a very memorable night, thought Victor.

At around 10 pm, Victor cleared his throat and gently pushed his chair from the table.

'What do you say to a stroll on the deck?'

'Yes, that sounds wonderful,' replied Esme.

The couple moved to the doors leading onto the deck and passed through. The chill attacked them immediately, particularly through Esme's thin dress. It surprised them at how quickly the weather had changed. It had dropped several degrees since the afternoon.

'Back inside,' laughed Victor, holding Esme lightly by the arm.

'There must be somewhere warmer,' she hinted.

'Let me see you to your cabin,' suggested Victor.

'That is very kind,' said Esme, leading the way, rather eagerly, Victor thought.

All traces of subterfuge disappeared at the cabin door. As Esme opened it, Victor followed her inside, where he took no time at all in helping to remove her dress.

She lay draped suggestively over the bed in the manner adopted by ladies of the night, and Victor hurriedly undressed to join her.

Only the dim light of a single lamp on the side table illuminated their torrid lovemaking. Victor had never experienced such intense feelings before, and the act left him exhausted, both mentally and physically. Esme smiled her gratitude as they lie side by side, arms and legs intertwined, slipping into a deep sleep.

Charlotte was also fast asleep, but not in her own cabin. She had made a prearranged tryst to meet her handsome steward, Alphonse, who had secured keys to a laundry room deep in the bowels of the ship.

Making a bed from towels and sheets, he led Charlotte into the improvised boudoir. She enjoyed his clumsy lovemaking. Although somewhat brutish, she responded with an ever-growing urgency, surprising him with her own outlandish demands.

Just a few seconds after 11.40 pm, anyone still awake would have been conscious of a scraping sound alongside the ship. The forward decks were showered with ice as the *Titanic* grazed the side of a massive iceberg.

By 11.50 pm, the icy cold North Atlantic Ocean was flooding into the forward compartments. A long gash had been scored beneath the waterline. Engines were ordered stopped, and the crew raced to survey the damage.

The news was grim. The *unsinkable Titanic* had a serious

flaw in her construction. Bulkheads separating various compartments did not extend to full height, meaning that the incoming water rose until it cascaded over the top into the next compartment.

Captain Smith ordered radio messages to be transmitted, asking for immediate help. In the engine room, stokers worked tirelessly to rake out coals from the boilers. A sudden meeting of ice-cold water and red-hot coal would cause an explosion.

Shortly thereafter, the captain issued the order to abandon ship. The *Titanic* was sinking. There was nothing that could prevent it.

The ship's metal structures began to groan as she settled in the water. The bow tilted down, and the stern lifted, causing dining room furniture to slide over the floor already littered with broken crockery and glasses.

Steerage passengers began moving upwards through the decks, racing upwards against the ever-increasing tilt as the stern began to rise out of the water.

First-class passengers were assembling at their prearranged stations, but crew training had been woefully inadequate; after all, the *Titanic* was thought to be unsinkable. Passengers roamed the decks looking for some direction from the crew, who were already panicking themselves.

Victor, Esme, Charlotte, and Alphonse slept on, exhausted from their nefarious trysts.

Charlotte stirred as icy cold water suddenly and dramatically covered her feet. Sitting bolt upright, she screamed,

'What's happening? Where is the water coming from?'

Water was pouring in through a louvred door and within seconds began to fill the room. Alphonse jumped to his feet, completely at a loss. The onboard lights were still on and, apart from the ingress of water, all seemed normal except for the tilt of the deck. He ran to the door and pushed against it, but it wouldn't budge. The pressure outside held the door fast and all the time inside, the water continued to rise.

Now, both standing, the water was already up to Charlotte's

chest. It would only be seconds before it covered her head. Alphonse lifted her so their heads were level. Each looked into each other's terrified eyes as the water rushed to cover them completely.

Alphonse released Charlotte, and holding his breath, made for the door. This time it opened easily, and he swam out. The torrent of water swept him along the passageway, and he appeared to be heading in an upward direction. Soon, he could touch the floor and waded with the current. Reaching a stairway, he climbed up and entered another deck, this one still dry. He ran as fast as he could, climbing up between decks until he emerged onto the main deck and the immediate terror of being trapped below left him.

Charlotte's fate never crossed his mind. Self-preservation had kicked in and he only thought of his own survival. It had finally dawned on him that the ship was sinking, and he was too young to die.

Charlotte's body swirled in the cold water below. Her unseeing eyes still wide open from the shock of her sudden end. It had taken only moments for her tortured lungs to breathe in salty water. From blind panic, she settled into momentary euphoria as she returned to the same sea from which her ancestors had emerged so many millions of years ago.

Victor and Esme were asleep in Esme's cabin, high in the first-class section. The noise of alarm bells eventually filtered through to wake them. Neither could believe that the captain would choose such an ungodly hour to hold lifeboat drill.

'You stay here, my dear, I'll find out what all the fuss is about,' said Victor, asserting that he would find somebody in authority and give them a piece of his mind.

He struggled with his clothes as Esme reclined on her bed, smoking a cigarette. He was finding it difficult to maintain balance. As his mind cleared, he realised he was standing at an angle. No wonder it was difficult to stand on one leg to put on his suit-pants.

The screams of other passengers rose above the annoying

chiming of the alarm as he opened the door to a scene of utter bedlam. Men, women, and children were running in both directions. Some upwards and others down, following the angle of the ship's deck.

Millie and Sophia were already on deck. They had heard the alarm and Millie immediately took charge, leading her young mistress out. She took the time to make sure they both wore warm coats, knowing that the night air would be freezing. As they left the cabin, Sophia grabbed her doll. She could never leave Cassey behind, but Millie grabbed it, plucking it from her grasp before Sophia had time to react.

'Leave it, we must get up on deck. Something is very wrong. Look how the deck is tilting,' she admonished.

'I'm not leaving without Cassey,' screamed Sophia defiantly.

Millie threw the doll back into their cabin and slammed the door.

'Sophia, leave the doll. I'll buy you another, but we must get to safety.'

Dragging Sophia by the arm, she struggled along the passageway heading upwards, rightly guessing that the ship was sinking and for them to head in the other direction would be disastrous for them.

It was difficult as the passageway was crowded with other guests milling about. A man rushed past, knocking Sophia to the floor. It was Alphonse, little knowing or caring that he had just knocked down his recent lover's child; he carried on running, still saturated and wheezing, fighting for every breath.

Victor and Esme emerged out onto the main deck, instantly aware of the situation and the impending fate of the doomed ship.

Esme's cabin was some distance from his own, and Victor worried for the safety of Charlotte and the two girls next door.

'I must find my wife and daughter,' he yelled above the ever-increasing cacophony surrounding them.

'You cannot go back,' said Esme, 'too many people are coming out, you will never make headway against them.'

'I must try,' said Victor, making for the door from which they had only just emerged.

It was no use; the passageways were now packed with people heading steadily towards the lifeboats. Some had already been lowered, but less than half full. Others dangled uselessly by a single rope as the vastly undertrained crew attempted to launch them.

There were insufficient lifeboats for all the passengers and crew because the ship's designers had considered this to be a waste of money.

The cry went up for women and children first, and mostly, this call was honoured. Class meant nothing at this stage and both well-dressed gentlemen and roughly clad third-class passengers helped women and children into the remaining boats.

Some men ignored the call, and many were seen, sitting in lifeboats, all classes, including some crew members.

Millie and Sophia were lowered into a boat. It was already crowded, but space was made for them. As they sat huddled together on a thwart, Millie managed a laugh.

'How did you retrieve the doll; I threw it back into the room?'

'I don't know,' replied Sophia, 'when I climbed into the boat, Cassey was already here.'

Millie put her arm around Sophia, both as a comfort and for warmth. The North Atlantic was no place to be out on the water at that time of year.

Sitting in the bow and looking out of place was Alphonse. He had secured a berth on the second attempt. The first time a gentleman passenger had grabbed him by the arm, pulling him away.

'Women and children only, and I recognise you, you're a steward.'

'Let me go,' screamed Alphonse, 'I don't want to die.'

'None of us want to die, but some of us must!' exclaimed the gentleman, punching Alphonse squarely on the nose and sending him backwards.

The man turned away to help others into the lifeboat, ignoring Alphonse. Just as they began lowering the boat down the side of the ship, he jumped, landing heavily on top of two women passengers. By the time the boat was in the water and the lifeboat crew had cast off, the steward had claimed a spot in the bow, risking the wrath of the forward crewmember. The two ladies he had struck on the way down lay in the bottom of the boat nursing injuries, including broken bones. Alphonse was no lightweight.

Victor and Esme stood beside one of the last lifeboats, already packed with people.

'Well, my dear. It has been such a pleasure knowing you, even for so short a time. I hope you reach safety and only ask that in future you think kindly of me,' said Victor.

'Won't you join me? I'm sure there is room for both,' said Esme.

'No, others are waiting and children amongst them. I shall stay here and take my chances,' said Victor. 'Look, the captain remains on the bridge. I can see him supervising.'

He helped Esme into the boat as others lowered children to join her. She gathered the youngest to comfort them. Most were terrified and alone; their parents lost already.

Victor saw the last of the lifeboats away and watched as passengers and crew alike plunged into the cold water, some wearing basic cork lifebelts.

He wandered to the stern, quite a climb as it gradually rose out of the water, the bow already submerged.

Wedged against the ship's fittings and sitting on chairs, the first-class orchestra remained to a man, playing soothing music. There was nothing to be done now but wait for the end, at least the music was superb. Victor hummed to one of his favourite pieces and gently swayed in time. Charlotte was nowhere to be seen, and he assumed she had either managed to get into a lifeboat, or he would soon meet her in the next life.

Lifeboats were well off into the distance when the *Titanic* gave one last enormous groan. The stern rose almost vertically, causing over 1500 people who remained on board to fall if they could not grab a rail. The mighty ship slid beneath the surface, leaving a massive swirl as the sea closed around her. None could survive the pull as the *Titanic* sank to her ultimate resting place.

The lifeboats drifted alone in the vast ocean, attempting to keep in sight of each other. Millie and Sophia, who still held Cassey, sat among the survivors, stunned at the dramatic end to the once mighty ship.

Millie leaned over the side, one hand in the water. It was freezing cold, but it gave her a hold on reality of sorts. Cassey's little porcelain arm shot out, and Millie disappeared over the side with a splash. Sophia screamed,

'No, Cassey, why did you do that? Millie was our friend.'

She saw Millie floundering in the water as they put the boat about. Like so many others in service, Millie had never learned to swim; she had never seen the ocean before the voyage. Sophia, beside herself with grief, jumped into the water to save her friend, leaving Cassey alone on the seat. Sophia was immediately in trouble herself; her clothing weighed her down and even though she could swim, the drag of her coat together with the icy water soon tired her. She reached for Millie and clutched her hand. The pair looked at each other and smiled, before disappearing under the waves, hand in hand.

The boat was very near as they sank, and a splash heralded an attempt to rescue them. It was Alphonse. Finally, he had showed chivalry, but the icy cold water claimed him just as it had the girls.

Cassey remained on the thwart, propped upright by another little girl, both eyes closed.

'I'll cuddle you and keep you warm,' said the girl.

Later that morning in the pre-dawn, the S.S. Carpathia steamed into the area, picking up those survivors who had made it through the night.

Leah clutched the doll as she sat with a hot drink. Her parents had drowned when the ship made its final plunge into the depths. She was an orphan now, but at least she had a new friend.

'I shall call you Cassey,' she said.

CHAPTER 9

Leah

L eah stood at the railing as the Carpathia tied up at South-ampton docks. People were waving at the passengers on deck, but on this occasion, they were not joyful signals but tinged with sadness as they greeted the survivors of the sinking. Many of the children, especially those survivors from third class, were destined for orphanages. Some, the luckier ones, had relatives that were willing to take them in.

Leah did not know what was to become of her. She gripped Cassey as the gangplanks were set up and the first passengers disembarked.

Soon, it was her turn, and she joined a queue of children, shepherded by crew members. Her legs felt funny as they met the stability of terra firma. She seemed to sway as if still on board. A crewman kindly assisted her,

'Don't worry, missy, the feeling will soon go away. Your legs think they are still on the ship.'

Out of the crowd appeared two familiar faces, Leah's aunt, and uncle. She broke into a grin as she spotted them and raised her arms, still holding the doll.

Ester and David Triggerboff smiled in recognition. David reached down and swept Leah off her feet.

'Oh, Leah, we are so sorry about your mother and father, but thank heavens you are safe; we are here to look after you now.'

David was also grieving over the loss of his brother, Leah's father, Samuel, but tried not to show it. He had made such a fuss about the impending voyage to America, where he was, he said, bound to make his fortune. His niece had more than enough grief of her own and didn't need to share in his.

Leah, like the other survivors, had no luggage, so their departure was relatively uncomplicated, and they made their way out of the docks to the train station.

A special London-bound train had been arranged for survivors with plenty of room, and they enjoyed a comfortable journey to the city. Cassey sat next to Leah as the little family dozed to the rhythm of the clickety-clack of wheels passing over joints in the steel railway lines.

Unseen by anyone, Cassey's gaze traversed the carriage, summing up her new family. They didn't seem so bad.

No. 43 Brick Lane loomed out of the chill evening mist. David opened the door, and they filed inside. Ester made for the kitchen to stoke the coal-burning range, which provided heating and the means of cooking for the small two up, two down terraced house in a long line of identical homes. There were several streets of the same design: no difference apart from the numbers on the front doors.

It was a working-class area, but not the bottom of the barrel. The ones at the bottom lived in squalid tenements; entire families occupying one room with a shared toilet servicing each floor.

Such was life in the East-End of London. David was a *cutter* in a large garment factory, a short walk from his front door. His task was to cut out layers of cloth to a specific design for others to sew together. It was a skilful job, and well paid.

They had two boys of their own, and with Leah, it made five mouths to feed. They made up a mattress for Leah by stuffing clean straw into a hessian bag. Covered in a sheet, it made a good bed for her. She weighed no more than a mid-size dog and would be warm and comfortable. Both boys, aged nine and eleven, shared a proper bed, but the old, lumpy mattress meant wiggling around until they could find a pleasant enough space in which to sleep.

The arrangement was not ideal. Leah was eight years old, and it would be better if she had her own room rather than sharing with two growing boys. Alternatively, they could put her in David and Ester's bedroom, but Ester was having none of that.

They might be working-class, but they were not reduced to sharing one room, as many of their co-workers accepted without a quibble.

Ester had a strict Victorian moral code which was exacerbated by her Jewish upbringing. Her and David's marriage had been arranged, and it was not until both families approved of the match, could they tie the knot. However, theirs had been a happy marriage and they seldom if ever argued. The entire family mourned the deaths of David's brother and his wife, and it was unthinkable that any offspring of the match would see the inside of an orphanage.

So it was that Leah spent her first night at number 43. She cuddled Cassey as sleep overtook her, little snuffles announcing to the world that here was an innocent sleeping peacefully.

Not so the boys. Full of mischief, they giggled to each other as they lay side by side in the lumpy bed.

'Go on, have a look,' Aaron said.

He was the eldest at eleven years.

'No,' nine-year-old Daniel replied.

'Come on, we'll both go,' said Aaron.

The boys crept out of bed. Leah's bed was only a few feet away in the small room, brightly lit by the moon shining through the undraped window.

They poised at her side, studying her sleeping form. She lay on her back as Aaron gently lifted the sheet. The next few moments passed in a blur of sheer terror for the boys. As he reached down for her nightie, the doll she was holding moved involuntarily. They looked on in horror as the head swivelled slowly around, the doll's hazel eyes staring into their own, hard, and penetrating.

In a fraction of time, they were back in their bed facing away from the doll. Clinging to each other, they whispered, swearing secrecy to each other. Nobody would believe them anyway.

The following morning, the boys sat at the breakfast table opposite Leah and Cassey. The girl was rested and ate with relish while the two boys left their food untouched. Aaron dared to glance at the doll. Its features remained stolidly neutral. It was only a doll, after all.

Weeks passed into months as life at No. 43 Brick Lane settled into a family routine. The three children attended a local school while David and Ester worked slavishly for the clothing factory.

The nights were the worst for the two boys. Never again were they tempted to satisfy their natural curiosity about the female form. They slept with their backs turned away from Leah and the doll.

Daniel, the youngest, but bravest of the two, had dared to peek twice across the room at the sleeping Leah. On each occasion, the doll had altered position, staring directly at him. He shivered and turned over to face the wall as an icy feeling of dread settled over him. Cassey never slept.

CHAPTER 10

August 1914

Summer in the East End of London was hot and dirty. There were no trees or grass, no cows lowing in fields, merely the same daily grind with the addition of heat. At first, they welcomed the warmth after the inhabitants' suffered months of a long, cold winter. Spring had brought with it an easing of the discomfort, but summer meant hot days with little relief. The terraced houses were constructed to keep occupants warm, not cool. Windows were thrown wide to attract any breezes, but it did little to ease people dressed in heavy clothing. Most had only one set of clothes, which did for all seasons. Nine months of the year were invariably cold and wet, with only the three months of summer showing the difference a little sunshine could make. Sometimes summer didn't bother to attend at all, in which case life went on under a dreary grey sky until moving once again into autumn.

However, the month of August in 1914 was the epitome of halcyon summer days. Many families had taken time off to celebrate the early bank holiday.

The Triggerboff family had been saving a few pennies every week for just this occasion. David and Ester grandly announced that the family would take the train to Clacton-on-Sea on the holiday Monday, August 3rd.

Aaron, Daniel, and Leah danced gleefully hand in hand around the kitchen table. Such was their excitement that the boys even ignored Cassey as they passed her, sitting on a chair, never far from Leah.

Monday morning found the entire family up and about very early. They would catch the earliest east-bound train, planning to spend the entire day on the beach, soaking up the sun and breathing in the bracing sea air.

Ester gently suggested that Leah leave Cassey behind for the day. She would be quite safe indoors, she assured her.

'You are ten years old now. Perhaps it's time to stop taking your doll everywhere. Very soon, you will join others of your age at work. Fourteen is not far off.'

Leah looked away. Part of her wanted to go by herself. Cassey was taking up a deal of her time lately. She talked non-stop, although none but Leah could hear her.

'All right, I will,' she said.

Ester was pleased. She had worried about Leah. She thought that maybe the tragedy of the *Titanic* sinking, and the loss of her parents, might have caused irreparable psychological damage. However, she noticed that Cassey seemed to have taken the place of her mother, and that was not healthy. Sometimes Leah looked at the doll and, scarily, it appeared to be looking back at her.

Leah laid Cassey on the bed and gently explained that she would not be going to the seaside with the family. The doll's features changed slightly, facial features hardening.

'You cannot leave me here alone.' Leah heard her say.

'I must Cassey, Auntie Ester says I can't take you,' she said out loud to the doll.

Leah left quickly, knowing that she could never win an argument against the strong-minded Cassey. The door closed on the doll, saving Leah from the sight of Cassey's rage.

The train journey was the highlight of the holiday for the children. Restricted to the dingy backstreets of East London, the sight of green fields flashing by at speed excited them, combined with the constant stream of steam and smoke passing their window.

By the time they reached their destination, the excitement had reached fever pitch. They walked beside David and Ester to the promenade where the sight of the sparkling sea entranced them. And there, right in front of them, was the yellow sand. As far as the eye could see, miles and miles of sand and all longing to be played upon.

With a word from David, the three children ran onto the sand towards the water. Leah thought she would die from excitement. Gone were the memories of that terrible night in 1912 when the *Titanic* sank with her parents entombed within. They flung off shoes and socks in their eagerness to sample the water. Even the prospect of entering the sea once again did not phase Leah. The boys' excitement carried her over the threshold.

For once, even Cassey was excluded from her thoughts. She felt strangely free. Not a worry in the world. Why had she held onto the doll for so long? Auntie Ester was right. It was time for her to let go of her toys and enter the real world.

They had such a wonderful day that when the time came to trudge back to the railway station; they were almost asleep on their feet. As soon as the train moved away from the platform, all three children were fast asleep.

It was late by the time they walked home from Liverpool Street railway station. The children went straight up to bed; Cassey lay on the bed where Leah had left her. She looked down at the doll with mixed feelings. Part of her regretted not taking her to the seaside, but she also felt that the doll was controlling her far too much. The day away from Cassey had changed her. However, now that she was back in the doll's presence, she felt an instant urge to gather her in her arms.

'You left me,' she heard the doll say.

'It was only for the day,' whispered Leah.

'You left me,' the doll repeated.

Sleep came quickly. They slept soundly until the alarm clock shrilled its unwelcome morning bell.

It was early, and the day appeared to be just another day in the endless weeks of work to come. The excitement of the holiday weekend was over.

Aaron was in his last year. He would leave school at fourteen to start work with his father to learn the skill of a garment cutter under his father's tutelage.

Noon arrived and workers and school children alike stopped for the traditional lunch break. That's when they heard the news. The newspaper vendors were beside themselves, shouting,

'England at war with Germany.'

David went down into the street to buy a newspaper; he normally never wasted money on the trivial gossip printed daily, but this was different. The war would change everything. Young men were roaming the streets chattering excitedly and chanting that the war would be over by Christmas and that they had better get a move on or they would miss out on the fun.

David wasn't so sure; he had an inkling of world affairs and knew this war had been brewing for a while. Crazily, it was first cousins against first cousins. Kaiser Wilhelm of Germany, The Tzar of Russia, and King George V of Great Britain were very close relatives.

That evening at the dinner table, the coming war was the centre of conversation.

'One good thing,' said David, 'I'm too old and Aaron and David are too young, so at least our family will be safe.'

'I cannot believe that so many young men are so eager to join-up,' said Ester. 'They seem to think it will be great fun.'

'Wait until they get to France and find themselves being shot at,' replied David. 'They won't be so keen then.'

In an adjacent street, in a room above a warehouse, an old man began to write. At first, he had written on paper, but when that ran out, he began writing on the walls. In the next room, an equally old woman increased the speed of her knitting. She was working on a multi-coloured scarf. It seemed she was not conscious of how long it should be, just kept knitting.

'Is this the darkness you spoke about?' She shouted.

'Yes,' came the gruff reply from the next room, '*The darkness is coming.*'

CHAPTER 11

World War One, 1914

Initially, things carried on as normal. Apart from a few articles in the newspapers, very little appeared to be happening overseas. Certainly nothing for the everyday citizens of England to worry themselves about.

But gradually things changed. The first telegrams arrived with the dreaded opening line.

'We regret to inform you............'

Young men were being killed and neighbours commiserated with the devastated mothers and fathers. More and more women began dressing in black as a sign of mourning. Men wore black armbands to testify that they had lost a son.

David thanked his lucky stars he was in an industry where he was of more value at home than fighting overseas. Heavily engaged in manufacturing vast quantities of army uniforms, his wages actually increased.

School continued for the children as before. Inside classrooms there was little or no sign of the war raging throughout Europe. Christmas had come and gone, without the predicted *quick victory.* The conflict had reduced to trench warfare, where neither side gained more than a few yards at the cost of many thousands of lives.

Posters were everywhere exhorting young men to join up for King and Country. The many widows that now roamed the streets on the look-out for men out of uniform would hand those unfortunates a white feather, branding them as cowards. Having lost their husbands and sons, they saw no reason others should not lose theirs too. Such was the stupidity of war.

The first anniversary of the war arrived, and the prospect of a quick victory had long since passed. In the second year, food became scarce. Long queues formed at shops for all items of food and Ester spent more and more time shopping. Aaron, too young to go to war, brought home a pittance as they considered him to be learning a trade and was of no value to his employer at that stage.

After their spartan dinner one evening, David and Ester were talking quietly by the small fire. They burnt the minimum amount of coal; it having also become scarce because of the needs of industry. Leah had fallen asleep in a chair snuggled close to Cassey, but the doll's eyes were open and reflected in the flickering firelight.

'We will soon starve at this rate,' said David gloomily.

'What can we do?' Ester replied, 'food is becoming scarcer by the week.'

'I don't want to sound uncharitable, but without Leah to feed as well as the boys, we would be better off,' he replied.

'We can't send her to an orphanage. That would be too cruel,' replied Ester.

'Cruel or not, we have to consider it,' murmured David, 'our boys come first.'

'We'll wait for a while. Maybe the war will be over soon,' she replied, unconvincingly.

Leah snored gently while Cassey stared at the couple, a rage building within.

David gently carried Leah upstairs to bed, Ester followed carrying her doll. She held Cassey as she would a child, one arm encompassing her body while her other hand gripped the stair rail. The odd thought crossed her mind that the doll's eyes should be closed as she lay almost horizontally. Instead, the eyes were wide open and staring directly up at her.

That night their street was bathed in the light of search-lights as they sought a massive German Zeppelin airship passing overhead. It was very high, and soldiers shot their rifles into the night sky with no effect. Two loud explosions shook the house as bombs dropped on the city. This was a new type of war.

One which involved not only trained soldiers, but defenceless women and children huddled below.

The following morning, the street was alive with the news of the previous night's air raid. The primary school had taken a hit, causing some minor damage, but would have to close for repairs. David and Aaron left for work, leaving Ester at home with Daniel and Leah.

'I have to go to the shops this morning,' said Ester, 'you two can come with me or stay here as long as you promise to stay indoors.'

'We'll stay here,' chorused the children; shopping meant long lines of adults waiting to buy what meagre rations were available. No fun for impatient children.

Ester left the house with a final caution for Daniel and Leah to remain inside. No telling what that Zeppelin thing had dropped besides its bombs. There had been tales of colourful packets lying on the ground after they had passed, which exploded in the hands of curious children, causing horrendous injuries.

Leah sat on her bed immersed in an apparent conversation with Cassey. To Daniel, it sounded one-sided, but Leah could hear every word the doll said.

After an hour or so, Daniel said he might go outside to play.

'No, you can't leave the house, Mummy said so!' Exclaimed Leah.

Daniel was furious. He was at that age when he considered himself to be a young man; stay indoors indeed!

'She's not your mum anyway, she's mine,' he retorted angrily.

'Who's *she*, the cat's mother?' Leah jibed in return.

This added to Daniel's fury, who, looking for instant vengeance, grabbed her doll before Leah could react.

'Give her back,' said Leah, her own fury at the affront bubbling to the surface.

Daniel made for the stairs, dragging the doll by one arm, trailing its legs along the floor. At the top of the stairs, he turned to face Leah.

'Me and the stupid doll are going out to play.'

'No!' Screamed Leah dashing forward.

She screamed in terror as Daniel tumbled down the steep stairs. He struck every step as he tumbled head over heels to the bottom.

Leah ran downstairs, tears coursing down her face as she stooped over Daniel. His legs were bent at an odd angle and blood was flowing from a wound in his scalp.

Opening the front door, she ran up and down the street screaming for help until neighbours surrounded her, demanding to know what was wrong.

'Daniel has fallen down the stairs,' she sobbed.

The neighbours found him just as Leah had left him. They shook their heads as the truth dawned. The boy was dead.

At that moment, Ester returned from shopping, dropping her basket in dismay as she saw the crowd at the front door.

She was inconsolable. Her youngest son lay at the foot of the stairs; his pale face surrounded by a crimson carpet of blood.

The police summoned David and Aaron from work, and they quickly made their way home, having been told the tragic news by a local constable. However, Daniel's body had been removed by the time they arrived, leaving only a large blood stain to mark his passing.

Ester sat at the kitchen table; the same table where only that morning they had met for the last time as a family.

She couldn't speak, stunned into silence by the enormity of her little boy's death.

Upstairs, Leah lay on the bed, still unable to comprehend that Daniel had died right before her eyes. She sat Cassey up beside her, propped against a pillow.

'He's dead, Daniel is dead,' she sobbed.

'But you won't have to leave now,' said Cassey.

'What do you mean leave?' Leah asked.

'They were going to send you away to an orphanage, said they couldn't afford to keep all three of you.' Cassey replied.

'What did you do to him?' Leah demanded.

'I didn't do anything, the stupid boy tripped,' said Cassey. 'He pulled me down with him and broke my eye in the process.'

Leah sensed the anger coming from within the doll. It frightened her so much that for once she pushed it away. She lay on her side, staring at Cassey, who stared back with her one remaining eye. The two stared at each other until a wicked grin began to spread across the doll's face.

'You killed him, didn't you?' Leah said, maintaining her frightened stare.

'Yes, I killed him, so what?' Cassey said, the grin widening even further.

'You are evil,' said Leah, her heart breaking at the thought she had been responsible for her brother's death. She lay back on the bed, her eyes closing, blotting out the harsh hazel eye of her hitherto friend before descending into unconsciousness.

That is where David found her, the doll having resumed its inanimate appearance. He panicked. Leah, his adopted daughter, appeared not to be breathing. He shouted down the stairs to Ester,

'Send the doctor upstairs, Leah has collapsed.'

An ambulance sped away from the house, bell ringing furiously as it conveyed Leah to hospital. Ester clung to David. Surely not two children in one day!

Leah never regained consciousness. The doctors said she had died of a broken heart, her frail body unable to cope with the stress of first the sinking of the *Titanic* with the loss of both parents, and then to witness the tragic death of little Daniel.

David carried the blame for both deaths personally. He became morbid and depressed, especially when looking at Leah's doll, which still occupied her bed. The constant begging by Aaron to get rid of Cassey did not help his state of mind. The boy complained endlessly that he couldn't sleep in the same room as the doll. It seemed to stare at him with its one eye always open, even when lying flat, and he begged his father to throw it out. But Ester saw Cassey as the last vestige of contact with little Leah. She had been the sole remaining member of David's brother's family.

The doll began to cause more conflict within the house and sent David into black moods. He was finding it harder and harder to cope. Making things even worse, every day now, the newspapers listed mounting casualties at the front. There was no relief.

Finally, things came to a head one moonlit night. Aaron's bedroom, which he now occupied alone, was bathed in a surreal light which woke him. He looked at the foot of his bed and went cold. Standing up and staring with her one good eye, Cassey seemed to smile directly at him. But it was not a friendly smile, thin lips were contorted into a grimace which very nearly stopped his heart, just as Leah's had.

His scream, when it came, began as a low howl, gradually rising to a high pitch, enough to wake the dead. David burst into the bedroom to confront the sight of his son sitting bolt upright, pointing to the foot of the bed.

'What on earth is the matter?' He asked.

'The doll, it was standing there looking at me,' mumbled Aaron, pasty faced and still shaking.

David glanced across the room at the doll, now lying innocently on Leah's bed.

'Right, I've had enough!' he shouted.

Dressing rapidly, he grabbed the doll and walked downstairs. He was deathly quiet as he walked out of the house and strode down the road. Ester, meanwhile, sat on Aaron's bed to soothe him.

'It was there. I saw it. The doll was standing at the foot of the bed, staring at me,' he cried to his mother.

David never wanted to set eyes on the doll again. His family had been pulled down into the depths of despair since it had entered their lives. Aaron was right, it was evil. Holding it by the arm, he swung it back and forth as he strode down the road, turning the corner into the next street.

Approaching an old warehouse standing beside a patch of empty waste ground, he stopped and looked around. He was alone with the doll, bathed in soft moonlight. Lifting it up, he looked into its face at the one open eye, which became brighter the more he stared at it. Feeling a strange power which seemed to emanate from within the doll, David found himself hesitating; perhaps he should keep it in Leah's memory.

Still holding the doll at arm's length, he was startled when suddenly and with no warning the closed eye flipped up, and he found himself looking into a pair of rage filled eyes.

Crying out, he flung the doll onto the waste ground and ran. He had no idea in which direction he was running. A dreadful fear was filling his soul, blocking out all reason and logic. Tears stung his eyes, limiting his vision as he ran tirelessly. Stumbling across road junctions empty now of traffic, he never wavered. Running like a man possessed. Running from evil.

He never heard or saw the steam locomotive; never felt the blow as it struck him. The feeling of peace came instantly. No more dolls, no more evil; David was free.

CHAPTER 12

Lizzie

The old couple in the warehouse rarely left the building. They appeared never to eat or drink and lived with a sense of urgency. She knitted; he wrote.

'The Darkness is coming.' The only words they ever exchanged.

It had been raining for days when the old lady suddenly announced she would go outside.

'Why?' asked the old man.

'Someone is calling. I have to go,' she replied.

Leaving the warehouse in the early evening, she walked outside with a sense of purpose. In her mind, she could hear a pitiful cry for help.

The cry led her straight to a rain-sodden doll. Its clothes were muddied, and she looked bedraggled. One eye was open, staring at the old woman, who gently reached down and lifted it to her bosom as if it were a human infant.

Returning to the upstairs section of the warehouse, she showed the old man the doll.

'She's back,' her only comment.

She carried the doll into her room. Scattered around the floor were many such dolls. All had damaged bodies. Some with an arm missing and others with no legs.

'I will try to mend you, little one, you have much work to do before the Darkness comes.'

The old woman replaced the doll's dress and attempted to repair its eye, with limited success. It appeared to function perfectly, and then for no apparent reason, the repaired eye closed. The one staring eye hard and bright compared to the bland look when both were open. The old lady tutt-tutted.

'It will just have to do, I suppose. Your new owner is wait-ing.'

The following morning, the old lady left the building be-fore dawn, clutching the doll under her coat. She walked for miles, traversing the city until she reached the more upmarket suburbs of the west.

Reaching an impressive looking Regency style house, she placed the doll on the front step and rang the bell, making a hasty exit from the scene.

Some paces away, she turned to watch, observing the door to the house open. A man ventured out and looked up and down the street, finally looking at the doll at his feet. The old lady thought he must be the butler because of his black suit. She smiled as he stooped to pick up the doll and retraced his steps back into the house.

The old woman had to get back to the warehouse. Daylight would damage her frail skin. She rushed along, seeming never to tire, or run out of breath.

'She is with her new owner,' she said to the old man, who never replied, but quickened his writing as if time was running out.

The butler stood downstairs in the kitchen, holding the doll at arm's length.

'I have no idea why I picked it up off the step,' he said to Mrs Bluff, the housekeeper, 'but for some reason I couldn't help myself. Some poor child will be missing her. Perhaps I should put it back on the step.'

'Let miss Lizzie have it. She loves her dolls and at least it will have a good home,' replied Mrs Bluff.

'You take it to her. I look silly holding a doll,' laughed Mr Dalrymple.

Mrs Bluff reached out for the doll and clutched it as if it were real, not a toy.

'I'll take it up to the nursery directly,' she said, making for the back stairs.

Lizzie sat in her usual place on the floor, surrounded by dolls. She knew each one by name and spoke to them as if they were friends. They were the only friends she had ever had. Her parents never allowed visits from other children.

General Ponsonby-Smythe, Lizzie's father, had very set ideas on the place of children in the greater scheme of things. He yearned for a son to take his place in the illustrious British army when the time came, but his long-suffering wife, Judith, had a frail constitution and doctors had advised them not to try for any more children.

His son, if they had been so blessed, would have gone to the best prep school, on to Eton Public School, then Oxford university, following in his father's footsteps.

Instead of which they had a daughter, completely useless in the General's opinion. A waste of money to educate; all she would need was a sound knowledge of the piano and embroidery. Her mother could guide her in the subjects of deportment and how to behave.

Lizzie seldom saw her father. He never passed the time of day with her, and certainly not at bedtime. That was Nanny's job. The General had not been aware of his own parents until it was time to leave the house for Eton Public School where he would be a boarder, even though it was no distance from home. Children, in his opinion, should be unseen and unheard. They resulted from one's need to procreate and carry on the family name. Although in his case, he knew well that the family name would stop on his demise because Lizzie would one day take her husband's.

Lizzie's eyes lit up when the housekeeper presented the doll. Somehow, she recognised it, surely; she had known this doll before, but she was as yet only eight years old. How could that be possible?

'Cassey,' she cried.

'How did you know its name?' Mrs Bluff said.

Lizzie stared up at the housekeeper, her smile disappearing instantly.

'Her name is Cassey, and I'll thank you to remember that in future.'

Mrs Bluff turned on her heel and left the room without further comment. That little hussy needs a good smack, she thought. Whatever is the world coming to? It must be this wretched war. People are changing and not for the better, in my opinion.

Meanwhile, Lizzie hugged Cassey to her.

'I won't lose you again, I promise,' she said.

'When the time comes, we might have to part again. But only for a little while.' Cassey replied.

Over the course of the following week, Lizzie felt herself bonding more and more with the doll. She took Cassey everywhere, much to her mother's annoyance.

'Really, my dear, must you take that doll everywhere you go? You have so many beautiful, well dressed, and well-turned-out dolls. That one, she said, pointing to Cassey, must be the ugliest doll I have ever seen.'

Lizzie stamped her tiny foot. 'Cassey is not ugly, Mother, you are!' she exclaimed loudly.

Her mother was speechless. Thank goodness there were no servants in the room. Whatever would they think? This was not like her Lizzie at all. Whatever had possessed the child to be so rude.

Lizzie skilfully avoided her mother from that day forward. She began to receive brief subliminal messages from Cassey. One morning, the doll told her she wanted to be alone for a while in her father's study. She was to be tucked away discreetly so that no one would notice her presence.

Lizzie did as she was told. Cassey had bent her completely to her will.

The General was sitting at a large table in his study. Those with him were in uniform or dressed as government ministers.

'We have had a communication from the German high command. The Kaiser believes we should discuss terms for an armistice,' said one minister.

General Ponsonby-Smythe grunted, 'It means we must be winning; the buggers would never sue for peace otherwise.'

'I'm not so sure that is true,' the minister replied. 'We have never before been engaged in this new trench warfare. Each side is dug in, and we fire on each other from fifty yards apart. It's sheer madness and a terrible waste of life on both sides. The prime minister has appointed me to open negotiations with the Germans at the highest level.'

It did not impress the General,

'In my experience, the only solution to war is to win.'

'But that might take forever,' replied the minister. 'We have already been at it for two years and neither side has made any gains whatsoever. At the current rate, we will run out of both men and money.'

The General was not convinced.

'I still think it's a plan by the Germans to lull us into thinking the war is near to an end. Just when we relax, they will launch a huge offensive and we will lose the whole of France.'

'Why are you saying that?' asked the minister, 'surely the opportunity to negotiate an honourable peace is better than sending millions of men to their deaths.'

The General sat back in his chair.

'Quite so, perhaps you are right.'

'Well, then we are in agreement. I will arrange talks as soon as possible, in the next two days,' said the minister, making his way to the study door.

'This war may be over by the end of the week gentlemen,' he said as he stepped out onto the pavement.

After the ministers had departed, the General spoke to his Adjutant,

'Gather my top officers here for a meeting. But mind, it must remain top secret. Not a word to those bumbling idiots at the ministry.'

Cassey sat at the back of the bookcase, listening to every word. She had focussed all her power on the General, putting words into his mouth. His trance-like state went unnoticed.

The following evening, at the hastily arranged meeting in the General's study, he put forward his plan of attack. As soon as the German forces stood down, the British would launch an all-out offensive along the entire battle line. There would be no customary pre-attack artillery bombardment. That would merely warn the Germans.

The attack would be under the cover of an early morning dawn as the two sides were sitting down to hammer out an armistice agreement. Stealth and surprise were the answer, not the usual mass shelling, which seemed to be useless on both sides. The trenches were deep and difficult to hit with the big guns at the rear.

'Remember, not a word until we go over the top,' urged General Ponsonby-Smythe, 'we'll finish this war with one monumental victory.'

Later that evening, the General relaxed in his study. He felt exhausted and took comfort in a decanter of single malt whisky shared with his adjutant, a young captain.

The younger man sipped his drink while the General waxed lyrical over the impending victory over Germany. Captain Brown wasn't paying too much attention. The General could be such a bore. The sight of a doll set deep into the shelf behind the General caught his attention. He stared into a pair of eyes that seemed to get brighter the more he focussed on them. His head became filled with compelling thoughts that were not his own. Captain Henry Brown recalled his youth, when as a young boy he had been known under a different name.

At last, the General signalled the meeting was over. The adjutant rose to leave as the General poured himself another drink. Heinrich Braun gently closed the door, making for the front door and the nearest telephone he could find. Cassey, only inches from the back of the General's head, smiled. Soon, the fun would begin.

The next day came and went. The General had left the house early before dawn could chase away the remaining darkness of night.

Lizzie made her way into her father's study, having woken up to the silent call from Cassey. Now, as instructed, she collected the doll from its hiding place and hurried back to her bedroom. Climbing back into her still warm bed, she cuddled the doll close.

That night, they declared a truce along the whole of the western front. The guns fell silent after two years of fighting over the same piece of ground, which now resembled a morass of clinging mud. Nothing remained of the lush French countryside it had replaced. Thousands of artillery shells fired from both sides had churned the soil more efficiently than all the ploughshares in the world.

Both sides met as arranged at an old chateau. They maintained the secrecy of the meeting, but as agreed, the guns remained silent.

They began the talks in the strangely peaceful atmosphere; even the dawn chorus from birds that had survived the carnage could be heard. Everyone felt their spirits lifted by the unaccustomed sounds of chattering wildlife.

One hour into the meeting, the doors to the room crashed open.

'They are attacking, the British are attacking!' Exclaimed a German officer.

The meeting was in an uproar. British negotiators did not know what was happening and voiced this to their German counterparts.

The German representatives, naturally, didn't believe a word.

'This means all-out war; you have no idea what you have just done. We will drive you into the sea and France will be ours; you are without honour,' screamed the German chief negotiator as he ran from the room.

Outside, they could hear the chatter of machine gun fire

in the distance before louder reports from artillery rent the morning peace.

The attack was a complete disaster. Somehow the German defences had got wind of the impending offensive and were prepared. Far from being taken by surprise, they waited until the approaching British and French forces were more than halfway across no-man's-land before opening fire. They met the unsuspecting attackers with a solid wall of bullets. Rifles and machine guns cut down the advancing soldiers in a swathe of destruction. The first four lines of troops lay dying as the fifth line wavered, looking for orders. Officers blew whistles, signalling the retreat, and grateful survivors turned back towards the safety of their trenches. They had not travelled far when the German artillery opened up, making the return journey as deadly as the advance. The air was thick with smoke and body parts, very few made it back to their own lines. As the barrage ceased, the few surviving troops had to endure loud cheering coming from the German trenches.

The following day heralded the recall of General Ponsonby-Smythe. He was ordered to attend headquarters immediately and knew what was coming.

Lord Mannerston looked up at him from his desk.

'What on earth were you thinking, man? We were about to end this bloody war!'

'I really cannot say, sir. I know it was foolish, but at the time it seemed the sensible thing to do.'

'Well, it wasn't. We have thousands of dead and wounded, and it has severely weakened our position. We can expect a retaliatory attack at any time.'

'I'm sorry and apologise for my actions,' was the only thing the General could think to say.

'You are hereby dismissed from your position, and I am considering a court martial. I'm sure you realise the outcome of that in a time of war,' said Lord Mannerston.

The General knew well what that outcome would produce. He would lose everything, including his life.

Desolate, he returned home. The servants already knew something had happened and endeavoured to steer clear of the master.

Upstairs, Lizzie sat with Cassey,

'I think I just heard the front door. Daddy must be home; would you like to go down and see him?'

Cassey slowly swivelled her head.

'Yes, take me back to the study.'

Lizzie carried Cassey downstairs, placing her in the same place as before, and left the room, climbing the stairs back to her room. Once in bed, she immediately fell into a deep sleep.

Later, the General entered his study with slow, reluctant footsteps. The conversation with his wife had not gone well. He had explained they might lose everything. Money, position, and even the house. They would be destitute, and all because he had made the wrong decision. He sat at his desk, still pondering how that had come about. Anyone in his right mind knew it was a formula for disaster. Especially as the enemy had been tipped off.

Well, it was too late now. There was only one honourable way out of the mess. He poured himself a large whisky from the decanter and sat for a while, contemplating the amber liquid before throwing it back in one gulp.

No point in stalling, he thought. Better get it over with before any interruptions.

Drawing his army issue Webley pistol from its holster, General Ponsonby-Smythe placed the barrel against his temple and closed his eyes. He knew he would have to pull the trigger quite a way before the hammer first drew back, revolving the cylinder so that a bullet was in line with the barrel. Then, at its peak, it would suddenly slam home against the base of the bullet, firing it.

It fascinated him as to how he could sense every fractional movement of trigger and hammer until, for a split second, he felt the trigger give as the hammer released. The .38 calibre bullet tore through his temple, exiting the other side and slamming into the wooden panelling. Most of the General's brains became a bloody smear on the floor.

Cassey watched the event from her vantage point. Everything had gone to plan. There would be no stopping the war now. Millions of men would die in the cloying mud of France and Belgium. The plans were coming to fruition, but it had taken so many years and so many wars; humans bred like rats.

CHAPTER 13

Lizzie stood at her mother's side as the undertakers removed her father's body. The authorities had been informed but did not seem surprised by the turn of events. Whatever else Ponsonby-Smythe might be, he was certainly a gentleman. He did the honourable thing by taking his own life in a manner befitting a man of his rank.

Cassey rested under Lizzie's arm, one eye closed, as the procession moved from the study. They draped the body with a black cloth. Once they had departed, a team of cleaners moved in.

For Judith Ponsonby-Smythe, the world had come crashing down about her ears upon the demise of her husband. There would be no more comfortable salary and she had very little money put away. Running the household with a butler, cook, and servants stretched resources to the limit.

Her first task was to inform the staff they would no longer be required. Faces hung long as she paid them off with a week's wage. The war had taken its toll on the working class. Jobs outside of the war effort were scarce and held on to tightly.

Judith sought the help of her parents, but after the disgraceful behaviour of the General they turned their backs. Judith had nothing. Their splendid house had merely been rented. A fact she was not previously aware of.

She had nowhere to go and nobody to turn to, so in desperation went to the local Catholic priest. Never a keen churchgoer, Judith felt guilty as the priest placed a comforting hand on her head.

'I will try to find a place for you, but in the meantime you and the child may stay here.'

'Thank you, father,' said Judith, almost collapsing with relief.

Father Martin placed a hand around Lizzie's shoulders to comfort her, noticing the doll for the first time.

'And is this yours?' He asked.

'Her name is Cassey,' replied Lizzie.

Father Martin reached down to touch the doll on its forehead but recoiled from the heat. He looked in amazement at his fingertips; they were bright red. The pain began as he stared at them. His face paled, and he recoiled from the girl.

'That doll has the look of evil about it. Look, it burned my fingers when I touched it,' he said, staring at his fingertips. As the words left his lips, the pain increased threefold.

'Out, get out of here. You cannot remain in the house of God for one moment longer. Either the child or that doll is cursed. Maybe both.'

Judith, Lizzie, and Cassey left under the watchful eye of the priest. He stared after them, blinking in surprise as the doll appeared to twist in the girl's arm. Its face stared back at him, both eyes wide open.

The end of the war came with a whimper. People were glad it was at last over. The government had promised the victorious British troops, 'A land fit for heroes.' Instead, the returned soldiers were confronted with massive food shortages.

Judith slumped in the corner of her squalid room. Whitechapel, in the East End of London, contained some of the worst slums. Judith had descended into poverty after her husband, the General, had committed suicide. Disowned and impoverished, she and Lizzie were reduced to the very basest of survival solutions.

In the latter stages of the war, she had no other option but to resort to the life of a prostitute. American soldiers were well paid and there were thousands pouring into the country prior to joining the fighting in Europe. There was only one way for destitute women to survive and it forced hundreds of widowed mothers into selling the only thing they had of value in order to support their children. There was no shame in that. A mother will do anything to protect her own. Lizzie, although now thirteen, clung to her last remaining possession, her doll, Cassey.

In 1918, *Spanish Flu* struck Europe. Millions of people died, their resilience to the virus weakened from years of deprivation caused by the war.

Half the occupants of London appeared to have contracted the virus. There was no cure or medication to ease the suffering, and victims had to suffer the crippling effects. They either survived or died. The pandemic showed no respect for class or money; rich and poor alike died in their thousands.

Judith knew she had been infected and Cassey was overjoyed. The signs were all too obvious. It began as an ordinary cold, rapidly changing to influenza and finally infecting her lungs to such a degree that death because of pneumonia became almost inevitable.

She was in the second stage and knew the end would be swift. She had witnessed many of her fellow slum dwellers die and accepted that her suffering would be great, although mercifully short.

Lizzie tried to comfort her mother, but Judith pushed her away.

'Keep your distance, Lizzie. I don't want you to catch it. It would be best for you to leave and look for somewhere safer.'

Lizzie slumped down against the opposite wall,

'I don't want to leave you here alone. I can look after you,' she sobbed.

With her strength failing, Judith pleaded with her to leave the following morning. It would give her the daylight hours to look for a place of refuge.

Lizzie nodded slowly. She had seen other residents of the building fall sick and die and knew what was going to happen.

The following morning, she woke to the sight of her mother

lying very still on the opposite side of their small room. Lizzie approached with some trepidation, reaching out to touch her mother's hand, but Judith was already cold; she had died during the night. Lizzie pulled away in fear as her hand touched the coldness of death.

A sound from the other side of the room startled her; it was Cassey, sitting up against the wall and laughing. A stunned Lizzie rushed over and grabbed her by the arm.

'How dare you laugh? My mother is dead,' she screamed at the doll.

Cassey stopped laughing abruptly, her eyes hardening,

'She's dead. They are all dead. Those that are not yet dead soon will be. *The Darkness is coming.*'

Lizzie had toughened up in the previous few years. She had seen far more than a delicate little girl should ever have been subjected to. A crash course in survival had taken care of that.

The shock of her mother's death and Cassey's outrageous reaction stirred her into action. Grabbing the doll by the hair, she ran to the window, opened it wide, and hurled the doll as far as she could into the street below.

Cassey landed with a crash on the cobbles as Lizzie returned to her mother's body. She looked down, feeling disgust at the strands of the doll's hair stuck to her fingers.

The doll lay in a heap of twisted limbs, its head showing bare patches where the hair had been ripped out by the force of Lizzie's actions.

There was nothing she could do for her mother, so Lizzie left the building. She knew she would eventually be found and buried alongside thousands of others in mass graves.

Without looking back, she walked away in the opposite direction to where Cassey lay. The doll remained in the street until night settled over Whitechapel.

By morning, a dull overcast sky revealed the empty street. The doll had gone.

CHAPTER 14

'Well, well,' said the old woman from inside the warehouse, 'she's back.'

Cassey was clearly visible from her grimy window. She lay in the street, looking up, both eyes open.

The old lady slowly made her way downstairs and out into the street, where she gently picked up the doll, wondering how it had managed to drag itself there with broken limbs. She cradled it in her arms, cooing softly,

'There, there, my precious one. I will soon have you better. What happened to your hair?'

The following morning, she was propped up against the wall. Encompassed in the ever-growing scarf, the old lady continued to knit. Nothing could be done about her hair, but her legs had been restrung. Cassey stared into the distance through unseeing eyes as morning light penetrated the window. The old couple never slept, carrying on their endless tasks, waiting for the final darkness to descend when they would be free at last.

Nothing changed in the room for several months until the old lady used the last piece of wool on the scarf. She sat disconsolately with empty knitting needles in her hand. The scarf wound around and around the room until it had covered everything in a thick layer of yarn.

The old man looked up with deep-set eyes as she stood in front of his desk.

'No more wool, and it hasn't happened. We have to begin again, from the start.'

The old man shook his head, looking around at the walls on which he had painstakingly written.

'I need ink,' his only comment.

'I will get more,' her brief reply.

Returning to her room, she sat in her usual spot and picking up the end of the scarf where she had only just cast off, began unravelling the yarn, remaking balls of wool as she went. As each ball reached the desired size, she snapped the yarn and started another.

The job would take ages, but there was now no immediate hurry. Peering out of the window, she knew the time had not yet come. Light still ruled the world. She sighed; would the darkness ever come to end their long stay in purgatory?

CHAPTER 15

Roslyn

1929

Days turned to weeks, months, and eventually years. She had knitted and unpicked the scarf several times before clocks struck midnight all over the world, ushering in the year, 1929.

As dawn broke, the old lady noted it was not as bright as usual. Her fear of the light made her conscious of even the slightest variation.

'It's time,' she announced loudly.

The old man grunted in reply.

'This time, or that time; one day you will be right, and it will be *the* time.'

He was busy scribbling over previous layers of writing on the walls. Incoherent to others, only meaningful to himself.

She left the building with Cassey tucked under one arm, heading toward Threadneedle Street in the City.

She was very early, needing to avoid too much daylight hitting her parchment like skin.

At the massive doors of the Bank of England, she placed Cassey on the step before scurrying off back in the direction of her home.

Big Ben struck 9am, and the doors opened. They would be closed again directly, as The Bank of England is not a general bank for use by the public. Rather, it is the central bank of the United Kingdom, dealing with government and other banks only.

However, each morning, it opens its doors as a custom before securing them once more. The security guard in charge of the main doors stooped to pick up the doll. He was not aware of what he was doing. Normally he would leave whatever was on the doorstep for the local rubbish collectors to sweep up, but on this occasion, he cradled the doll in the crook of his arm before stepping back inside and securing the doors.

Harold Fletcher was middle-aged, running to fat, and fond of his undemanding job, which was relatively well paid and secure. At home, he had a wife and six children. Five of the six were the product of his first marriage, his wife, Gladys, having died suddenly during the flu epidemic. He had met a younger unmarried girl, who had a child of her own, and married her at the local registry office.

Their marriage was symbiotic rather than a love match. He needed someone to care for his five children, and she needed a husband to remove the slur of *bastard* from her own child. Having a child outside wedlock was nothing short of disastrous. There would be no help forthcoming from the government, and a young single mother had very little choice. It was either hand her child to the authorities as a waif and stray to live in a home, pending adoption, or taking to the streets as a woman of the night. She had no intention of taking the latter road, as that is how she became with child in the first place. The former alternative she dismissed instantly. There was no way she was giving up her child for adoption.

Harold, having been a widower for several years, had taken to the odd bit of relief now and again with the local prostitutes, from which there were many to choose from.

One evening, as he walked along the street where the local girls hung around waiting for business, he saw a rather attractive young woman who didn't seem to fit in. She looked completely out of place amongst the gaudily dressed prostitutes, and intrigued, he approached her.

'How much?' He asked casually.

She turned on him, giving him a healthy round of abuse and how dare he mistake her for a common tart.

After much apologising on Harold's part, she saw the funny side, and they both burst into laughter. He invited her to join him in the pub for a drink and so they began a friendship which quickly developed into an intimate relationship.

Lizzie egged him on with some speed, seeing a way out of her dire situation, while Harold enjoyed the charms of a much younger woman with the bonus of finding a new mother for his children. That she already had a child meant nothing to him. It merely meant there were six children instead of five. Her daughter, Roslyn, was young, and he quickly adopted her as his own after they married. She had a sweet nature and a quick smile.

The neighbours were very accepting of their marriage despite the difference in ages. After the war, and then the catastrophic flu epidemic, there were so many widows and widowers, it seemed logical that the survivors should pair up and get on with their lives.

The doll Harold had found sat in a spindle backed chair in his little office by the front door. At the close of business, he carried it home for little Roslyn. It looked a little scary, with tufts of hair missing and one lazy eye, but he knew the girl would adore it. In the coming years, he would come to regret the decision, but at the time, he thought only of his newly adopted daughter's joyful reaction at being presented with the doll.

'Daddy, daddy, is it really for me?' Screamed Roslyn in delight when Harold presented her with the doll.

'Yes,' he replied, 'she is your very own, nobody will ever take her away from you.'

Unsure why he had made such a firm commitment to the girl, he called his wife.

'Come, and see Roslyn's new friend,' he called.

The door opened and Roslyn's mother walked in, pausing when she saw the doll in Roslyn's arms.

'Isn't she beautiful, Mummy? I will call her Cassey.'

'Of course you will,' replied Lizzie quietly.

Cassey's closed eye popped open when Lizzie came into the room. She felt the latent power emanating from the doll and shivered, already feeling the power from Cassey as their eyes met. Somehow, the doll had found her, and now Lizzie's daughter had taken her place. She knew Roslyn would not be able to resist the doll, as she herself could not.

The doll had taken on an even greater evil appearance, thanks mostly to the ripped-out hair. Lizzie remembered that sickly feeling of the doll's hair on her fingers after she had thrown it out of the window, thinking that she would never have to look at it again.

Cassey seemed to read her thoughts. She had imperceptibly moved her head to be facing Lizzie, the malevolent stare frightening in its intensity. Lizzie was unable to maintain her own stare and quickly looked down.

The other children filed into the room to see what all the fuss was about. They ranged in ages from sixteen down to eight. Roslyn was only six years old.

The oldest, Ralph, looked at Roslyn, holding the doll.

'It's ugly,' he said. 'Where did you find it?'

'Cassey is not ugly,' screamed Roslyn, shocking the boy with the loudness of her rebuff.

'Now, now,' said Lizzie, startled by the sudden change in her daughter's usually kind nature, 'don't be unkind to your brother.'

She remembered the capabilities of the doll and attempted to placate it. 'I'm sure he didn't mean what he said.' One look at Cassey's face told her she had failed.

'I am not her brother,' shouted Ralph, biting back at Roslyn.

'Stop arguing, we are all one family,' said Harold, regretting bringing the doll home in the first place. He couldn't even remember why he had. Ralph was right, the bloody thing was ugly.

He was happy for the first time in years until this toy arrived, delivered by his own hand. It was already coming between them, dividing them.

Roslyn, hugging the doll, ran upstairs to the bedroom she

shared with the other children. There were two double beds, one for the girls and one for the boys.

The others joined her and with the six of them in the room; it became rather crowded. Cassey had pride of place, sitting up in Roslyn's bed. One eye was open wide, but the other adopted its closed position, giving the doll a very eerie look.

'I think she is nice,' said Brenda, one of Harold's daughters.

'Thank you,' said Roslyn. 'Cassey was very pleased to hear you say that.'

'How did you know?' Asked Brenda.

'She told me; didn't you hear her?'

'No,' said Brenda, 'why, did you?'

Roslyn looked around at the others.

'Did any of you hear Cassey speak?'

Ralph laughed,

'Of course not, she's a stupid doll, she can't talk.'

'But I heard her,' whispered Roslyn, herself afraid now. How could it be that Cassey spoke only to her?

That evening, the family gathered around the table for dinner, only they referred to it as *tea*. Only posh people had dinner in the evenings, and what they referred to as *lunch* was known to the working class as *dinner*.

Lizzie called Roslyn to one side, speaking quietly.

'Why don't we buy you a brand-new doll? You can choose her, and she will be just yours, and yours alone, wouldn't that be nice?'

'No!' Roslyn exclaimed, her face darkening. 'Cassey is mine now, and she is beautiful.'

Lizzie was shocked at her daughter's reaction. She had always been such a sweet child but had changed overnight. It was Cassey, and Lizzie knew she had an evil nature.

As the family sat down to eat, Lizzie slipped upstairs. She gingerly picked up the doll and carried it out of Roslyn's bedroom. She had to get rid of it.

The doll turned its head to face Lizzie, the one open eye gleaming brightly,

'Put me back or you will never see your daughter again.'

Lizzie stopped in mid-stride, shaking inside, recognising the doll's voice from long ago.

'You cannot hurt my daughter; I will destroy you first.'

Cassey's lips twisted in a snarl.

'You fool, you do not know who you are dealing with. I am invincible. No matter what you do to this body, I shall remain, and it will be your daughter who will suffer. Now, put me back.'

Lizzie felt a deep sense of foreboding. She couldn't win. She believed that the day she had thrown the doll out of her window and watched it crash onto the road would be the end of their relationship. However, Cassey was back. Maybe the doll was right, maybe she was invincible. Deciding she couldn't take the chance with her daughter's life; Lizzie reluctantly returned the doll to Roslyn's bed.

Cassey spoke in her soft voice,

'There, that's better, and as a reward I will enrich your life; you will come to love me again as you did in the past.'

Lizzie left the room, seriously doubting that Cassey could give love.

Harold was lecturing the children on the wonderful state of the world's economy. There had never been so many millionaires created in so short a time. The stock market was booming both at home in Britain and across the Atlantic in America. It was a unique phenomenon. Everybody appeared to be smiling. Shops were doing good business, and manufacturers were finding it hard to keep up with demand. The many private banks were happy to lend vast sums to a new breed of stock market entrepreneurs, who seemed to know just what stocks to buy, turning a huge profit in a matter of weeks.

Harold Fletcher was normally by nature a cautious man, but as he sat in the kitchen across the table from Roslyn and her doll, he had an idea. He couldn't help overhearing a conversation the other day about a certain company which was about to be listed on the exchange. He knew it was privileged information and that he should not act upon it, but as his eyes met the one open eye of the doll, it seemed to brighten in intensity, and his mind was made up.

Harold had all his money squirrelled away in a private bank located around the corner from The Bank of England. He had always been a frugal man and had saved every spare penny for a rainy day.

He made an appointment to see his bank manager the following day and laid out his plan to convert his savings into shares. Greed was rife, and the manager insisted upon knowing the company in which Harold would invest, using the excuse that he was merely looking after his interests.

He looked up the company in question and immediately offered to lend Harold double the money he had on deposit so he could make more money. The manager would also invest his own cash; all of it. This was his big chance to join the ranks of the many millionaires who used the bank, he was envious of their quick rise to wealth. One day they came in smoking a cigarette, the next a big cigar, and he wanted to join their ranks. He and Harold sat together as they placed their orders with the bank's brokers. Within minutes, they both owned pre-issue shares, the manager becoming a major stockholder for the soon to be listed company.

Harold went to work afterwards, feeling nervous but also tingling with excitement at the prospect of perhaps doubling his money.

The weeks that followed saw his investment double, then triple, and finally run away in value. On paper, he was a millionaire. He knew his bank manager would by now be a multi-millionaire.

It was breakfast in the Fletcher household. Monday 21st October. Harold sat opposite Roslyn, as usual, who held Cassey on her lap. His eyes were drawn across the table to the gaze of Cassey's one good eye. It seemed to glow brighter, and Harold was about to pass comment when he heard the voice in his head,

'Sell all your shares today and deposit the money with The Bank of England.'

He continued to look at the doll. Surely, he hadn't heard it talk. Why should he sell his investment when it was bound to double in value over the coming months? How bizarre.

The more he stared at the eye, the brighter it appeared until it shone into his eyes like the sun on the brightest day.

Breaking the stare with difficulty, he grabbed his coat and made for the door.

Arriving at the Bank of England, he sought an audience with the general manager, begging him to allow his lowly employee to deposit the proceeds of an impending sale of shares.

The manager said he could oblige him, as there was an arrangement whereby any employee of the bank was allowed an account.

Harold's next task was to contact the broker directly and instruct him to sell all his shares at market price, forthwith. The broker questioned the wisdom of his decision, saying his shares were already rising steeply that morning and did he have inside information? He could hardly say that he was acting on information received from a child's doll and instead used the excuse that he considered he had made enough money and wished to convert his holdings into cash.

His shares were snapped up immediately by greedy investors, and in a few days, the cash would be in his newly opened account with the Bank of England.

A strange peace enveloped him for the rest of that day. It was as if someone had lifted an enormous weight from his shoulders. He stopped on the way home to buy an enormous bag of sweets for the children and a bunch of flowers for Lizzie.

During the usual boisterous family time at the table that evening, he caught Roslyn's eye. She was smiling at him in a special way, and on glancing at her doll, he caught the same expression. Both Cassey's eyes were wide open.

That Wednesday, they confirmed his deposit at the bank

from the sale of his shares. Harold was a cash millionaire. He entered the manager's office and tendered his resignation.

'I cannot say that I blame you, Harold, or should I say, Mr Fletcher. You no longer need the small wage we pay you. Good luck, I say, and I will be happy to advise you regarding investing your newly gained wealth.'

Harold left the bank, almost dancing a jig as he walked down Threadneedle Street. He made the announcement at the dining table that evening that he no longer held a position at the bank and would, from that day forward, live the life of a gentleman of leisure.

Lizzie sat opposite later that evening.

'I'm glad you sold the shares; something is not right.'

'How do you mean?' Harold asked.

Lizzie paused before answering,

'I don't profess to understand the complexities of high finance, but surely things cannot keep going up. There must be a point when they reach the top of the mountain and begin to fall down the other side.'

'Very profound, my dear,' said Harold. 'I have witnessed so much greed in the past two years. It's a kind of madness. Nobody wants to be left out of this astonishing boom, but as you say, it cannot last forever. Maybe I jumped out too soon, only time will tell.'

'Well, at least we do not have that worry any longer,' said Lizzie, 'the only thing we have to do is to plan the rest of our lives, preferably away from the dinginess of London. Somewhere in the country would be nice.'

They retired to the privacy of their bedroom in the small house, both excited at the prospect of a new life funded by Harold's newly gained fortune.

Lizzie had purposely avoided looking at Cassey since their conversation about Roslyn, fearing the power that she knew the doll was capable of. However, she was equally sure that Cassey had promoted their recent good fortune. Maybe the doll had turned over a new leaf. Perhaps she was trying to make up for the past?

The morning began as usual. Breakfast routine never varied apart from the fact that this morning Harold did not rush out, making his way to work at the bank. The children had caught the fever of newfound wealth, and each had a list of things they desperately needed and simply could not do without. Harold laughed good-naturedly.

'Settle down, you lot. Your lives will certainly change, but maybe not in the manner of your choosing. The first priority is to find a bigger house, and the second is your schooling.'

This was met with groans of displeasure from all the children.

They trudged off to school while Harold settled down to read the morning paper.

He eagerly scanned the financial section, but everything appeared to be normal. The mass hysteria still centred on buy, buy, buy.

He was not used to sitting around the house and becoming bored, announced they should get dressed up and go into the city.

'It's a long walk,' said Lizzie.

'Who said anything about walking?' Laughed Harold, 'We'll walk to the main road and hail a cab.'

'I've never been in a taxi,' said Lizzie excitedly. 'that's only for the wealthy folk.'

'Lizzie, now we are the wealthy folk. Get dressed up and we'll go into the city for lunch.'

'Don't you mean dinner?'

'No, we call it lunch now, my dear. Us wealthy people always refer to the midday meal as lunch,' smiled Harold, 'and while we are on the subject, in future, I will address you as Elizabeth.'

'Oh, my,' whispered Lizzie, 'we will sound posh.'

An hour later, they were in the back of a cab, heading for the city.

When they arrived, they could see something unusual was

unfolding. Threadneedle Street was packed with men running back and forth. Not working men, but city types, dressed in smart suits. They had in common the shared look of anxiety.

Harold stopped a man and asked what was going on. The man threw up his hands, almost in tears,

'The market has crashed. It began in America overnight and now it has hit here. Share prices are tumbling, there are no buyers. I'm ruined!'

Harold led Lizzie around the corner to his old bank and was pulled up short by a crowd of angry men.

'Get in line, we all want our money. Wait like the rest of us,' one of them snarled.

Leading Lizzie to the relative safety on the other side of the street, he paused to watch.

A man who he recognised as the manager appeared at the door waving his hands.

'The bank is closed, we have no more cash, I'm sorry.'

The crowd rushed towards him as he retreated inside, slamming the solid doors closed with a bang.

Grown men now stood unashamedly in tears as they realised that in a moment, their savings had disappeared into thin air. Shares were worthless, and it had reduced many banks to a state of bankruptcy themselves.

Inwardly, Harold congratulated himself for having had the wisdom to deposit his cash with the Bank of England. A stray thought crossed his mind as the face of Cassey flashed into his consciousness. Surely not? He thought.

The weeks following the stock market crash were difficult for everyone. Except Harold and Lizzie. They had to witness their friends and neighbours endure the loss of jobs and loss of wages.

Feeling not a little guilty, Harold planned to move as soon as possible. He had no wish to witness the agony of his desperate neighbours and, with a distinct sense of self preservation, kept the secret of his wealth to himself, admonishing Lizzie, and the children to say nothing lest they become the targets of desperate folk.

One dark and rainy night, they decamped en masse from their rented home, settling into a reasonable hotel on London's fringe.

They had a suite of rooms with separate bedrooms for themselves and the children. Lizzie no longer had to cook meals. They ate as a family in the hotel dining room, waited on by deferential servants.

Over the course of the following days, the family disposed of their clothes, exchanging them for completely new wardrobes. They were, apart from their diction, part of the newly risen class of people that had money. A rare commodity in the latter part of 1929.

Harold and Lizzie explored the suburb of Hampstead Heath, leaving the children in the care of hotel staff. The area was literally a breath of fresh air to the couple. Wide open spaces with grassland and trees dominated the area. It was such a juxtaposition to where they came from that they stood staring for some while, turning around in circles, marvelling at the view.

Walking along a wide street lined with four story mews houses, they could only stare and wonder. They stopped at a sign advertising the property for sale. It stated boldly that it was a *mortgagee sale,* and Sidney assumed the owner was one of the many well-heeled people who had suddenly fallen on hard times because of the world financial crisis.

He noted the telephone number of the agent. Lizzie stared at him.

'Surely, we cannot possibly afford this?'

Harold chuckled,

'This and many like it, my dear. I will contact the agent to arrange an inspection.'

'Oh, my,' replied his wife, 'this must be a dream and I shall wake in a moment.'

'It's no dream. We will spend the rest of our lives in luxury,' he laughed.

The following day, they met the agent at the address and

arrived promptly.

'Are you sure you can afford this?' Richard Melville asked them rudely.

He was the senior partner in the estate agency handling the sale on behalf of the bank. A bank that had managed, so far, to ride out the storm, but they needed to claw back as much cash as they could from defaulting borrowers to meet the demands of depositors lining up every day to withdraw their savings.

Similar signs to the one under which they now stood were popping up all over the country as the jobless grew in number. No job meant no wage, which led to no mortgage repayment.

Harold raised himself slightly on his toes as he replied.

'Can you afford to be rude to a man with one million pounds lodged with the Bank of England?'

He knew it was rather gauche but couldn't resist putting the pompous agent down.

Richard realised his error of judgement; he was still adjusting to this new era of the *Nouveau Riche.*

'I'm so sorry, sir. One has to be careful these days, one never knows who one might be speaking to.'

He was merely digging the hole deeper, and Harold smiled gleefully as the agent recognised his faux pas.

'Let's go inside,' said the red-faced agent, 'please call me Richard.'

'Thank you, Richard, you may call me Mister Fletcher,' replied Harold glibly.

This casual remark finally reduced the agent to adopt a servile attitude. He needed to make a sale and was now aware he was already offside with this potential buyer.

However, once inside, Harold and Lizzie resumed their previous station in life. Totally in awe of the rooms and furnishings, they could only stumble from room to room, speechless.

Richard was once again in his element.

'The property is for sale fully furnished, walk in-walk out, so to speak.'

'How much?' Harold asked.

The agent cleared his throat, juggling figures in his head. What sum could he extract from this jumped-up nobody who had so rudely put him down?

'Two thousand pounds, and it's a steal at that price,' he said.

Now, Harold might have been a lowly security guard at the bank, but he had spent many years eavesdropping around important clients and their discussions. In short, he was familiar with the cut and thrust of dealing and recognised that the man standing before him was attempting to extract a large sum of money for a property that a bank was desperate to sell.

'Rubbish,' said Harold, 'I will contact the bank direct and find out how much they require to clear the debt.'

Richard could see a healthy commission rapidly sliding from his grasp and ran after him who, with Lizzie in hand, was exiting the house rather quickly.

'Let me contact the bank and negotiate on your behalf,' he pleaded.

Harold turned to face him at the entrance.

'Sir, you have lost my trust. I would rather deal direct. In that way I know I will pay a fair price.'

'But you don't know the bank that holds the mortgage,' said Richard, desperate to save the situation he had himself created.

'A call to my bank will soon solve that conundrum. I'm sure the mortgagee will be glad to have a cash offer. Especially with no agent's fee involved.'

They left the speechless agent at the house. Harold had at first merely intended to give him a fright before making an offer, but the man's superior attitude had annoyed him. He was even more annoyed that the man had completely ignored Lizzie. How dare he.

She had never witnessed this new quality in her husband and hardly recognised him. Harold had effortlessly morphed from doorman to the super wealthy in a flash. She hoped she could keep up and not disgrace him with her common approach and appearance. Even though she now wore fine clothes, she felt that the transformation was not complete. Underneath, she was the same East Ender.

The next day, Harold called his old boss. He could feel the tension through the receiver.

'Things are not good,' began his old employer. I lost everything. Every penny I had put away, and more besides. The bank will close its doors permanently at the end of the week. They and I are flat broke.

He felt genuine pity for Ernest Balham. The manager had always been good to him and had helped him buy the shares in the first place. The fact his own greed had consumed him didn't matter. Thousands were in the same position. Harold had been lucky enough to sell just before the crash. The more he thought about that, the more he believed he was blessed with good fortune. Cassey's advice had completely disappeared from his mind.

Harold explained he needed to talk to whichever bank was selling off the house in Hampstead Heath. A thought struck him, and he added that naturally there would be a hefty cash commission in it for Ernest. That would be a way to help his old employer without the rankle of charity.

Ernest was no fool and guessed the generous intentions of his old employee. However, he needed money to support his family so readily agreed.

'Call me in two hours. That should be long enough for me to get the details and give you a price, and it will be the best price, Harold, I assure you.'

'I know that Ernest, I trust you,' said Harold.

Two hours later, he had the necessary information.

The mortgagee would be more than willing to deal directly with him, and the suggested amount was a real bargain. Harold planned to transfer funds and later that day he conveyed the news to Lizzie that they were the proud owners of a luxurious mews house in Hampstead Heath.

In two weeks, they entered the house clutching a full set of keys. The bank had hurried the transaction through, desperate for funds. As the furniture and fittings were included, they had no need to do anything except settle in. The children were amazed. They had come from near poverty in the East End to up-market privilege in one fell swoop.

Harold and Lizzie had hastily arranged two live-in maids and a cook, positions were becoming scarce and there were many applicants for the positions. The new members of the household started the same day. Their rooms were at the very top of the house, and a narrow set of stairs at the rear led up from the basement kitchen.

Roslyn, Brenda, and Amie shared a bedroom while the three boys, Ralph, David, and Cedric, shared another across the hall-way. Lizzie and Harold had a bedroom each joined by a connecting door. That, as he explained, was how the wealthy chose to spend their marriage. He, however, insisted they occupy one bedroom. He enjoyed cuddling up to his wife every night and had no intention of changing.

Lizzie laughed as he explained the sleeping arrangements of their supposed betters.

'Little wonder they have such cold natures,' she said.

Harold smiled in agreement.

CHAPTER 16

Lizzie was deliriously happy. All her wildest dreams had come true. She was now in a position far beyond any expectation she may have fostered as a young girl. Life was perfect. She was making a distinct effort to correct her speech, gradually changing her diction from the East End parlance to that of the wealthier upper middle class of the *better* suburbs. Harold didn't bother. While being aware of his wife's efforts, he preferred to stick to his roots.

The children, however, were encouraged to improve their own diction to better fit in with the new surroundings and the new private schools they were about to attend.

Then something happened that would forever change the situation. Harold, always wanting to spoil Lizzie's daughter, even at the expense of his own children, arrived home one day with a fancy wrapped box.

Presenting it with a flourish to Roslyn, he made an announcement.

'Out with the old, and in with the new. This shall be the way we live now.'

Paper wrapping was torn asunder in her eagerness to get at the contents. None of the children could remember receiving presents, let alone wrapped in fancy paper.

At last, the box was exposed, and Roslyn sat hugging the exposed box amidst the carnage that used to be wrapping paper. Harold laughed,

'You enjoyed that, didn't you?'

Roslyn smiled up at him,

'Yes, Daddy, thank you so much.'

Harold's children looked on, unsmiling now. Where were their presents, and Roslyn shouldn't call father *Daddy*?

Harold and Lizzie were so intent on watching Roslyn that neither noticed the change in atmosphere. A coldness had enveloped the room.

As the lid of the box opened, the youngest of their shared children beamed.

'Oh, Daddy, she's perfect.'

Roslyn carefully wrapped her arms around a new doll and lifted it from its container. It was of the very best quality that money could buy. A porcelain body, with a pretty head covered in golden curls. Soft blue eyes looked out onto the world, seeming to spread joy into the room.

Harold rocked back and forth on his heels, enjoying the moment.

'A new doll for a new life. That ratty old thing upstairs can go to the dump. We, or rather you, cannot be seen carrying a dirty, broken doll around this neighbourhood. It just wouldn't do.'

Roslyn didn't hear one word. She was in love with her new doll.

'I shall call her Antoinette,' she announced, 'a beautiful name for a beautiful doll. Thank you, Daddy.'

Ralph clenched and unclenched his fists in pure anger. He didn't trust himself to speak, instead leaving the room to make his way upstairs.

As he passed the girls' bedroom, he thought he heard a voice. It wasn't a child's voice, and he assumed it was one of the newly engaged maids.

'I gave them everything and now I'm to be thrown away.'

Ralph hesitated, opening his sister's bedroom door, and peering inside. Roslyn's old doll, Cassey, appeared to be sitting up in bed looking straight at him.

Ralph remained silent but could not break the stare of Cassey's one eye.

'Come in, don't just stand there,' she said.

He stepped into the room, closing the door behind with a soft click.

Inside he was terrified. The doll talked. He wanted to run from the room, downstairs and out of this house. But he simply couldn't make his legs work. Instead, he walked towards the doll.

'You will look after me, won't you?' Cassey ordered him.

Ralph broke out in a sweat as he slowly nodded his head.

'You will have to hide this *ugly old doll*, but you and I shall remain together,' she said.

Ralph approached her and gingerly lifted her off the bed. Her warm body surprised him. It was only a porcelain doll. There should only be coldness, not warmth. The doll felt human to his touch, and he almost dropped it in surprise.

'Don't drop me you fool!' exclaimed the doll angrily, 'hide me, they must not find me.'

Holding the doll, Ralph descended the stairs, passing the parlour and ignoring the sound of Roslyn still admiring her new doll. He left through the back door, making his way into the small rear garden to a wooden shed. Opening the door and spying a solid looking box in the corner, he lifted the lid and placed the doll inside.

'You will be safe here,' he said, barely able to believe he was talking to a doll. The open eye stared back at him, and he once again heard the raspy female voice. It came from the doll, the small porcelain lips somehow moving, sending cold shivers down his spine.

'We will talk again, you and me. I hate being let down, and they all need to be punished, starting with the new doll; that will be your task. Make sure you do a good job.'

Ralph left the shed, pausing to slide a large nail through the hasp, securing the door. He assumed the doll could not move by itself but wasn't taking any chances.

Opening the parlour door quietly, he slipped inside. Roslyn sat in a chair with Antoinette perched on her lap. The other children looked on, their jealousy clearly on view but apparently unnoticed by his father and stepmother. Putting an arm around

Brenda's shoulder, he whispered.

'I'm sure they will get you something nice as well.'

Brenda looked up at her older brother, a tear slipping down her cheek,

'I wish I had a beautiful doll.'

Ralph could feel his anger building. How dare they ignore the rest of the children? Why should Roslyn get everything? It had been the same since the day she had walked into their lives. He was aware he was overreacting and that Roslyn, up to this point, had not received preferential treatment but could not quell the anger bubbling dangerously to the surface.

Before things could get out of hand, the group broke up. Harold and Lizzie retired to the sitting room, while the children made their way upstairs to prepare for the evening meal, or dinner, as they had come to think of it. Delightful smells were already creeping upstairs from the kitchen, which made them eager to change and return to the dining room, that had by now already been laid out by the servants.

Roslyn proudly carried her new doll to the bedroom and sat it on her bed, leaning Antoinette against the pillows.

Looking around the room, she frowned. Where was Cassey? In her excitement, her old doll had slipped her mind completely. Where was she?

Entering the boys' room, she asked,

'Have you seen, Cassey? She's missing.'

Ralph replied without looking up,

'Maybe it heard you downstairs with your pretty new doll and left,' he hissed.

Roslyn searched the entire floor and then downstairs, but Cassey was nowhere to be seen. Cook and the maids listened to her plea patiently before replying they were sure the doll would turn up somewhere. They had work to do, the family would soon sit down for dinner, and it had better be ready.

The meal was a sombre affair. The ill feelings of the other children had negated the excitement of Roslyn's new doll. Harold attempted to lift the mood by promising them a special treat, but the damage had already been done.

After the meal, the children were sent to their rooms. Harold wanted some time with Lizzie and even though this house was so much larger than their old home, they never seemed to get the opportunity to spend time together. If it wasn't the children, it was the maids. They entered and left rooms without so much as a by your leave, which annoyed Harold to the point of distraction.

He had settled into the comfy overstuffed lounge settee and reached out for Lizzie, needing her company and warmth urgently.

A loud scream from upstairs shattered the moment. Jumping to his feet, he raced upstairs to find Roslyn staring at her bed, still screaming.

'My lovely new doll. Who could have done such a thing?'

Harold looked beyond her to the bed. The new doll lay spreadeagled on the bed. Its arms had been torn off together with one leg. Someone had roughly pulled out her hair and one eye had been pulled out. It lay grotesquely on the bed, even its clothes were ripped and dirtied.

Harold put a comforting arm around Roslyn, remaining silent. What could he say?

The other children stood quietly at the bedroom door. Roslyn turned to confront them, pointing an accusing finger at Ralph, who stood, pale faced with fingers nervously twitching at his sides.

'You, it was you. I know it was. You are jealous of me because Daddy loves me more than you!' She exclaimed in a burst of anger.

Harold was about to issue a vehement denial, but before he could utter a word, Ralph lashed out with his fist, catching Roslyn full in the face. Her nose disappeared in a cloud of foaming blood, flattened against her pretty face.

Harold saw red and delivered a massive blow to his son. Ralph dropped like a stone, remaining still.

Lizzie looked on in horror as Brenda and Amie screamed

in terror while David and Cedric bolted downstairs, fearing the wrath of their father. They had never witnessed this side of his nature.

The sight of Ralph laying comatose quickly brought Harold to his senses, and he knelt by his side. Ralph appeared to be lifeless as Harold gently slapped his face to bring him round. When that didn't work, he slapped harder until Lizzie shouted for him to stop. She had stilled the girls' screams by pushing them into the boys' bedroom.

'Harold, stop!' she yelled, kneeling beside Ralph. She felt for a heartbeat and when none could be found, she looked into her husband's anguished face.

'He's dead, you killed him.'

Harold walked downstairs, his head reeling from what he had done. He had killed his own firstborn son with a single blow.

Roslyn, trailing blood, crawled across the floor and into her mother's arms. Lizzie looked down at her flattened nose and cried. Up to that point she had been too shocked, but now the first tears cascaded down her face, dropping onto her daughter, mingling with her blood.

David and Cedric had collided with one maid in their desperation to escape their father.

'Father has killed Ralph,' said David, Cedric nodding his head vigorously in agreement.

The maid, horrified, ran into the street shouting, 'Murder,' at the top of her voice.

This was not a common occurrence in Hampstead Heath, and her cries quickly brought neighbours out into the street. Somebody called the police and within minutes they were on the scene.

Harold had entered a trancelike state and wandered off across the heath. Dusk was coming on and he walked aimlessly, blind to the enormity of what had just happened.

'My husband hit his son because he hit my daughter,' said Rose, showing the police officers her daughter's bruised and bloodied face.

'No matter the reason, the boy is dead, and that is murder,' said one officer, 'where is the father now?'

Lizzie shook her head, 'I don't know. He is distraught. Harold never meant this to happen. He would never purposely hurt any of the children.'

The officer knelt beside the boy to examine him.

'The blow crushed his face. I would say that death would have been instant, but the coroner will know better after an autopsy.'

At the mention of an autopsy, the finality of death suddenly struck Lizzie and she once again dissolved into tears. Brenda and Amie rushed from the boys' bedroom and wrapped their arms around her. Shielding Ralph's body from them as best she could, Lizzie led all three girls downstairs, where the two maids and cook stood, staring at the floor.

David and Cedric made their way outside via the back door, neither speaking as if by mutual agreement, walking along the path towards the rear gate. They had no plans but didn't want to return to the house where their brother lay.

Passing by the shed, David glanced at the window and froze. Framed in the grimy pane of glass, Cassey stared at them with her one good eye.

Cedric bumped into him and, following his brother's gaze, looked directly into the brightly shining eye.

The boys bolted, leaving by the gate, and running without looking back.

CHAPTER 17

Dawn broke over the heath as Harold woke up with a raging headache, having fallen asleep near a pathway. He had not gone unnoticed by early morning walkers, and getting to his feet, began walking again. But where should he go? The events of the previous day had become cloudy in his mind.

The sight of two police officers startled him, and he turned in the opposite direction. It was enough to arouse their suspicions, and they followed him.

Glancing back, Harold spotted them striding purposely. Increasing his own pace, he looked back to see they were gaining on him. He broke into a trot, then a full run. Police whistles blared out their ear-splitting sound and his legs turned to jelly. Yesterday's tragedy had finally registered, and he knew he was done for. Sinking to the ground on his knees, he waited for his pursuers.

'What's the hurry?' A police officer asked.

Harold couldn't answer.

'Why did you run away?' Insisted the police officer.

'Scared,' mumbled Harold.

'Been sleeping rough, by the looks of it. You had better come with us,' said the other police officer, reaching down to help him to his feet.

Harold walked between the two officers, realising that they didn't know who he was or what he had done. That knowledge gave him strength.

When the police officers least expected it, he broke free and ran away. They stood, looking at his fast disappearing back, and shrugged their shoulders. Another vagrant sleeping on the heath, nothing new there.

Harold headed home, Lizzie and the others would need him. He walked forlornly into the line of mews houses, noticing a lone police officer standing at the door.

He tried to walk past the officer but before he could get the door; the officer challenged him.

'And who are you?'

Harold looked at the man with a quizzical look,

'I'm Harold Fletcher, I live here.'

The police officer clamped a big meaty hand onto Harold's shoulder.

'In that case, I am arresting you for the murder of Ralph Fletcher.'

Harold's fuzzy mind couldn't understand.

'Murder, but Ralph is my son. What do you mean, murder?'

'Was your son,' the police officer said unkindly, 'until you beat him to death.'

Lizzie appeared in the doorway, her eyes red from crying.

'Harold, what have you done?' Lizzie said, breaking into tears once more.

'I don't know,' mumbled Harold, 'this man said I killed Ralph. Surely that can't be true.'

Lizzie cried louder as she shouted,

'Of course, it's true, you hit Ralph and killed him.'

Harold's shoulders slumped, and he quietly allowed the constable to place him in handcuffs. The reality of what had happened slowly sinking in, the terrible memory of the previous day's incident beginning to resurface.

In the days that followed, the two missing boys returned, having spent a few nights wandering the streets. They had been afraid to return after Cassey's face appeared in the shed window. The look she gave them had been murderous, and they were too scared to risk repeating the experience.

Ralph had not disclosed where he had hidden the doll, so she remained in the shed. Cassey simply stayed where she was and watched the drama she had caused unfold from a distance. She was still angry at being replaced. How dare Harold introduce a shiny new doll after all she had done for him. Now they would all pay the price.

It especially upset Roslyn in that not only had she lost the new doll, the remnants had quickly been disposed of in the bin, but now Cassey had disappeared as well.

Weeks passed until Harold's trial was due to begin. The matter was serious enough to be heard at the Old Bailey. The highest and most famous court in the land.

Harold stood high up in the dock, above the jury and spectators. He looked the worse for wear, dressed in prison drab and shackled at both wrists and ankles with heavy chains.

He had spent time alone in a cell on remand and felt his remorse weighing him down to the extent where he had lost the will to live. To be responsible for the death of one's own child was a terror seldom visited on any parent, and Harold couldn't cope with the guilt. Standing in the dock, he had the look of guilt and when he was asked whether or not he pleaded guilty to the charge of wilfully murdering his own child, he nodded and whispered, 'Guilty.'

Because of the guilty plea, they released the assembled jury. Sentencing was to be announced in the afternoon, and Harold was locked in a cell under the courtroom awaiting his fate.

He stood once again in the dock, facing the judge, his eyes cast to the ground. The judge looked directly at him as an assistant draped a square of black cloth over his wig.

The judge began the sentence with a stern order that the prisoner was to look at him while he spoke.

'You have admitted to this court and to the world that you did viciously and wilfully murder your own firstborn son, Ralph Fletcher. The only sentence I can give you is that you will be taken from this court to a place of execution where you will be hanged by the neck until you are dead. May God have mercy on your soul.'

Harold had been expecting it, knew that it was what he deserved, but nonetheless, when the judge read out the sentence, he shook so much the noise from his chains reverberated around the cavernous courtroom.

'Take him down,' the judge ordered.

They escorted Harold down the underground tunnel that led back to the holding cells beneath the building, wondering how much of this precious life he had left. As he sat with his head in his hands, he recalled how happy they had been when poor and living in the East End. He, with his security job and small pay packet at the end of each week. They had been thrust into the world of the rich, believing that a new life awaited them, a life of riches and plenty. But it was not to be. He had killed his son, lost the love and respect of his family, and would soon be executed.

As he lifted his eyes to the dark green, painted brick wall and the small, barred window above, a vision of that blasted doll came into view, the eyes bright and hard. In that moment, Harold realised she was the real culprit. Cassey was responsible for all this heartache, but who would believe him? How could an inanimate object be responsible for what had happened?

Cassey's vision continued to stare at him with an impish grin spreading across the hard, porcelain face.

Then she was gone, and he was alone, more alone than he had ever been in his life. He hoped the execution would proceed without delay. He had no further use for this life.

Lizzie, meanwhile, had taken control of Harold's fortune, to which she was wholly entitled. The mews house was immediately placed on the market. She could not, in all good conscience, remain there for one more night. Together with the children, she moved to a hotel until such time that a new home could be considered. Not the same hotel as before. She could not wear the shame of her husband's crime together with the fact that he was about to be executed in the time-honoured fashion.

The house was left just as they had purchased it. All furnishings were to be yet again included. She engaged an estate agent to handle the sale, who would work in tandem with her solicitor.

Lizzie had attempted to visit Harold as he awaited trial, but he would not see her. The shame was just too much. Lizzie accepted his wishes, part of her glad she would not have to deal with the pitiful sight of her husband sitting in jail awaiting the end that was already a foregone conclusion.

The house stood cold and empty. Some would say colder than normal for this time of the year. Upstairs, a young boy wandered from room to room, calling for his brothers and sisters. As he shouted their names, a cold mist came from his mouth, but he did not feel cold.

Descending the stairs, the boy left the house. It amused him that he could pass through the closed door with ease, and he smiled. The garden shed appeared in the evening gloom, and he paused at the door before passing through it into the interior. There, at the window, stood Cassey.

'Hello, Ralph,' she said.

'Why aren't you in the box where I put you?' Ralph asked.

'I'm afraid of the dark,' lied Cassey.

It was a chill, dreary day. Lizzie stood outside the prison where her husband was being prepared to meet his maker. She had left the children in the care of the hotel staff with strict orders not to let them out of their sight.

There was an enormous clock set in a tower adjacent to the prison gates, and she watched the minute hand grind slowly in its upward arc.

At precisely nine o'clock, a bell rang once within the prison, sounding the death knell for Harold Fletcher. As the bell sounded, he dropped through a trapdoor into the void below.

Lizzie walked away, a widow, alone with the children. However, she was a wealthy, independent woman and would make her own way in the world.

CHAPTER 18

The mews house had stood empty for far longer than expected by the estate agent. Every inspection had been a disaster.

Most people did a quick walk through and exited at speed, complaining that it was far too cold within.

The agent knew they were not referring to the ambient temperature inside. There was something bad in the house, something malevolent that everyone felt as soon as they entered.

He had remained on one occasion as his clients beat a hasty retreat, determined to investigate. The house had been on his books far too long and had seen many price reductions until it was now a bargain. Even though the Great Depression had struck hard in terms of employment and the stock market, property prices had remained largely unaffected.

Wandering through the house, upstairs and down, and even through the servants' quarters in the attic, he was aware the coldness was uniform. To the point where he noticed wisps of vapour coming from his mouth when he breathed.

However, nothing appeared to be out of order, merely an unwelcoming feeling. He walked out into the small rear area, noting that the man hired to keep it tidy had failed miserably in the task. It was overgrown and unkempt; he would have words with him on his return to the office.

Stopping at the garden shed, he attempted to peer through the grimy glass window. It was dark inside and difficult to make any direct observation, so he cupped his hands on either side of his face, peering in intently.

The sudden appearance of a face directly against the glass

from inside nearly stopped his heart. He remained rivetted to the spot as a pair of bright eyes held him transfixed. Slowly, one eye closed, making the appearance of the other so much brighter.

Through the haze of the grimy window, he recognised it as a doll's face, and remained glued to the glass, unable to break the baleful one-eyed stare.

The doll's head receded into the background as the head drew back. The agent felt a momentary sense of relief; shattered when the face smashed against the glass.

He fell back onto the paved path, relieved to be free of the doll but conscious he had voided his bladder. Getting to his feet, he made for the back door, racing through the hallway and out through the front into the blessed sunshine. Looking back at the house, he realised there had been no sunshine at the rear, only a gloomy, misty light.

Returning to his office, he shakily picked up the telephone and dialled the number of Lizzie's lawyer.

'I'm returning the keys; Mrs Fletcher's house is completely unsaleable.'

The lawyer had never heard that from an agent before and interjected.

'Just get me an offer. That cannot be too hard, surely,' he said.

'No,' replied the agent, 'I'll send the keys over by messenger,' breaking the call before the lawyer could say another word.

Lizzie had put the house to the back of her mind. She concentrated on bringing up the children and purchased another home far away from Hampstead Heath. The single life suited her, although she had some ardent suitors. A few saw her as a prize catch. Still attractive, and obviously wealthy, made her a target for many men, especially those who had once enjoyed the privilege of wealth.

Two years after Harold had so dramatically left this world, Lizzie did become attracted to a gentleman. He had once been *something in the city* as his clothes bore testimony, although he now relied on the generosity of friends to survive.

He was older than her, but she reacted positively to his subtle overtures. Patrick appeared to like the children, although professed to have none of his own. Business had hitherto occupied him to the exclusion of even finding time to marry.

He became a regular visitor, and Lizzie began to look forward to his visits. The children, especially the boys, were at first suspicious but began to accept him as a regular addition at evening meals.

One evening, after the children had retired to bed, Patrick dropped to one knee and begged Lizzie for her hand in marriage. It had impressed her he had never tried to take advantage of her either physically or mentally and was so touched by his entreaties that she consented.

Things moved swiftly after that. Patrick Doherty had never been one to sit on his hands, and his patience with Lizzie was testing him. She was an attractive woman, no question about it, but Patrick's motivation was more about money than genuine love.

Patrick was and always had been an opportunist. He may have adopted the appearance of a city gentleman, but in fact was at the opposite end of the spectrum. His parentage was questionable, and he had been raised by a bevy of women in the south of London. As he grew older, he realised they were all *ladies of the night*, and his role in their lives became one of general servant; culminating in standing guard while they carried out their *duties.*

On one such occasion, he had been guarding an older woman when her cries for help rang out. Patrick smiled to himself as he leaned against the door, listening to the activities on the other side. Elsie was known for her crying. Men seemed to enjoy it when she feigned distress. She had instructed Patrick to ignore her first cries. It normally earned her a higher fee from the *client.*

But this time, her cries became louder and louder, and Patrick, deciding that enough was enough, opened the door of the dingy bedroom, exposing a bacchanalian scene.

Elsie was covered in blood and screaming. Patrick stared before being able to react, shocked at the dreadful scene. In three strides he was across the room and taking hold of the man, beat him with the small truncheon he always carried.

As the man fell beneath the blows, Elsie reacted by beating Patrick with her fists.

'Leave him, you oaf. He is the best paying client I've ever had.'

Patrick stopped his onslaught and stared at her.

'But you're covered in blood and were screaming for help. I'm only doing like you said!' Patrick exclaimed.

'Get out, you idiot,' screamed Elsie, stooping to comfort her own assailant.

Patrick left that same night. He had nothing to stay for. Elsie had been his substitute mother but had now revealed herself to be nothing more than a whore, willing to suffer any indignity to get her hands on cash. Any respect he had for the fairer sex had been snuffed out like a cheap penny candle. He would go out into the world to seek his fortune.

He soon found out that fortune was very hard to come by. This was the era of the Great Depression, and millions of men worldwide were out of work. Both men and women would sell their souls for a good meal, and he was reduced to at first begging, then to offering himself to any taker for the price of a bed and something to eat.

He put up with this life for a year until at eighteen he was approached by a smartly dressed man who did not beat about the bush at to what was required.

However, Damien was generous and paid for a smart suit and coat, allowing Patrick to stay with him in his home. Naturally, it all had to be paid for, but in his case, it was paid for *in kind.*

The *arrangement* continued for twenty-two years, Patrick enjoying the luxurious lifestyle bestowed upon him by a generous lover. Until Damien discovered Patrick's numerous affairs. The fact that he had been sleeping only with women did nothing to appease the hurt, and he threw him out. Patrick was once again penniless and back on the streets.

It was under these circumstances that he first met Lizzie.

They were married at a registry office, with only two witnesses plucked from the street and the children in attendance.

David, Cedric, Brenda, and Amie looked on as their stepmother married once again. They had no connection with this unknown man and would never bear his name. Roslyn, however, being Lizzie's daughter, could and probably would adopt her mother's new name. Roslyn Doherty sounded quite lyrical as the girl toyed with the idea.

Patrick moved in and assumed the role of master of the house. He decreed it was far too small for their needs. They would sell it and buy a bigger house in a better area.

'But I already have a bigger house, in Hampstead,' declared Lizzie, adding, 'but I don't want to go back there.'

'Nonsense,' declared her new husband, 'I shall inspect it tomorrow.'

Lizzie remained silent. She had been so happy on her wedding day, but that mood had been extinguished the same night. The honeymoon had been a disaster. Patrick had merely moved into her bedroom, asserting that to go away on holiday would be to squander money unnecessary.

That had been only the first change in his nature that Lizzie had been obliged to witness. That first night when they retired to the marital bedroom proved to be the second. Patrick unceremoniously stripped off his clothes and climbed onto the bed, bidding her to join him. Lizzie had been used to the tenderness and decorum Harold had always exhibited. Now, her new husband lay leering up at her, making her feel dirty and uncomfortable.

'Couldn't we wait for a while?' Lizzie asked quietly, 'I'm exhausted, it's been quite a day.'

'Don't give me any of that hogwash,' said Patrick, 'we need a baby to cement the union and we may as well start now.'

Lizzie gritted her teeth silently as she suffered his rough lovemaking, wondering how a man could change so quickly in one day.

When he had finished with her, Patrick rolled over with his back towards her.

'There will be a repeat performance in the morning, so don't be in a hurry to get up,' he said.

Lizzie spoke, in tears,

'But the children will need their breakfast.'

'You had better wake me early in that case. An opportunity missed is one never to be reclaimed,' he replied, before immediately falling asleep.

Lizzie lay awake for the entire night. What had she done?

Patrick set off for Hampstead Heath with keys in hand the following morning. Lizzie wasn't asked to accompany him and, in any case, preferred to stay behind. The morning's lovemaking had been as cold as the previous evening. Lizzie sensed her husband had not enjoyed the experience and was merely intent on getting her with child to ensure his own future.

The key turned stiffly in the front lock of the mews house in Hampstead Heath. Patrick pushed gently, but the door refused to budge. He pushed harder, but still the door remained obstinately closed. Standing back two paces, he shoulder-charged it and the door finally gave up its struggle to exclude him and swung open, crashing against the hallway wall. Inside, the entrance smelled damp. Wallpaper had peeled and hung down in strips. The house reeked of decay, but it did not put Patrick off. It was more than he could ever have aspired to. This was a posh suburb, and all the surrounding houses were well maintained, the exterior walls painted a uniform colour to complete the grandness of the curved line of mews.

Walking through the downstairs rooms, Patrick was

amazed at the size and grandeur. However, the entire interior would need redecorating. He had his own ideas but guessed that a professional interior designer would be needed. He did not want others to look down their noses at his common efforts to exhibit respectability.

Upstairs was much the same. The bedrooms were damp with peeling wallpaper and paint. The furniture had also suffered. It had never been covered and was thick with dust and speckled with mould. Everything would have to go. Once again, he would engage somebody to furnish the house in the correct style. His new wife had plenty of money. He had demanded to inspect her accounts and when her vast estate was revealed, he had difficulty hiding his surprise. Patrick had struck gold; his future was guaranteed.

Lizzie quickly found out she had no say in the matter and reluctantly left everything to her new husband. Patrick did his best to ignore the children, stating the old maxim that *children should be seen and not heard.* In his case, they could remain hidden as well. He disliked children and lacked the ability or desire to communicate with them. He insisted on making love to Lizzie at any opportunity to get her with child as soon as possible. On completion of that chore, he would insist on his own rooms in the new house. Lizzie was unaware of that intention but would have been gladdened if she had known earlier. His onerous attentions were becoming insufferable.

Three months later, the family stood at the threshold of the newly refurbished mews house. Patrick grandly swung the door open to reveal a completely new interior. Lizzie could not help being impressed; the team of designers had not failed them in any way.

Walking through every room in the house, she hesitated only upstairs at the site where Ralph had been felled by his father. There was no sign of damage or blood. Everything smelled of fresh paint and newly manufactured furniture.

Patrick led them through the house to the rear. The boys refused to enter the small backyard, staring at the shed in fear.

'Come on, you two, don't lag behind,' insisted Patrick.

They knew better than to disobey. Without Lizzie's knowledge, he had delivered blows to both boys when they refused his commands. David and Cedric had stood together in defiance just after the wedding and had been rewarded with a stinging slap that was so forceful it knocked them off their feet. There had been no further disobedience from them since.

Reluctantly, they followed their new stepfather down the path to the shed. Patrick threw the door open and ushered them inside.

'See, nothing to fear. I've had the place cleaned, and the contents taken to the rubbish dump.'

'What about the wooden box that was over there?' said David, pointing to where the dreaded box containing Roslyn's old doll used to stand.

'Everything has been taken away. We shall begin again in our new home,' said Patrick, encircling Lizzie's waist with his arm.

'My, my, putting on a little weight, my dear?' Patrick said, as she tried to wriggle free.

'I believe you may have your wish in a few months,' whispered Lizzie into his smiling face. His smile broadened as he looked down at her, noting the lack of expression on her own countenance.

Days turned into weeks as they settled in. A cook and two maids were employed as before. Patrick and Lizzie occupied separate bedrooms with individual dressing rooms, much to Lizzie's relief. Patrick's insistence on his brutish lovemaking had ceased once her pregnancy had been confirmed.

David and Cedric shared a bedroom, as before. Brenda and Amie shared a bedroom, while Roslyn had her own smaller room next to her mother. It pleased Lizzie, as their rooms had an interconnecting door. Mother and daughter were at last reunited.

On the landing, a small cupboard was set into the wall. The decorators had been unable to open the solid door and instead had merely wallpapered over it. It was far too small to be of any actual use, so they never gave it another thought. The door virtually disappeared, the thin line delineating the outline hardly visible.

Inside the musty interior sat a figure propped against the far wall. Cassey's eyes were closed as if she had been sleeping. As the house settled into night, her eyes slowly opened.

CHAPTER 19

David woke to the presence of someone in the bedroom. He sat bolt upright, staring at the figure at the foot of the bed, too shocked to cry out. He couldn't see any features; the diminutive figure was framed in moonlight streaming through the window. He could only see a dark, solid shape, but the fact that it was diminutive added to his terror. It was like his worst nightmare, but somehow, he knew this wasn't a dream. His worst fears were realised when his brother woke. Cedric sat upright. His bed was next to David's, and he could also see the figure. This was no dream. David had paled, his lips moving slowly but with no sound coming out.

To the horror of both boys, the figure walked between their beds, approaching them slowly. It was no ordinary walk. The legs appeared to be moving jerkily and its torso swayed gently from side to side. It turned to face David, and he tried to scream. Cassey was only inches from his face, illuminated by bright moonlight. One eyelid drooped and the other glowed brightly.

They remained speechless as the doll slowly retraced its steps, walking clumsily out of the bedroom.

Morning arrived as weak sunshine, casting a soft glow into the boys' bedroom. They both lay supine; still pale, their shallow breathing gently moving the bedcovers.

Lizzie opened the bedroom door and was about to remonstrate with them over their tardiness in getting up when she noticed their appearance.

'Whatever is wrong with you two?' She asked.

David moved his lips a few times before any words came

out.

'Cassey was here last night.'

'Cassey?' Lizzie repeated, 'What was she doing? Who brought her in?'

'She was just here, and she walked,' said David. Cedric nodded rapidly in confirmation.

Lizzie knew the doll had certain powers from the days when it was her own and sat on the bed, taking David's icy hand in her own.

'Don't be afraid, she was my old doll too and I'm sure she will not hurt me, or anybody close to me,' she said, uncertain.

Later in the day, Lizzie searched the house from top to bottom but could find no trace of Cassey.

Patrick had taken to going out every evening, not returning until dawn on some occasions. Lizzie cared nothing for his nightly sojourns. She was pleased he now left her alone.

Patrick could not resist commenting one morning,

'Cooking nicely, soon be here.'

'Don't be so crass!' Exclaimed Lizzie.

Patrick's reaction took her completely by surprise. She didn't see the blow coming and felt no immediate pain, only a strange ringing inside her head. She was on the landing next to the stairs and held onto the rail to steady herself. Patrick ran downstairs and out through the front door, shouting over his shoulder,

'There will be more of that to come if you don't button your lip.'

Lizzie dragged herself to her feet, supported by the rail. How could he hit her when she carried his child? She was almost five months pregnant.

'How I wish this child hadn't happened,' she said quietly. 'I would do anything to rid myself of him.'

Out of the corner of her eye, she sensed movement behind her. Turning, she didn't see anything out of the ordinary, so made to walk downstairs. As she took the first step, something hit her very hard behind the knees. Screaming in terror, she tumbled headlong down the stairs, turning over and over until she reached the hallway.

Lizzie momentarily blacked out. When she came around, she was staring up into the face of Roslyn.

'What happened, Mummy?'

'I must have fallen down the stairs,' said Lizzie, her memory of the event clouded by the fall.

'I heard that man shouting at you,' said Roslyn. She always referred to Patrick as *that man*. She had no love for her new stepfather, she never had. There was something false about him that her mother seemed unable to see.

Roslyn studied her mother's face. The bruising caused by Patrick's blow was slowly turning her cheek a dark blue.

'He hit you, didn't he?' Roslyn said, not waiting for her mother's confirmation. 'Then, he pushed you down the stairs.'

Lizzie couldn't think to reply, she was studying her bloodied hand. There was a dark stain growing beneath her. She looked down at her stomach, a hand automatically feeling for her unborn child.

'The baby,' she cried, her voice rising in panic, 'the baby is coming.'

Roslyn ran down to the basement kitchen, yelling for help. The staff were quick to join Lizzie in the hallway; Cook guessing what was happening. Lizzie was losing her baby and might well lose her own life. She instructed the others to telephone for an ambulance while she attempted to make Lizzie comfortable.

Upstairs, a soft click sounded as the small hidden cupboard door closed. Inside, Cassey resumed her usual sitting position, as if a child had sat her in place.

Later that evening, Lizzie lay in a hospital bed staring at the ceiling. She felt guilty. A part of her mourned for her lost child, but deep inside she felt relieved that Patrick would not get his way this time.

He had visited but stayed only minutes before leaving, an

annoyed look on his face.

'I suppose you told them I'm responsible,' he snarled.

Lizzie could not answer. Had he pushed her? Surely, he had gone by then. Her memory was still hazy. However, the thought of being with him again terrified her.

After a broken night's sleep, Lizzie woke to a fresh morning. She was no longer pregnant, Patrick nowhere to be seen, and the sun was shining.

Doctor Snell assured her she had survived the miscarriage, although the outcome could easily have been so different. He had taken it upon himself to report the matter to the police. Her facial bruising showed she had been the victim of an assault, and he considered it his duty to report the matter.

Mid-morning saw the arrival at her bedside of the children. Roslyn led them in, rushing to her mother's side. Brenda, Amie, David, and Cedric hung back in deference to Roslyn's role as Lizzie's natural daughter.

She was having none of that and held out her arms to them.

'Come, give mummy a hug, we are all one family.'

David approached the bed but spoke for them all.

'What about Patrick? We don't like him. He hit you and pushed you down the stairs.'

Yet another confirmation that it was indeed her husband responsible for her fall. Lizzie was beginning to believe it herself. It must be the truth.

The children were told to leave after one hour.

'Quite long enough for a visit,' said the ward sister, 'the police are waiting to interview your mother.'

The children filed out quietly, passing the waiting police officers.

David was the last to leave and murmured under his breath to the police.

'Her husband did it. He beat her all the time. He never wanted the baby, so got rid of it.'

The lie slipped easily from his mouth; he had no idea what

he was saying. Leaving the hospital, he wondered where the idea had come from.

Lizzie sat up in bed as the police officers stood on either side, one of them with an open notebook.

'Your husband did this?' The senior officer began.

'Yes, I suppose he must have,' answered Lizzie

'Suppose he must have? Or he did it. You cannot have it both ways.'

Lizzie realised this was her opportunity to rid herself of the loathsome husband she had hitherto welcomed with open arms.

'Yes, he did it,' she whispered.

'Are you willing to testify that he pushed you downstairs?' asked the officer.

'Yes,' answered Lizzie, embracing the lie with open arms. There would be no going back now.

One week later, she was home. The children and staff lined the hallway as she made her way in. Of Patrick there was no sign. He was languishing in a prison cell, remanded in custody on several charges, including attempted murder. Police could not charge him with the murder of their unborn child as, in law, they deemed the foetus not a living independent human being.

The trial attracted the press and as Lizzie stepped into the witness box; it surprised her at the attention she was being given by the public gallery, who were firmly on her side. Patrick was already reviled as a child killer and made worse by the fact the child was his own. The prosecution emphasised the fact that he had married a wealthy widow to gain control over her considerable estate. They said Patrick saw the unborn child as an impediment to his future, rather than the truth; that he wanted the baby to secure his future with Lizzie and her money.

Lizzie found it difficult to meet his eyes, looking at him standing in the dock. She answered the prosecutor's questions quietly, averting her eyes as each lie emerged. The only time she looked straight at him was when she was asked to describe the moment he had punched her in the face. She stared at her attacker coldly; he returned her stare, hatred etched into his face. The jury was quick to see his reaction. This was not going well for Patrick.

In the end, the jury found him guilty on all charges. The judge looked kindly upon Lizzie, seeing a very vulnerable mother, before turning to Patrick. His countenance changed as he addressed the prisoner.

'You are a fellow of low morals and an even lower respect for women. I find your actions against this lady, your wife, despicable beyond imagination, robbing her of her child in your clumsy attempt to better yourself. I sentence you to twenty years in prison with hard labour.'

Patrick turned white. He might not survive that length of sentence. Hard labour entailed exactly that, crushing rocks into small stones in some quarry. Quite unnecessary but seen as a just form of punishment. It would be a very long twenty years.

Lizzie's lawyers assured her that the marriage would be dissolved quickly, Patrick had no defence. The divorce would free her, and this time she would remain so.

The house she detested so much went onto the market immediately. Occupied as it was by her, the children, and staff, the coldness stopping previous purchasers was no longer apparent. A sale was secured quickly, and she hastened to move out as soon as she could find another property, promising the staff they would move into the new home and remain with the family.

When the noise of the removalists had finally ceased and the front door slammed shut for the last time, Cassey stirred. A wicked smile passed over her face. It was time for her to move on as well. There was work to be done. She must hasten the Darkness.

CHAPTER 20

Lilith

Cassey sat propped up in the secret cupboard above the stairs. She was merely a vehicle for the spirit of the demon, Lilith, who had lived from the beginning of time. God had created her for Adam as his wife, but she refused him, believing that as a couple, they were equal in every way. However, Adam, believing himself to have been created in God's own image, maintained that he and he alone was the superior being on earth. Things got out of hand and Lilith flew off in a rage, transforming into a demon.

Lilith bore witness to the beginning of the age of mankind and watched as men insisted that their wives maintained the subordinate role. She passionately believed that women were at least the equal of men, if not superior, and was not ashamed to show it. After all, wasn't she also God's creation?

But women continued to be subjugated by men and as age followed age, she railed against it, adopting many identities.

She had spent so many years brooding, planning death and destruction, assuming many identities, but always falling short of her goal. In desperation, Lilith divided her spirit into many parts. Each would inhabit an innocent looking inanimate doll. What better way to inveigle herself into households around the world? Surely the opportunity would someday present itself when she could complete her plans for the destruction of the entire human race.

The first world war had not even come close, only some thirty-five million had perished.

The flu pandemic which followed killed many millions more, but still she was not satisfied. They all had to die.

The old couple in the dingy warehouse had been with Lilith for a long time now. They were part of a world-wide network distributing children's dolls to young innocents. The dolls were constantly recycled as they fell into disrepair, but all had one thing in common; they all possessed the evil spirit of Lilith. Every country now had a supply of the dolls, and they were strategically placed where they could inflict most harm. No human could detect which dolls were evil or were mere toys.

Lilith carefully selected her contacts to repair and distribute the dolls. Once lured into her clutches, there was no way out. The promise of everlasting life tempted even the most righteous; after all, wasn't that God's promise to the faithful? They inhabited a lonely world, shunning contact with others as their bodies began to decompose. Inside, their spirit lived on, but it was a living death.

CHAPTER 21

Bernard And Hilda

Early 1939

Cassey's eyes flicked open. The house had a new family. She could hear laughter downstairs, recognising the voices as that of a man and woman. They were speaking English at first, but constantly changed to German.

'Only English, my love. We may be tempted to slip up outside and that would never do.'

'Very well, Bernard, but I detest speaking in Englander. Our pure language is so much better,' replied Hilda, 'soon we will be able to expunge it completely.'

'We have put up with it for two years. This will be the last leg. Victory will soon be ours,' replied Bernard.

'But the Führer would rather not go to war here,' said Hilda.

'No, they are ill prepared for war over here as we have been observing and reporting,' said Bernard. 'The English will welcome the opportunity to side with the Fatherland. When they are safely ensnared, the glorious Reich will absorb them completely.'

In the cupboard, Cassey smiled; these were the ones she had been waiting for.

During the following two days, she heard furniture being moved around. Then the sound of footsteps as the couple made their way to the bedroom for their first night in the mews on Hampstead Heath.

Cassey eased open the cupboard door. It was pitch dark in

the hallway as she made her way towards their bedroom. The door pushed open easily, framing her in the subtle moonlight creeping through the curtained window.

Bernard and Hilda lay entwined in bed, snoring softly as Cassey silently approached. Her head was level with theirs as she studied the sleeping forms. She had to find a way to help them.

A few days later, lying once again in the hall cupboard, she heard their conversation clearly. They were sitting up in bed smoking.

'The time is rapidly approaching,' said Bernard, 'the naïve English are refusing our offers. Soon, very soon, Poland will fall with the help of our new allies, the Soviets. The Führer hates them almost as much as he hates Jews, but they will serve our purpose well. England is isolated; even the Americans have deserted them. We will crush Europe, then walk into England; victory will be ours in less than twelve months.'

The couple in the bedroom had no idea they were being used. Lilith was not the only demon. Adolf Hitler could equally use others to pave the way to his goal of world domination. Cassey smiled to herself at the interesting juxtaposition. No doubt Hitler had been pleasant enough as a child, but no one had any idea what was coming; what demonic terror and suffering he would inflict upon the world.

Bernard and Hilda had been careless. They were on the brink of war, but people still chose to party, ignoring all the signs. The depression was over, and people had embarked on years of celebration; even the prospect of war could not dampen their spirits.

The German couple certainly knew what was coming. The mere thought excited them beyond reason, both mentally and sexually. They had been selected years before in Germany for their fluency in English. Both were married, but not to each other. They travelled under the guise of marketing agents for a company in Berlin. The firm was a front for the SS. They had been sent to England as a married couple where they would be deeply buried as moles with the assurance their respective spouses would be looked after.

Once they were securely in England, the SS took care of their spouses. Neither had children, so it was a simple case to make them disappear forever.

The one time they had slipped was crucial. It was in a pub, of all places. The drinks were flowing freely and, typically, for a London pub, a piano was churning out all the popular songs. Bernard was well into his cups, sitting alone at a small table whilst Hilda was being entertained by a stranger in a dark corner of the bar. She was in a state of heightened sexual arousal and easy prey for a local who sat with her on his lap.

The piano finished its rendition of *Pack up your bags* to the thunderous cheers of the patrons.

The next tune began in silence until Bernard suddenly broke into song. He sang perfectly and loudly to the dumb-founded patrons. The piano player had chosen *Lili Marlene* and Bernard was singing it in perfect German.

He sang with his eyes closed, remembering his younger days in the Munich taverns. He was completely unaware that other patrons were not joining in. How could they? He was the only German in the bar.

Hilda pulled the stranger's hand away and jumped off his lap. She approached Bernard, still singing loudly with eyes closed, and slapped him hard across the face. The attack stunned him, and he rocked back in the chair, falling over backwards. Grabbing his hand, she rushed from the pub. They ran until they could hail a taxi. Once home in Hampstead Heath, Hilda rounded on him.

'You idiot!' She exclaimed, 'all that we have worked for almost up in flames.'

'I'm sorry,' said Bernard lamely, 'but everyone was drunk, so no harm done.'

'You had better hope that is true,' said Hilda.

They went up to bed and lay in the darkness, listening for any strange noises which might foretell a raid by the authorities.

They both knew the secret service would watch out for any German nationals now that war was imminent. Bernard had blown their cover built up over the preceding years.

He reached over and touched her.

'Should I finish what that other fellow started?'

Hilda's answer was to violently slap his hand away.

'Go to sleep, you are useless to me until you sober up.'

It was in the early hours of the following morning, that time when sleep has taken its firmest hold on the mind, when a figure crept slowly upstairs, conscious of every small squeak from the stairs. Reaching the top of the stairs, a man looked along the landing, searching for their bedroom. Guided by sounds of deep breathing and gentle snores, he turned towards them.

He felt a thump as something hit his leg, followed by a searing pain as a knife blade appeared from the front. Someone had driven it hard, completely penetrating his right leg.

He tried to suppress the scream but failed. The sleeping forms in bed rolled away from each other, hitting the floor simultaneously. Months of training coming to the fore.

Hilda was closest to the door and reached it, crawling on hands and knees. As she entered the hallway, she came face to face with the still moaning man. He was clutching his leg, blood pouring from the wound.

Guessing the purpose of his visit, she drew the knife she held across his throat, pressing deeply so it severed his windpipe. She was careful not to nick the carotid artery. The resulting mess would take ages to clean.

She lay over him to hold him in place while he died. Bernard stood up, but she pulled him back down beside her.

'There may be more; they usually work in pairs.'

Bernard nodded. She was right, but then she usually was.

He cautiously made his way to the top of the stairs and peered down. All was quiet below.

Cradling the brutish-looking Luger pistol in one hand, he

felt his way downstairs one tread at a time; taking the same care as their failed attacker.

A search downstairs and of the basement revealed that the man had been by himself. Or perhaps his partner had beaten a hasty retreat when he heard the screams. Bernard wouldn't have blamed him; he had very nearly died of fright himself.

Returning upstairs, he joined Hilda, looking down on the corpse that had once been a potential assassin. They were sure of his intention. Bernard's stupidity in the pub guaranteed them a visit from the Secret Service. They merely didn't expect it quite so soon.

Hilda and Bernard were set to complete a vital role in the coming war. The information they had gathered would ensure their glorious Luftwaffe would wipe out every airfield in the land. German intelligence already knew many, but there were others safely hidden away with hangers full of the newly developed Hurricane fighters. Preparing for the invasion which most denied, but those in power knew all too well was imminent.

They had to get the information out quickly. Bernard had almost ruined it, and they might still be in danger.

They were so engrossed in their close encounter with the enemy they had not thought of the obvious.

'Who stabbed him?' Hilda asked.

Bernard looked down at the body.

'There must be someone else here.'

'But who would want to stab him and help us?' Hilda whispered, thinking the man's assailant might well still be in the house somewhere.

The small door beside them opened with a click, loud in the surrounding silence.

They both turned as the door slowly opened, revealing Cassey.

'It's only a doll,' gasped Hilda.

'Scared the life out of me,' agreed Bernard.

A thought entered Hilda's mind, 'We can use the doll to hide the location map.'

Bernard nodded; it was as if they had experienced the same idea simultaneously, and they laughed nervously.

'Great minds think alike,' he said.

They plucked the doll from the cupboard and took it into the bedroom, closing the cupboard door. The bloodied knife remained behind; Cassey had no further use for it.

It was morning by the time the pair had dragged the corpse downstairs and out into the garden shed. They would dispose of it later. They had to make haste. There was no telling when the next unwelcome visitors might arrive.

Hilda carefully pulled up the doll's dress, exposing a delicate hinged door. Opening it, she saw the workings. Cords joining the arms, legs, and eyes. Skilfully engineered to give the effect of movement when played with by a child. The folded sheet of paper containing the bearings of the secret airfields slid inside and Hilda pulled the dress down. A good hiding place, she thought, patting herself on the back.

'We must leave,' hissed Bernard, 'there are two cars parked down the road and they were not there a few minutes ago.'

'The body,' said Hilda, 'they'll see it. Quickly, we can escape through the back before they surround the place. There's a laneway there.'

They pulled a heavy hallstand in front of the door before exiting from the back of the house. Bernard paused at the shed. Inside, he began pouring a can of petrol over the Secret Service man's body. Outside, he liberally scattered the remains of the can around the base of the shed. There was a loud *woof* as the petrol ignited, burning Bernard's hand in the process.

He yelled out in pain, and Hilda slapped him hard,

'Be quiet, you idiot, can't you do anything right?'

She led the way, clutching the doll. Being much fleeter of foot than the overweight Bernard, she soon left him behind, taking a sharp left turn at the end of the lane.

Bernard was huffing and puffing on shaky legs and nursing his burned hand. He had his head down with the effort and did not see the two men standing in his path. Running into them pell-mell, it brought him up short, too exhausted to fight them off.

The handcuffs on his badly burned wrist hurt so much he thought he might faint. But the Secret Servicemen ignored his pleas.

Hilda made it to the next road and, glancing back, saw that at present she was free and clear of pursuit. She spotted a small shop ahead with an unattended baby's pram, and without breaking stride, grabbed the pram and continued running, much to the consternation of the tiny occupant, who began screaming loudly. Hilda dashed around another corner with the baby's mother in hot pursuit. She pushed Cassey into the pram, exchanging the doll for the baby, which she unceremoniously flung by the arm into a garden.

This action stopped the mother in her tracks, who cradled the now silent baby, tears streaming down her face.

Hilda ran on until the suburb melded into the city proper. She could now walk calmly and serenely, her baby tucked up in a blanket, hiding its face.

Inside the pram, Cassey grinned. Once again, she had saved the day.

CHAPTER 22

Bernard slumped in his chair.

'I am not a spy, I'm simply a travelling salesperson,' he whimpered. The burns on his hand had received no treatment and hurt with the chafing handcuffs.

'What about the body of our agent in the shed? Burned beyond recognition, but we know who it is, or was,' the interviewer corrected himself.

'What agent? I know nothing about any agent.' Bernard had adopted the accent of an East Ender. He was good with accents.

However, when the man standing behind him twisted the skin on his burned wrist so that it tore free, his accent changed.

'Nein, nein bitte tu mir nicht weh,' he screamed.

The interviewer smiled coldly,

'It won't hurt for long. Now, tell me about your mission?'

Hilda walked for miles through the city, heading for a rendezvous which had been arranged months before. The darkening sky of a September evening cloaked her passage as she wandered among the myriad narrow streets of the East End.

Stopping at the door of a nondescript terraced house, she tapped out a precise series of knocks. The door opened almost immediately, and she was ushered inside. Eager hands pulled the pram in behind her.

A single bulb illuminated the front room, heavy curtains

giving assurance of complete privacy.

Three men occupied the room, the smallest of the three, a diminutive blond-haired man who looked no older than a callow youth, spoke.

'Well?'

Hilda knew she was addressing the leader of their cell but gave no sign. She matched him for coldness, and the other two men stepped back a pace. The power between Hilda and Heinrich was such that both were transfixed.

'Where is the map?' Heinrich asked, thin pale lips smiling. Anyone who knew him recognised that there was no warmth in his smile. There never was.

Hilda nodded her head triumphantly,

'Here, as ordered, I deliver into your hands the complete layout of the English secret airbases and their precious fighter planes.'

She picked up the doll and roughly tearing the dress upwards, revealed the little hatch on the back. She didn't notice Cassey's expression of hatred.

The bitch has torn my new dress!

Heinrich held out his pale hand for the paper. Hilda glanced at his thin fingers, feeling instant revulsion at the mere thought of them touching her.

'Where is Bernard?' He demanded.

'I don't know,' replied Hilda, 'he was running behind me, but I lost him.'

'If he is taken, he will reveal the purpose of our mission and all will be lost,' said Heinrich coldly.

'He won't talk. He is loyal to the Fatherland,' said Hilda.

'Rubbish!' shouted Heinrich, 'give me any man or woman and I would make them talk in minutes.'

Hilda shuddered at the thought of what this man was capable of. He had an unenviable reputation for cruelty.

'Bernard will talk. We have wasted our time,' he said, grabbing the doll and throwing it into a corner of the room.

Cassey lay crumpled with limbs in disarray, her face contorted with the fury she held pent up inside.

Heinrich pulled out a pistol, and with no further comment, shot Hilda in the face. She had no time to react as the bullet tore through her cheek, exiting through the back of her head. Blood spattered the wall around Cassey, who crawled across the floor towards the man holding the gun.

Heinrich didn't notice the doll approaching, but a second man did.

'The doll, it's moving by itself,' he yelled, pointing, and waving his arms wildly.

Heinrich mistook the flailing arms for a threat and shot the man twice in the chest.

Carefully approaching the man, he had shot, Heinrich tripped on Cassey's body, falling headlong.

Stunned, he remained sprawled over his victim's body as the doll edged towards his face.

Heinrich came to his senses; the gun was lying on the floor some distance away.

He gazed hazily into the face of the doll. He was trying to make sense of the fact that the doll's face was contorted. How could that be?

For a split second, he saw a stubby porcelain finger before it painfully entered his left eye, extinguishing the light completely.

Heinrich screamed but had no time to move before his second eye popped in a miasma of blood and intraocular fluid.

Blinded, he struggled to his feet. Feeling his way with outstretched arms, he eventually found the door and made his way along a hallway towards the front door. He almost made it. The thud of a bullet entering his back and severing his spinal cord forced him to slump against the door. There was no pain, no feeling whatsoever. It reduced Heinrich to the state of a lifeless doll.

Cassey lay in the hallway. The recoil of the gun had broken the strings connecting her arm to her body, and both gun and arm were now some distance away.

Meanwhile, Bernard sat in the chair stolidly refusing to answer the questions put to him. His burned wrist was now devoid of flesh, and blood covered the floor around the base of the chair.

The blow to the side of his head was unexpected, and he screamed involuntarily.

'Talk,' said his inquisitor, 'you will in the end, so you may as well save yourself any further suffering.'

Bernard remained silent, guessing the man who had hit him was wearing knuckledusters. He could feel his face swelling and guessed his cheekbone had been shattered. Waiting patiently for the punishment to continue, he was rewarded with yet another blow to the other side. He knew he was finished as the other cheek bone crumpled into pieces inside his mouth.

Bernard opened his mouth, but no words came out; he was incapable of talking.

The glass ampoule containing cyanide secreted inside his cheek before they captured him had burst under the impact of the blow. The men questioning him stood back, contemplating their next move as he died before their eyes.

'We will never know now,' said one man, roughly cuffing the dead man's head.

Bernard had not talked, had not given away their mission, but it was to no avail. The sheet of paper with the carefully gathered information lay crumpled in a ball beside a wall. No one would even notice it.

Cassey lay fuming. She had done her best to make sure the information reached the Germans, resulting in the world being plunged into chaos. Hitler's Third Reich would have become the new Roman Empire, his dream of complete European supremacy, so close, yet so far away. Only Britain stood in his way and, with their secret defences revealed, they would have had no chance.

Two weeks later, the bodies were discovered. The atrocious smell alerted passers-by who contacted the local council with a string of complaints.

Secret Service agents quickly took over and in the depths of the night, disposed of all traces of the German spies. The sheet of paper with so much valuable information was swept up and thrown away. Cassey, it was assumed, had been left by the previous tenants. A broken doll, no doubt once treasured by a little girl and now nothing more than rubbish.

CHAPTER 23

Madge

Mid-1939

Cassey was in complete darkness. The metal dustbin's heavy lid blocked out all light. Cassey sat amongst the refuse from the house, her broken arm beside her along with some disgusting rotten food scraps from neighbours.

Noise outside made her open her one good eye. She could hear children playing. How she detested them. The sound of their laughter sent chills through her broken body.

'Come on, I dare you,' shouted a boy.

'I'm not scared,' replied another.

'Let's tip it over and run for it,' said the first boy.

Cassey felt her world move dramatically as they pushed the bin over into the street. The lid came off with a clang and she, together with the refuse, spilled from the bin in an unholy mess.

Laughter faded as the two boys ran along the street, disappearing around a corner.

'What happened to you?' said a sweet voice.

It was a little girl dressed in careworn clothes, kneeling beside the broken doll. She held Cassey gently in one arm, the other holding the missing limb with strings still attached.

Madge had never owned a doll. The closest she had come was to gaze at one through a shop window. Few girls from the area had a doll to play with. Money was always tight and with the prospect of an imminent war, things could hardly be worse. Here was a doll somebody had simply discarded. It may be a broken wreck to the previous owner, but to Madge, it represented a

140

dream come true. She would take it home, give her a bath, and ask her father to fix the arm.

Maud shook her head good-naturedly as her daughter stood in the cramped kitchen of their rented house, clutching the broken doll.

'Please, may I keep her, Mum,' Madge pleaded.

'It's broken and filthy,' said her brother unkindly, 'put it back where you found it.'

'Now, now, Reggie, don't be unkind to Madge. She has never had a doll and your dad will be able to fix the arm,' said Maud.

Reggie stormed out of the room; his little sister had been the favourite since the day of her birth. His reign of being an only child had come to a sudden end on that fateful day.

Madge's father, Cecil, arrived home at tea-time. The familiar clump of his heavily built-up boot making its familiar rhythmic sound in the hallway. As a child, other children had ridiculed him mercilessly because of his withered leg. During the depression, nutritional food had been scarce, resulting in many children suffering from rickets, and worse. One leg was so much shorter it forced him to wear a special boot. In adulthood, the authorities had seen fit to give him one boot, with an ordinary boot to match. They were his only pair and had been to the cobblers frequently. Cecil wore them everywhere, including a local factory, where he had a job sweeping floors, the only job available to a handicapped man.

However, Cecil was, in fact, brilliant with his hands and set too immediately to repair the broken doll presented to him by his treasured daughter, Madge. She was the apple of his eye, and he adored her.

'What are you going to call her?' He asked.

Madge thought for a moment until a name popped into her head.

'I shall call her Cassey,' she said, beaming as her father re-strung the arm back into place.

'There, that's the arm back in place, but I'm blessed if I can sort that eye out. It seems to have a mind of its own. One minute it's open and before I can blink it closes. I've checked the mechanism, and everything appears to be working.'

'Never mind,' said a delighted Madge, taking the doll from her father's lap, 'she is perfect, and I love her already.'

Madge's idyllic life with her new doll lasted only a few months. As bombs fell on London, the government deemed it appropriate to move vulnerable children to a safer location, far from the city. Night after night German bombers arrived over London, dropping their deadly cargoes of munitions onto the helpless people below.

The Blitz decimated the city. Commercial docks were the priority, but most bombs missed their targets, instead falling on civilian homes, killing thousands.

Madge stood on the station platform clutching her mother's hand, tears in her eyes.

'I don't want to go, Mummy. Why can't I stay here with you?'

Her mother knelt beside her, stemming the flow of tears with a handkerchief.

'All the children are leaving. The Germans are dropping bombs and it's safer for all the children to leave. You will stay with a nice family in the country where it is safer.'

Madge doubted she would be happy with strangers, and what if a bomb hit her parents' house?

'Why don't you come, too?' She asked, sobbing.

Maud stood up, still holding Madge's hand firmly.

'You and Reggie will be company for each other. Mummy and Daddy must stay here with all the other parents. We can't all leave.'

Maud forced a laugh. She was not feeling very good about sending her children away for who knew how long, but the government had insisted.

'You have Cassey too. She will look after you,' added Maud. For some strange reason, she had a strong feeling that it should be the other way around, but she dismissed the thought as a whistle sounded and shouts of *all aboard* rang out along the platform.

Madge stood peering through the grimy carriage window, clutching Cassey tightly as the train pulled out of the station.

'Here, let me hold your ugly doll for you,' said Reggie before they had even cleared the platform.

He grabbed at the doll and tore it from Madge's grasp. She shrieked in protest, dissolving into tears; her brother was truly horrid.

'Give it back,' said a voice behind.

'Why should I?' Reggie snarled back over his shoulder. 'She's my sister and I can do anything I want.'

He didn't see the fist approaching, his head exploding with coloured lights as it connected. Madge's doll bounced on the carriage floor as Reggie let it slip from his grasp.

Madge stood transfixed as a boy approached, holding out her doll. She took it from him gratefully, unaware of the doll's bloodied fingers.

A scream from the carriage floor threw passengers into a panic. At first, heads looked out of windows, searching the sky for enemy aircraft. It was well known that the Germans like to shoot at trains. But the sky was clear. The screams had by now reduced to a whimpering and as Madge looked down; she saw her brother writhing on the floor clutching his face with both hands. Blood ran between his fingers as at last an adult supervisor knelt beside him.

'It's his eye,' said the lady, 'something must have penetrated it.'

They sat Reggie up and closer examination revealed the horrible mess that used to be his left eye.

The boy who had punched him became distraught.

'I didn't do that. I punched him because he was being nasty to her,' he said, pointing at Madge.

Other children volubly agreed that the boy had merely punched Reggie and he must have struck his eye on something as he fell.

That is precisely what had happened, or something akin to it. Reggie had indeed fallen to the floor with the force of the boy's punch, but the eye injury had happened shortly afterwards. As he lay stunned on the floor, a tiny porcelain finger had stabbed him in the eye. He was speechless with shock and Cassey had been handed back to his sister before real pain set in.

Children tumbled out of carriages as the train came to a halt in a tiny village deep in the Sussex countryside.

They were lined up, labels pinned to their outer clothes stating their full names and addresses as lines of adults waited to receive their temporary wards.

An ambulance awaited Reggie. He was being transferred to the local hospital for treatment as Madge, still holding Cassey tightly, stared at the older couple standing before her.

'She will be all right, but the boy is now useless,' the old man said.

'She will do for the kitchen. Maybe we can change him for another?' His wife replied.

'He's my brother. We have to stay together,' blurted Madge.

'Have to nothing,' said the old man in a strange drawling accent, 'if he isn't any use, we have no room for him. There's a farm to run and all the men have buggered off to the war.'

The couple picked up Madge's small cardboard suitcase containing all her worldly possessions and walked towards the station exit.

'What about my brother?' Madge asked, following behind reluctantly.

'What about him?' Replied the man unkindly.

The farm was only a few miles from the train station and the three made the journey in a small trap pulled by a horse. Ordinarily, Madge would have found it exciting, but all she could think about was her brother. She felt so alone.

Her face fell as they pulled into the farmyard. It was nothing like she had imagined a farm would look like. The yard was thick with mud and chickens scurried away as the horse trudged up to the house. It appeared to be in worse condition than their small, terraced house in Whitechapel.

Inside was no better, the filthy furniture covered in a film of dust.

'Plenty for you to do to earn your keep,' said the lady. 'You can call me Mrs Snipes.'

She escorted Madge to a small room and deposited her case on a bed. There were two single beds, and she assumed the other would be for her brother when his eye had been fixed.

When Mrs Snipes left the room, Madge collapsed onto a bed and wept. She had never been so unhappy in her short life. Cassey sat propped up on a pillow, a little smile touching the cruel lips.

Reggie never returned. A nurse sat Madge down in her room to explain that whatever had penetrated her brother's eye had carried an infection which the hospital could not contain, and that her brother had unfortunately passed away. The authorities had informed her parents of the tragedy, but because of the increasing intensity of the German bombings over London, Madge would have to remain where she was.

She was heartbroken. Reggie had never been nice to her, but he was her brother, and she was relying on him to help her now that her parents were so far away.

Mrs Snipes kept her busy cleaning the house and afterwards, Mr Snipes insisted she help in the yard, feeding the chickens and collecting their eggs. Madge had no free time to mourn the loss of her brother, and the unfeeling couple made sure she would be occupied every minute of the long days.

Cassey, however, spent her days lying in the small bedroom not caring for her isolation and unable to formulate any kind of a devious plan for her own future. The war was in full swing, and she could contribute nothing positive toward it. Lilith hoped her peers were doing better. She had divided herself into so many dolls that her knowledge on their progress was, at best, confused.

The war was to drag on for five long years, and Madge grew into a robust young lady. Her looks were plain and never having anything to smile about, her demeanour remained sullen. Mr and Mrs Snipes treated her as an unpaid skivvy. There was always plenty to do and precious little time to complete her many daily tasks.

CHAPTER 24

M adge spent her days working on the farm. A system had been in place to monitor the evacuated children, to ensure they were properly looked after and attended school. But some slipped through the cracks, and Madge was one of those unfortunates. Child evacuees were returned to their homes at war's end, but not Madge.

Days turned into weeks as the daily grind continued unabated. Madge worked until dark and, after a bland meal, retired to her small bedroom. Her only solace was Cassey, and she spent hours talking to the doll.

Cassey listened to her idle chatter, wishing the girl would shut up. She was not at all interested in the girl's life or problems. Her one aim in life was to cause chaos in the world and ultimately engineer the end of the despicable human race altogether.

Eventually, Madge drifted off to sleep, knowing full well she would be summoned downstairs at 5am. Farm life began at dawn, but the family had to be up and fed before first light.

Cassey waited until Madge's breathing changed, indicating she was in a deep sleep before easing herself out of bed. Sliding to the floor, the doll began to walk awkwardly. The strings attaching her legs were too tight, and inwardly she cursed Madge's father, Cecil, who had kindly repaired her. The oaf might have made a better job of it!

The bedroom door presented its usual obstacle. The silly girl always closed it before getting into bed. Cassey liked to wander abroad in the night to alleviate the frustration of being cooped up in the tiny bedroom. An old crate located next to the door enabled her to reach the handle, which was fortunately a lever.

Gaining entry to the hallway, Cassey clumsily made her way along towards the top of the stairs. She had almost reached the top step when a door opened, and Mrs Snipes appeared.

'Who's there?' She whispered nervously.

Encased in a voluminous nightdress, only her feet could be seen protruding from the hem as she tentatively took a step into the hallway. She was staring through the darkness, looking left and right; failing to notice Cassey, who remained still. The old lady took another uncertain step and almost bumped into her. Sidestepping, Cassey grabbed at the thick nightdress and pulled hard. Mrs Snipes screamed as she began the long and painful descent to the foot of the stairs. They had never been carpeted and offered no protection from the soft body bouncing down.

Mrs Snipes lay at the foot of the stairs, her head twisted at an awkward angle and blood trickling from her mouth. Cassey made her way back to Madge's bedroom and pushed the door closed with a soft click.

Mr Snipes, a heavy sleeper, was none the wiser and continued snoring.

He awoke at 4am. The clock in his head accurate to the minute as usual. Not noticing he was alone in bed, Mr Snipes pulled on his outer clothes over his pyjamas. He could see no point in letting in the cold by taking them off. At night, he would simply remove his outer clothes and would be ready for bed.

Half asleep in the still dark house, he trudged downstairs, almost falling over his wife's body.

Trying to rouse her, Mr Snipes reacted in disgust as her head flopped to one side.

'Stupid bloody woman, now I'll have to get my own breakfast,' he said, shouting, 'Madge, rouse yourself, I want my breakfast!'

He unceremoniously dragged his wife's lifeless body into the little used front parlour, shutting the door with a slam.

'I must get on to the insurance people. I'm sure we had a policy; might get a few shillings for her.'

Madge came downstairs, still half asleep.

'Where's the missus?' She mumbled.

'Gone and killed herself falling down the bloody stairs, stupid cow.' Mr Snipes muttered.

Madge was stunned,

'You mean she's dead?'

'As a doornail, she was never much use to me, anyway. Now, get me some breakfast, there's plenty to be done today.'

Madge couldn't believe the man's callousness but set to and prepared the usual early morning breakfast.

Between mouthfuls, Mr Snipes said he would contact the undertakers later in the day, when he had a spare minute.

'I suppose those leeches will want plenty to bury her.'

'Where is she?' Madge asked, looking around.

'In the front parlour, leave her be. It's not a pretty sight. Mind you, she never was pretty when she was alive.'

Mr Snipes sniggered at his own crude joke and went out into the yard.

Madge couldn't resist looking and opened the parlour door. Mrs Snipes certainly was not a pretty sight. Her husband had taken no care to place her neatly on the floor. She was exactly as he had left her, sprawled out with her head at an even more acute angle.

Closing the door gently, Madge retreated upstairs to the sanctity of her room. Without thinking, she began to relay the story to her doll. Cassey had always been her silent confidant.

So engrossed was she with the telling of her story, she didn't notice the wicked grin on the doll's face.

Later, Madge watched in silence as two men in dark suits removed Mrs Snipes from the parlour. They placed her in the back of a green van and with a wave to Mr Snipes, drove off. He turned on his heel and walked back inside, muttering that those bastards at the insurance wouldn't pay. They had patiently explained to him that as he had not paid any premiums since 1935;

the policy was null and void. He kicked the door shut in anger and shouted up the stairs.

'Madge, get yourself down here. You'll be taking her place.'

Mr Snipes studied the girl standing before him. He had never taken much notice of her whilst his wife was alive. She was merely the unpaid servant. Now, though, he saw her in a different light and Madge felt uncomfortable; he had never looked at her that way before.

Feelings, long dormant, were rising. He felt alive again. But to Madge, he was an old man, unattractive and grubby.

'You will have to do her work as well as your own,' he said. 'Maybe I can give you a small wage to make up for it.'

Madge was more worried about the look in his eyes than the possibility of an income.

That evening, after a gruelling day's work, she collapsed into bed. Cassey, lodged on the pillow, smiled in satisfaction. Lilith liked nothing better than human suffering, and her plans seldom failed.

Madge was asleep as her head hit the pillow. She had been too tired even to undress and lay on the bed fully clothed.

Her door swung silently open as Mr Snipes peered into the darkened room. He couldn't resist running a hand through Madge's unruly hair. It had never seen a pair of scissors and fell to her waist.

She was lying on her side facing away from him and he was able to slide onto the bed beside her. The doll lay on the floor where Mr Snipes had thrown her in his eagerness to cuddle the supine body.

Madge was unaware of his evil intentions until she felt a sharp pain tear through her body. She awoke with a startled cry, the only sounds coming from Mr Snipes. He was moaning and panting as he held her tightly, forcing himself into her.

With a final deep sigh, he pulled away from her, saying nothing, merely retreating through the door. Madge pulled herself to the side of the bed and lit the stub of candle on a small side table. Her clothing was in complete disarray, and she cried out in fear as she looked down to see the sheet tinged red with blood.

Gathering Cassey in her arms she cuddled the doll tightly, crying in anguish. Cassey remained rigid. An ancient primeval satisfaction had taken hold of her, and Lilith was in ecstasy.

The following morning, Madge woke to the knocking on her door.

'Get up, I want my breakfast,' Mr Snipes shouted.

He sat at the table as she put the food in front of him together with a mug of tea.

No mention was made of the night before. Madge sat opposite with a mug of tea.

'Not hungry?' Mr Snipes grunted.

'No,' she whispered.

He left the table with a clatter of cutlery, making for the door. Outside, dawn was breaking.

'I'll be in at 10, have my morning tea ready.'

Madge set to and cleared the things away. Later, she would feed the chickens and collect the eggs.

The day passed in its usual monotonous way until the farmer came in for dinner. Madge had prepared a rabbit stew. There was always plenty to be had as the local farmers trapped or shot them regularly. They hung behind the pantry door until it came time to skin and prepare them for the pot.

The time to retire came early that evening. Mr Snipes seemed to be in a hurry to finish his meal.

Madge made her way to her bedroom, wishing that the door had a lock. She lay on the bed, fully clothed, not daring to close her eyes. The stub of candle flickered in an unseen draught. It had only an inch or so to go before even that faint light disappeared.

She froze as the door lever began to go down, gripping Cassey tightly, using the doll as a shield against who she knew would be coming through her door.

Mr Snipes stood framed in the doorway, unclothed, and

Madge looked on in horror as she saw for the first time a man's naked form.

She curled up into a tight ball as he approached. Tearing the doll from her grasp, he flung it to the far side of the room. Madge was beside herself with fear and crying uncontrollably, but Snipes was deaf to her protests. The fire was in him as he reached out and slapped her face savagely.

'Do as you are told,' he snarled.

Madge was lost. There was no way she could fight him, so in the end she lay quietly while he took his pleasure, hating every moment.

In the morning, again, nothing was said, no mention of his attack.

The nightly invasion became habitual, and Madge grew numb. She no longer protested but waited each night for the inevitable intrusive visit.

Madge knew this was how babies were made and feared the inevitable. Day after day she looked for signs of her period, but nothing showed. Snipes didn't realise and didn't care. He carried on with his relentless attention, rarely missing an opportunity.

After many anxious weeks had passed with still no sign of her period, Madge knew she would have to tell him she was pregnant, fearing his reaction.

Such was her trepidation and fear, the news about the end of the war didn't register. All she could think of was her condition and Snipe's reaction.

He stood inside the barn up in the loft area, using a pitchfork to transfer stored hay to the floor below.

'Can I please talk to you, Mr Snipes?' Madge asked from below.

'What now, girl? There's always something for you to gripe about.'

'Please, sir, I have to tell you something important.'

'Climb up here, I can't hear you from down there.'

Madge climbed the vertical ladder at the side of the loft. As she emerged level with the loft floor, Snipes spoke angrily,

'Ok, go ahead, spit it out!'

He hadn't been to her room for three nights in a row, a rare occurrence. A cow had been having trouble birthing and cows were valuable. By the time he had seen to its needs, it had been early morning, the same thing for three nights now.

His lust rose to fever pitch as she stepped onto the landing. Reaching for her, he threw her onto the loose hay and unbuckled his belt.

'Please, Mr Snipes, I'm going to have a baby,' she cried.

Snipes laughed, 'The first of many, perhaps.'

Madge was horrified, he didn't care; he was going to do it again, here in the barn!

Something inside her snapped. A red mist dropped over her eyes, and she became calm. Snipes had dropped his trousers and was walking clumsily toward her.

Standing at her feet, he gave a disgusting leer,

'My wife couldn't give me children. It's never too late, is it?'

Madge reached beside her for the pitchfork she had nearly fallen on when Snipes threw her to the floor. Gripping the handle with both hands, she drove it upwards as he lunged forward, the prongs driving through his chest. Snipes had a surprised look on his face as he continued falling, driving the prongs deeper into his heart.

Madge kicked up as the body fell towards her, skewing it to one side. She lay, panting, still on her back.

Looking sideways, she stared into the farmer's bulging, wide-open eyes.

Her calmness deserted her. What had she done? The involuntary scream carried across the farmyard, but there was no one to hear it.

Struggling down the steep steps to the floor below, she saw her doll lying in some loose straw against the wall. She didn't remember bringing Cassey with her and walking towards it leaned down to pick up her doll. As she did so, that same strange calmness once again enveloped her.

'He was a nasty man,' Madge told Cassey, 'very nasty.'

She didn't return to the farmhouse, walking instead out of the farmyard and along the lane. She had no idea where it led, only that it would get her away from this accursed place.

Cassey nestled comfortably under her arm; finally, she had found her ticket out of this place and could continue her own personal war against the entire human race.

Madge walked out of the lane and onto a main road. She turned left, no reason. Either direction would have been right. As dusk approached, she snuggled down under a hedge. She would be cold and starving, but at least she was free. Free from what? She asked herself. Shrugging her shoulders and keeping Cassey close by as she drifted off to sleep, her mind was blank. The horrors of the past few years finally catching up with her and blocking her memory.

Rain dropping onto her forehead woke her as the early morning light promised a miserable day ahead. She was now also wet as well as being cold and hungry.

Madge walked for a good part of the day. There was little or no traffic on the road, mostly army trucks which didn't stop, busily ferrying troops from the recently ended war.

Eventually, a car stopped, and the driver enquired if she was all right. It was a local doctor, and he knew she was very definitely not all right by both her manner and physical appearance. Madge gratefully climbed into the warm interior of the car.

'Where are you going, young lady?' The doctor asked.

'Cassey and I are going for a walk,' replied Madge.

The doctor headed straight for a local hospital. His passenger needed help and not only in the physical sense. He thought she may have decamped from an institution, as it was unusual for a young woman of her age to be carrying a doll. Especially as she constantly talked to it and paused to listen, as if expecting an answer.

CHAPTER 25

Blackthorne hospital welcomed Dr Wright as a regular. The girl submitted to an examination, but only after a female nurse held her hand.

'She is pregnant, about five months, I'd say,' said the examining doctor.

'I have no idea where she's from. It's hard to get a word out of her,' said Dr Wright. 'I'm worried about her state of mind too.'

'I suggest we keep her until we can properly evaluate her,' suggested the hospital doctor.

'That could be some time, I fear,' said Dr Wright.

Cassey had been left propped up in a chair not far from Madge. She was not happy, cooped up on the farm for the entire war had left her no chance to further her cause, and now this. She had to get away, back to London.

As Madge left the room, escorted by a nurse, she reached for her doll. Unseen by the nurse, Cassey's expression turned venomous. She had no intention of spending the next few years locked away in a mental hospital. Propelling herself off the chair, she avoided Madge's outstretched hand.

'Oh, dear, you've knocked your pretty doll onto the floor. Let me get it for you,' said the nurse.

A desperate scream startled everyone. Nurse Dilly looked at her hand in shock. Something sharp had severed the top of her index finger. Her legs buckled as she fainted and crashed to the floor alongside the doll.

'She must have caught it in the doll's mouth,' said Dr Wright, examining Cassey's mouth. 'These little teeth are razor sharp. Why on earth would a toy maker do that?'

Cassey had failed. She was handed back to Madge, who gripped her tightly as she was led away. Madge liked her room. It had only one single bed, so she assumed she would be left in peace. That night she slept peacefully for the first time in years, tucked up and warm. A radiator heated her room and as the nurse closed the door with a soft click, she slipped into a deep sleep, unaware that it was the medication taking effect.

The doll lay nestled under her arm. Cassey was livid. She didn't take kindly to defeat and would once again have to bide her time.

Madge withdrew further into herself, and the doctors feared she might never recover. The bulge in her tummy became more and more obvious as the weeks passed.

Cassey became frustrated with Madge, who would sit for hours, cross-legged on her bed with the doll sitting up in front of her. Occasionally Madge would talk, but it was all meaningless. She had truly lost her mind. The authorities still had no idea who she was. The day Mr Snipes had collected her from the train station was the day she effectively disappeared from records. It was as if she had never existed, which was something of a blessing as unknown to Madge, both her parents had been killed during the Blitz. If she was privy to those horrific details, it would simply push her even further out of reach.

Cassey, in desperation, began to talk to the girl when they were alone. She told Madge she was a fallen angel, and that God had placed her on earth for the salvation of humanity. Madge had no idea what the doll was talking about but listened intently to every word.

'The people in here want to keep you from the rest of the world,' said Cassey. 'They know you are here for the good of humanity, but they will do and say anything to keep you locked away. When your baby arrives, it will be taken away. You will never see it again.'

Cassey never let up, repeating the story over and over until Madge was totally convinced the staff were her enemy.

Doctors were puzzled. Madge appeared to be physically

healthy and almost ready to deliver her baby. Her mental condition, however, was still a mystery. Enquiries as to who she was had reached a dead end. So many people were homeless and the number of children without parents had tested the system to its limits. Refugees were now pouring into the country from devastated Europe, adding to the confusion.

Madge gave birth to a baby girl one rainy morning. It was a dreary day and summed up her feelings exactly. She held her baby tightly, suspecting that at any moment it would be plucked from her hands, and she would never see it again.

She had insisted Cassey accompany her to the little surgical room and the doll now sat perched on a chair watching the birth with morbid satisfaction. Cassey felt a sense of ownership, as it had been under her influence that Snipes had fathered it. In fact, the whole episode after the death of Mrs Snipes had been engineered by the doll. She had taken over Snipe's mind completely using his weaknesses to subdue any moral recriminations he may have felt at the time. She had planned to escape from the farm and used him to further her aims.

Snipes lay dead in the hayloft for a long time. The animals became neglected and if it was not for a neighbour noticing that the dairy cattle were in extreme discomfort from not having been milked, he may have lain there for months.

The police were called when the body was finally discovered. However, there were no clues as to who might be responsible for the grisly death. Everyone was convinced that he lived alone since the death of his wife some time before. With the countryside swarming with European refugees, it could have been anyone. The baffled police labelled the case as *murdered by person or persons unknown* and filed it away to gather dust with other unsolved cases.

The baby lay on its mother's chest, eyes blinking at the harsh overhead light in the centre of the room. Its bleary gaze traversed the room until it connected with Cassey's single eye. A connection was made. One that would last forever.

As expected, the baby was taken away one night when Madge was asleep. She spent the following day screaming for her newborn until a doctor administered a sedative.

Madge didn't fall asleep, merely became quiet. Inside, she was still screaming, but no sound came from her mouth. A strong idea came to the forefront of her mind as Cassey wormed her way into her subconscious.

Madge's quiet voice surprised the staff.

'Can my baby have the doll?' She pleaded.

The doctors conceded that it might calm her if she knew the baby had at least one thing of hers and relented, taking the doll away from her to give it to the baby.

Madge had nothing now, no baby, and no doll. She was alone in a harsh world. Cassey had told her there was no future for her on earth and that one day she should make her way back to God.

Six weeks later, Madge appeared to have turned a corner in her recovery. There was no more talk either of the baby or her doll and doctors were pleased with the speed of her apparent return to sanity.

She asked to be allowed a little more freedom and it was decided she could leave her room, but she must stay in the building.

The staff became used to seeing Madge wandering through the different wards and began to ignore her. It appeared she was beginning to return to normality.

In time, Madge found her way to the roof by a seldom used stairway. She had wandered all the wards, seeking but not finding a way out of the place until trying the door at the top of those stairs. It led onto the roof and without hesitation, she made her way out, closing the door behind. The roof was flat with a low parapet, and she made her way to the edge. Dusk was fast approaching, and she decided to wait until full darkness before making her way back to God, as Cassey had instructed.

Downstairs, the nursing staff were panicking. Madge

should have been back in her room, and they searched high and low for her, fearing she may have found a way to leave the building. Doctors informed the police, who confirmed they would carry out a search the following day at first light.

Madge looked over the parapet into the darkening woods as a vixen suddenly gave its harsh cry. The girl took this as a signal and knelt on the parapet, gradually rising to her feet.

The fox's cry sounded once more, and Madge stepped into space. Cassey was right. It was time for her to return to God.

CHAPTER 26

Sally

1950

Madge's funeral was a lonely affair. As a suicide, she could not be buried in consecrated ground, so she lay with other ungodly souls just beyond the graveyard wall. No minister would attend the funeral, as self-murder was still a crime.

Her baby, however, fared better. A suitable couple was found, and she was adopted. The happy couple fussed over their new daughter, dressing her in new clothes and determined to give her a privileged life.

The one thing they did not want was the doll. It was ugly with dirty clothes, torn hair and one eye which refused to open.

'What shall we call our baby?' Daisy asked.

'Should we name her after your mother?' replied Tom.

Daisy smiled, 'That's a good idea, mum will be pleased, Sally it is then.'

And so Sally was christened in the village church. The Youngs had tried for years to have a family with no success and both now in their early forties, had given up hope entirely. They had studied the adoption process a little late as older couples were generally overlooked, but with the number of children with no parents stretching government resources to the limit, it was decided to ease the regulations.

Baby Sally seemed to have a mind of her own, a very strong mind, demonstrating it to the full when her new parents tried to take away the doll. With surprising strength for one so young, she clung to Cassey relentlessly.

In the end, they decided the doll was important enough to remain with them. Sally rewarded their generosity with a big watery smile, and the Youngs were completely won over.

'At the very least we can get the doll new clothes,' said Daisy.

'I don't know what we can do about the hair or that bloody eye, it fair gives me the creeps,' said Tom.

'It does look rather gruesome, but Sally loves it,' laughed Daisy.

Cassey began to exert her control over both the child and parents. It took her a year to instil the idea that the family should move to London. Cassey needed to get back. She could create more chaos there and the old couple would be wondering where she was.

Tom and Daisy looked bleakly at their new home. It was one in a long terrace of rented workers' houses in the East End. Cassey tried to contain herself. The old couple was so close.

Furniture came from second-hand dealers and, although obviously not new, created a pleasant home for the Youngs and their new baby. They never revealed Sally was adopted. Nobody knew or even suspected, so why go into lengthy explanations. The baby's mother had died, and the father was unknown. Sally Young was theirs and that was that.

Two nights after their arrival, Cassey was able to slip out unseen. Her small stature made that easier, although walking on her stubby legs was awkward.

She lay outside the door of the warehouse. The stairs to the old couple's flat above were never cleaned and the door at the top looked as if it had not been opened in years.

Sarah paused, an inner sense alerting her to Cassey's presence. Rising painfully to her feet, she made the long journey slowly along the hallway to the door. It was stiff with lack of use, and it took some time to ease it open on dry hinges. Struggling downstairs, one step at a time, pausing before attempting the next, she eventually reached the external warehouse door; on opening it, a smile creased her worn features. Cassey looked back at her with her one eye, but there was no warmth of welcome. Cassey did not know the meaning of warmth. Coldness had surrounded her entire history. It suited her and her purpose in life.

'Take me upstairs,' was all she said. It was an order, not a request.

The old woman bent down to pick her up, and the doll recoiled at her touch. The wrinkled skin was dry, and she smelled as if her flesh was already putrefying. Cassey had adopted many human traits over the years, including the sense of smell, something she regretted as the old lady carried her upstairs.

Lionel Plunkett sat at the same desk, still scribbling meaningless words to everyone except himself.

'Tell me about your travels,' said Sarah, thirsty for any information to relieve the boredom of her small world.

The doll ignored her plea. She had her own needs,

'I need you to find out what is going on in the world. I have been locked away for years,' said Cassey.

'Yes, of course, anything you say,' replied Sarah, feeling fearful. Cassey had come into their life many years before, when she and Lionel were merely an ordinary couple, lulled into her clutches by false promises. They had no idea that Lilith inhabited the doll they knew as Cassey.

'Take me back to that insipid child,' demanded Cassey. 'These legs are almost useless; it took me ages to get here.'

Sarah hurried to obey, carrying the doll back to the Young's house and leaving it outside the front door. She knocked loudly on the door before making her way back to the warehouse. On the way, she mused that at least she occasionally saw something of the outside world. Her husband had never left the warehouse in all the years since they had known Cassey.

Tom warily opened the door. The loud knock had disturbed his sleep, and it was some time before he was awake enough to realise it was someone at the door. Staring out into the gloomy night, he studied the empty street.

'Bloody kids,' he said aloud, beginning to close the door. Out of the corner of his eye, something caught his attention. Reaching down, he gripped the doll by its arm and lifted it from the doorstep.

'What the hell are you doing out here?' He said aloud.

'Who are you talking to?' Daisy said from the top of the stairs, 'who is it?'

Tom laughed, 'It's only the bloody doll; she's had a night on the tiles and come back late.'

'Be serious,' said Daisy. 'How did it get outside?'

'How the hell would I know,' said Tom. 'Sally must have forgotten to bring it in, and somebody returned it.'

'It's very late,' observed Daisy. I wonder who it was?'

Tom walked upstairs carrying the doll by one arm. 'Don't think she would have got lucky with any handsome boy doll. It's the ugliest doll I've ever seen. It really ought to be thrown in the bin, but our Sally loves it.'

He laughed again as he placed the doll back in Sally's bedroom. 'There you go, ugly duckling, back where you belong.'

Fortunately for Tom, it was still quite dark, and he was unable to see Cassey's expression. If he had, he would not have been so jovial. The doll's face was dark with anger, her little rosebud mouth twisted into an ugly gash.

Two weeks later, Cassey once again slipped out. She sat propped against a wall in the flat above the warehouse as Sarah brought her up to date on the world news.

The war in Korea made her smile. At least the fools had not learned anything from the preceding two world wars. Humanity thrived on conflict and the vast amounts of money generated. While many fought and died, a few sat back, counting the spoils of war. The same kind of people proliferated on both sides, supplying the needs of battle, and making vast profits, the deaths of so many innocents viewed as necessary collateral damage.

It gladdened Cassey's heart, or at least it would have done had she a heart in the first place.

The best news, though, was of the development of the atomic bomb and of how it was used against Japan at the end of the Second World War. How she regretted missing that event instead of being stuck in the country with that stupid girl. What a waste of time that turned out to be with no unsuspecting victim available to transport her to a better vantage point.

She tried to imagine the destructive force of a single atomic bomb dropped on a heavily populated city and of the thousands killed. She conjured up images of the carnage bigger, more powerful devices could inflict; this was getting closer to her aims.

Sarah went on to explain that currently there existed what the press called a *cold war*. Its two protagonists were known as *superpowers*, America, and Russia, both of whom possessed a huge arsenal of atomic weapons ready for deployment at a moment's notice.

'I hope they use those bombs again,' said Cassey wistfully.

Once again, Tom was woken by a sharp rap at the front door. He stared in disbelief at the doll lying on the step.

'This beggar's belief,' he said aloud, 'I must be going mad.'

Traipsing back upstairs with the doll, he opened Sally's door and threw it inside.

'Keep your doll inside in future,' he said, closing the door.

Sally stirred, wondering what all the noise was about as Cassey bounced on the hard linoleum covered floor, ending her short flight lying awkwardly against a wall.

'You have to go,' she said to Arthur's back as he shut the door, 'and go you will!'

'Where have you been?' Sally asked sleepily.

'Nowhere,' said Cassey, quietening her tone, 'go back to sleep.'

Life in the small, terraced house settled into a routine.

Tom worked in the East India Docks as a clerk and Daisy became an outworker for a local factory, making up clothes on her sewing machine. She used the front parlour as a workroom as it was seldom if ever used, usually reserved for entertaining important guests or for the laying out of a dead member of the family. Neither event thankfully occurring too often.

Sally grew into a rather plain young lady, attending the local school, full of working-class pupils. However, unlike other girls, she never grew out of her doll. Cassey occupied pride of place in her bedroom and the first thing Sally did on returning home from school was sit and relate her entire day.

Cassey was becoming impatient again. To her disappointment, nothing positive came out of the Korean War. It had fizzled out after years of conflict, costing only a few thousand lives. A complete waste of time, in her opinion. The new atomic bombs had not been used and the opportunity for more destruction lost. North Korea had been supported by China, who also had the weapons at their disposal. Cassey wondered why the other dolls had not been more successful in influencing matters. Maybe the spirit of Lilith, her own spirit, was spread too thinly. She would suggest to the old couple that they contact other helpers and arrange to consolidate the dolls, to increase the individual power of a few. Cassey, as the leader, possessed more of Lilith than the others, but so far, all her efforts had been for nothing.

CHAPTER 27

With one eye open, the doll sat propped up on the bed. Sally had omitted to close the door as she raced downstairs and out the front, joining the crowd of children heading for another day in school.

In the front parlour, Daisy sat at her sewing machine, engrossed in making up a part of a dress. Every outworker was supplied with pieces of a garment to sew. It was far more efficient if only one piece was stitched by each machinist. In that way, the operator could almost do the job blindfolded, churning out vast quantities. It very often took many such machinists to complete a single garment, but the result was worth it. Each day, teams of workers ferried the pattens and materials to the various houses.

Daisy became very efficient at her job and made a good living. Together with Tom's wages at the docks, they were considered to be one of the better off couples in their street.

The clatter of the sewing machine began to irritate Cassey. Her lazy eye popped open, both eyes staring into space. She had lived through this with another family and did not need to repeat the experience. The noise must stop.

They were alone, Daisy and Cassey. The stairs were a struggle as usual, but she managed to slither down, getting to her feet, and wincing as the loud clatter of the sewing machine assaulted her through the open door of the front parlour.

Daisy had her back to the door. An occasional glance through the window in front of her, the only relief from the tedious and repetitive sewing.

The machine was an old Singer that had been fitted with an electric motor. It worked through a foot pedal and was quite fast.

Daisy was adept at using it and rarely made an error.

'Bugger!' she exclaimed as the machine over ran a seam.

Angrily she began to unpick it, grumbling to herself that it would slow her output.

Putting the two pieces of cloth together under the foot of the machine, she took extra care to make sure they were lined up before pressing the footswitch.

Daisy concentrated, focussing on the machine as it roared into life. She watched as the cloth on which her hand was resting pulled her fingers under the foot of the machine. The needle was punching holes through her fingers, threading cotton through in a lockstitch. She kept lifting her foot in a vain attempt at stopping the machine, but it carried on until three fingers were sewn together.

The scream when it came shook the walls. She looked down at her foot switch, but the machine had already stopped. Cassey was already making her way upstairs one step at a time, reaching the top by the time a neighbour, alarmed by Daisy's screams, ran through the front door.

Tom, with Sally in hand, stood beside the hospital bed.

'I've told you a hundred times to slow down, but you wouldn't listen, would you?' he said, shaking his head from side to side.

'I don't understand what happened. My foot was nowhere near the switch, it just started on its own,' mumbled Daisy.

'Well, they don't run themselves, do they? Tom remonstrated, 'you were going too fast and pressed it by mistake.'

Daisy, convinced she had not pressed the foot switch herself, was puzzled by the entire episode. In any case, there would be no more sewing until her hand healed. The surgeon had done the best he could, picking the stitches from her fingers just as she had the pieces of cloth. Her fingers ached despite the aspirin a nurse had administered.

Cassey sat in her usual place on Sally's bed, basking in

weak sunlight and enjoying the peace and quiet.

That night, Sally relayed the events of the day to her doll, including the terrible accident downstairs. Cassey maintained her blank stare but inside she was ecstatic. Things were going to plan.

With Daisy unable to work, money became tight and nightly arguments became a feature of the household. However, they were not the only couple to argue. Most of the neighbours seemed to engage in loud name calling and swearing. The camaraderie of the war years quickly disappeared, to be replaced by violence of a different kind. Domestic arguments often resulted in altercations between husband and wife, most often the wife coming off second best.

Sally would spend most evenings lying on her bed listening to her parents' downstairs together with neighbours on either side also going at it hammer and tongs. Thin walls left very little to the imagination.

On one such occasion, she clutched Cassey in fear as she heard her mother racing upstairs. The heavy footfalls of her father following made her cringe. This was a fresh development, and she was afraid for her mother.

Putting Cassey to one side, she opened the door to peek out. Her mother lay prostrate in the hall, her father looking down at her.

'Now look what you made me do!' He exclaimed.

There was no movement from the figure on the floor, and Sally couldn't stop herself from crying out.

'Mummy, wake up,' she shouted.

Tom's anger dissipated immediately.

'Go back into your room, Mummy will be fine, she slipped, that's all.'

Sally retreated to her bed but left the door ajar. Picking up Cassey, she bit her lip to stop herself from crying.

'She didn't slip, he hit her,' said a voice beside her.

Sally looked down at the doll; surely, she hadn't spoken?

'Probably killed her,' said the voice, 'let's go and see.'

Holding the doll close, she warily opened the door wide enough to slip through.

'See, she's dead,' said the voice.

'No, she isn't,' cried out Sally in reply.

'No, she isn't what?' said her father, still looking down at the still form of her mother.

Sally realised only she was aware of Cassey's voice.

'Mummy isn't dead,' she hissed.

Tom's anger had returned. He had been drinking, which had caused the argument in the first place.

He slurred a reply.

'The silly cow fell and hit her head.'

'No, she didn't. He hit her,' said the voice in Sally's head.

'You hit Mummy,' said Sally accusingly.

Tom's guilt made him overreact.

'Get back in your room and shut the bloody door!'

The next few moments became a blur to Sally, never being able to accurately recount what happened next.

When the neighbours rushed in, she was sitting ashen faced on the top stair, looking down at the crumpled body of her father at the foot of the stairs, quietly singing an old nursery rhyme,

'Ring a ring of roses, a pocket full of posies. Atishoo, atishoo, we all fall down.'

A police officer gently led her away, still clutching Cassey.

Upstairs, Daisy lay with the side of her face crushed against the skirting on the landing, bleeding from a fatal blow to her temple. She had died instantly when her head struck the sharp corner after Tom's fist caught her by surprise.

Tom had not seen the doll coming until it was too late. Sally had swung Cassey by the legs, so the doll's hard porcelain head connected with his own.

Sally was alone in a sombre room. She studied the walls, green from the floor to halfway up, then cream to the ceiling. She sat on a simple iron bed with a thin mattress and hard sheets.

169

A single blanket covered her to the neck, beneath which her doll lay at her side.

Cassey was furious with herself. She had not meant to kill Tom, but her temper had got the better of her once again. Now, she was stuck in a new institution with another insipid girl. Her plans once again stymied.

CHAPTER 28

Sally remained institutionalised until her eighteenth birthday. The authorities had tried on numerous occasions to place her with other families, but none would accept her. She had matured into a young lady; however, the doll was never far from her side. Prospective foster parents felt disquieted by this young woman sitting with an old, battered doll on her lap. The one piercing eye a terrifying sight as it appeared to follow them around the room.

Sally had grown accustomed to this way of life. Nurses and doctors were kind and for some reason she had slipped through the cracks of the system. The institution had become her home. She was able to go out into the surrounding streets, returning for meals and in the evening to a comfortable bed. No one bothered her, not even for medical check-ups until the day dawned when an official picked up the error.

It was deemed appropriate to send her off to another facility. Her files were suitably adjusted so that it appeared she had always received medical attention. It was merely that she had reached an age when she should be moved on.

As the van transporting her passed through the secure gates of her new home, Sally realised this was not the same environment she had grown used to. She shuddered at the wording on the ancient, faded sign at the entrance which, in an age of increased awareness of political correctness, should have been removed years before,

"Eastern Counties Asylum for Idiots, Imbeciles and the Feeble-minded."

She assumed the sign was a leftover from the nineteenth

century, but its appearance lived up to the wording. The building displayed Gothic architecture, conjuring up images of tall towers, gargoyles, shadows, and a genuine fear of what might go on behind its walls.

The new sign attached to the wall did nothing to dispel her fear and Sally clung to Cassey with all her strength.

"Eastern Counties Mental Hospital"

The cavernous entry hall was noisy, every word uttered echoing and bouncing back at the speaker. Four wide arches led off in different directions. It was like the spokes of a wheel and from each hallway came more noises, presumably made by patients. The cacophony of noise made Sally clasp her hands over her ears. Cassey lay trapped between her knees.

'Come now, miss, it's not that bad. You will soon get used to the noise,' said a man dressed in a white uniform. He at least seemed friendly, and Sally managed a smile.

While the attendants saw to the paperwork, Sally wandered away, looking up in awe at the height of the ceiling, wondering if the place had been purpose-built or had once been a stately home. She didn't see a figure approaching until she felt a light touch on her arm.

'Hello, I'm Diana, and I'm looking for my baby. Have you seen her?'

Sally looked into the vague bloodshot eyes and stammered that she hadn't.

Without warning, the woman grabbed for Cassey.

'Give it back, give my baby back!' She screamed.

Sally held onto Cassey as the woman tried to pull the doll free.

'She's mine. You can't have her,' yelled Sally.

Diana lashed out with her free hand catching Sally full in the face.

'Give me my baby, you thieving bitch!' Roared Diana.

The sudden intensity of the blow made Sally release her hold on the doll and Diana, shrieking in victory, grabbed it and ran back along the corridor from which she had emerged.

Sally was incensed and began shouting after the woman. She was further distressed when she realised the attendants, far from helping, appeared to be amused. They thought the incident very comical. Anything which could engender laughter was welcome in this house of misery.

The friendly man approached Sally and assured her he would return the doll.

'Diana does it all the time. Her own baby died, and she has never come to terms with the fact. She will soon tire, and I will be able to get your doll back. Aren't you a bit old for dolls?'

Sally cast her eyes down before answering,

'Cassey is my only friend.'

'Well now, how about I become your friend, a special friend?'

Sally nodded, 'But I still want my doll back.'

Wilf was well satisfied. This young lady was different from the rest. She was attractive and appeared as almost normal, something of a novelty in this hospital.

The attendants, mostly male, were able to satisfy their strange sexual tastes as they pleased without fear of discovery. The authorities shunned the hospital, happy to leave its unfortunate inmates to their carers.

Sally entered a dormitory with a seemingly endless line of beds. She lost count as she tried to work out with how many she would be sharing the room.

'There are only women and girls in here,' said Wilf. 'The males are in another dorm, safely away from you. Don't worry, I'll be looking after you.'

Sally was beginning to feel the first feelings of doubt about her new *special friend*, although she was still innocent in many ways. The glint in his eyes foretold of things to come.

The first few days were a nightmare. She found it difficult to cope with the almost constant noise. The other women in her ward were, she was convinced, quite mad and spent hours talking to people who were obviously not there.

One evening, her nightmare became worse as Wilf glided

into the ward late in the evening when most had at last suc-
cumbed to sleep with a little help from the white pills dished out
to all and sundry. Sally had learned to slip hers under her tongue
and spit it out at the first opportunity.

'Hello, Sally,' he whispered, 'why don't you come for a little
walk with Uncle Wilf?'

Sally was too scared to speak. She knew he expected her to
be drowsy and didn't want to spoil the illusion, in which case he
might force her to swallow more of the pills, and then she would
really be out of control.

Leading her by the hand, Wilf quietly left the ward and
walked toward a smaller room. He opened the door and slipped
inside with Sally in hand.

The room lit up with a subdued light as Wilf flicked a
switch. It was, she surmised, an examination room. He led her to
a table and began to gently undress her. She had on only a nightshift, so in an instant she was standing naked before him.

'Hop onto the table, Sally, so Uncle Wilf can get a better
look at you.'

She did as he asked,

'Please don't hurt me, Uncle Wilf,' she murmured.

'I won't hurt you, I promise,' said Wilf as he began to shed
his own clothes, 'you are so pretty, Sally, Uncle Wilf would never
hurt you.'

Wilf was beside himself with passion. He had never encountered such a beauty. This girl was different, almost normal.

He had one leg on the table and was about to assuage his
evident passion when a series of high-pitched screams rent the
air.

He stopped, reacting to what sounded like a riot coming
from the men's wing. Hurriedly donning his clothes and arran-
ging Sally's nightshift, he cautiously opened the door to peer
out. The sight that met his eyes would have done justice to the
original asylum, Bedlam. The word had entered the English language as a description of chaos, and tonight it was completely
justified. Male patients were running in all directions, scream-

ing, and pointing. The few attendants on night duty were no match and were falling beneath blows haphazardly delivered by crazed inmates.

Quickly, Wilf led Sally back to her bed and with a quick peck on the cheek, he couldn't resist this one gesture of his unrequited passion, ran out to join the melee.

Cassey lay by her side. The doll felt warm to the touch, as if she had been running, and the smile of satisfaction lighting her face was unmistakable.

Sally lay awake, confused, and scared.

When Wilf had first approached Sally's bed, Cassey knew what was to come. She didn't care if the girl lost her innocence, either willingly or by force. Her hedonistic desire for revenge was all that mattered, and she could see an opportunity to cause unrivalled mayhem, her chief pleasure.

Clambering awkwardly from the bed, Cassey followed Wilf and Sally down the corridor, watching as they slipped into the room.

Making her way silently across the cavernous reception area, the doll was able to slip unseen into a ward filled with men. They were all in a mildly drugged state and when one of them sat up in bed to be confronted by an ugly doll snarling at them, the place erupted. Others could see the doll apparently waving its arms, panic setting in immediately. To some patients, it was a fantasy brought to reality. Many had long suspected that inanimate objects could spring to life and take them. This only served to confirm their worst fears. The doll from *Hell* had arrived to carry them away.

The inmates began running back and forth falling over each other, which only increased their collective panic. Attendants, drawn by the screams, could do little to pacify them. They were not dreaming or imagining this. The doll was there, in front of them, real and frightening.

Cassey lowered herself from the inmate's bed. He was in a catatonic state of shock and would probably never recover.

Making her way unseen back to Sally's bed was not diffi-cult. Two patients caught a glimpse of her en route, but Cassey merely waved her small stubby arms, creating more chaos, as they too joined the throng of panicking inmates.

By the time Sally had returned to bed, Cassey was already in place. Hot from both the physical effort and excitement.

It was some time before the ward returned to what for it was *normal*. Sally slept soundly for the first time in weeks, and Cassey was once again in control.

CHAPTER 29

It was inevitable that Wilf would try his luck again. He seemed to be there every time Sally looked over her shoulder. However, the doctors had by now taken an interest in Sally. They couldn't understand what she was doing in a mental hospital. She certainly didn't appear to be insane. Apart from her obsession with the doll, she appeared to be quite normal. The attention of the doctors kept Wilf at bay, at least in the short term.

Sally kept herself to herself. There was not, she thought, one sane patient with whom she could converse. Until, that is, the arrival of a man who at least appeared to be normal. Lacking the twitching features and constant verbal tirades exhibited by many others, he smiled at her as if recognising a kindred spirit, and she smiled back.

It was a few days later that their paths once again crossed. Sally was seated at her usual table, tucked away in a corner when he approached.

'Is this seat taken?' He asked politely.

'No,' she replied hesitantly.

He drew out a chair and sat adjacent to her. As their knees touched, she felt a thrill go through her body, and instead of drawing away, pressed her knee into his.

Feeling her face beginning to flush, she pulled her knee away, but he pursued her with his until they were touching again.

'I have no idea what I'm doing in this place,' he said. 'One moment I was walking along the road and the next I'm banged up in here.'

'Same with me,' Sally replied. 'I'm not mad, not even

slightly.'

They laughed. At least they had found each other. She had finally found someone she could talk to.

Wilf, standing at the far side of the room, noticed them laughing and couldn't stop the sneer spreading over his face as a twinge of jealousy crept in.

Brad and Sally managed to meet every day after that. She at last had something to look forward to and the mornings seemed brighter somehow. She even began to leave her doll in the bed, under the covers. Cassey wasn't pleased about that. She needed Sally to get her out of this place, she couldn't pursue her evil intentions stuck in yet another institution.

Outside her bedroom was a courtyard with a small garden, and Sally had often looked out, wishing she could feel fresh air on her face. She had accustomed herself to the unpleasant odours of the wards but longed for the crispness of the open air.

Risking another meeting with Wilf, she approached him with her request.

'You can certainly go into the courtyard, but I will have to accompany you. Nobody is permitted to leave the confines of the hospital alone,' said Wilf, grudgingly.

Sally decided it would not be too much of a risk. After all, it would be in the daytime, and they could be observed from the dormitory.

So, it became a daily routine unless it rained. Sally and Wilf, side by side, walking around and around the courtyard. At first, conversation was stilted and a little awkward, but as time passed, they became easier with each other, and looked forward to their mutual outing.

However, Brad was not so happy. He looked on Wilf as competition and unfair competition at that. But there was nothing he could say or do. He was a patient, an inmate, with no rights whatsoever.

On Wilf's part, he gained a new respect for Sally. He no longer thought of her as an easy target for his personal satisfaction. His passions were easily assuaged by others not so compos mentis as Sally.

She became happier with her days. Inside, she had the company of Brad and outside, Wilf. In her innocence, she considered them both merely good friends. Anything else never crossed her mind.

So easy going was her relationship with Brad that she happily followed him around the hospital without a care in the world. He was a strong, handsome man, and she felt safe, guarded against others who, before, she had carefully avoided.

Brad, however, was not what he seemed. Inside ran a streak of dark cruelty that only a few had witnessed, and none had survived. He was in a mental hospital because the authorities were unsure of his sanity. His name had cropped up in a few murder investigations, but so far, the police had not been able to prove he was in any way responsible. He had been committed for observation under an obscure clause in the mental health act.

Sally chuckled at one of his jokes. She had heard it before, but it still amused her. Brad had run out of funny stories and repeated them endlessly, forgetting he had already told them to the attractive girl at his side.

Without realising it, they had wandered farther than usual to the end of a corridor. The lighting was dim, but the room at the far end was used only for the storage of items long since forgotten.

'Let's see what's in here,' suggested Brad, trying the doorhandle.

It opened easily, and they peered inside. Shelving was attached to the walls on either side and was full to overflowing with dusty discarded items.

Sally thought they shouldn't go in and voiced her fears.

'We aren't allowed to go into closed rooms,' she said, appealing to Brad with her doe-like eyes and intimating they should return to the main hall.

'Nonsense, where is your sense of adventure?' Brad answered, tugging her by the hand.

A single dusty light illuminated the room as Brad flicked the switch. As she passed in front, he deftly closed the door. They were alone.

Sally froze as Brad slipped a burly arm around her waist. She tried to pull away as his lips sought hers in an uninvited kiss. Twisting away, she shouted,

'No, Brad, I don't want to.'

Her head rang as his open hand connected with the side of her face.

Terrified now, she felt her clothing being torn off. Brad slapped her even harder as she screamed, reducing her to sobs as he flung her to the floor. Sally felt him drop on top of her.

Gritting her teeth, she was forced to listen to his guttural groans as he ground into her. His hands around her throat squeezed as he continued, and she felt her windpipe collapsing under the pressure of his thumbs. Darkness invaded her senses as she lapsed into unconsciousness.

Brad was now in total control, the state of mind he thrived on, needing always to be the master of his own destiny.

He never felt the blow to the back of his head and continued to strangle Sally. Now that he had satisfied his base instincts, she was of no further use, and he felt the compelling need to kill again.

The second blow was delivered with all the strength Wilf could muster. Brad's hands relaxed as his staring eyes clouded. Blood cascaded down over Sally, but she neither saw nor felt a thing.

Wilf, himself jealous of the attention Sally gave to her fellow inmate, had followed them, becoming aware of her danger when he spied them entering the disused storage room. He was at the far end of the hallway and quickly made his way to the closed door. From inside, he could hear Brad's grunts and guessed as to what was going on. Whether it was voluntary or not did not matter. Close fraternisation was forbidden, so he was quite within his rights to open the door on the unsuspecting couple.

The sight which met him left no doubt in his mind that the act was not consensual, and he picked up an old rusty spanner, bringing it down on Brad's head.

Sally was clearly unconscious and Brad's grip on her throat threatened to extinguish her life if he had not done so already.

The second blow, delivered to the same part of his head, succeeded in shattering Brad's skull, his blood raining down over Sally and almost hiding her face.

Several days later, Sally regained consciousness. Mercifully, she had no recollection of the events in the storeroom. It became clear that she had suffered a complete memory loss, blocking out the horrors of her ordeal.

Wilf had been by her side the whole time, sitting beside the bed holding her pale hand, talking to her endlessly, hoping to bring her out of the coma.

He had been exonerated over Brad's death, who was by now a confirmed rapist, and responsible for the deaths of at least five other women. In stopping Brad, Wilf had undoubtedly saved Sally's life.

Considering the new circumstances, the authorities were forced to reconsider Sally's future. Awkward questions were being asked in high places, and it was decided that Sally should be placed in a safe house where she could adapt and learn to lead a normal life. At last, the authorities had established that she was of sound mind and should no longer be locked up.

When the staff remade Sally's bed, they discovered the doll. It became a figure of amusement, and they wondered how anyone could possibly love the hideous thing. Wilf took it away, meaning to dispose of it, because Sally clearly had no memory of her precious doll, and he considered it best if it disappeared altogether.

Wilf stood in front of the furnace door. It was constantly alight, ready to dispose of hospital waste, and he thought it the best place for Sally's doll. Holding it by a leg, he opened the furnace door, taking a step back as the fiery heat reached out for him.

'In you go,' he said, as he attempted to throw the doll into the furnace.

The momentum of his action, coupled with the heat generated by the fire, threw him off balance and his head caught the edge of the hot door. Screaming in pain, Wilf tried to stand, but the doll seemed to be fixed to his hand. The doll appeared to be in total control as Wilf stared into two baleful eyes, blood beginning to flow from his shattered brow; his mind going blank as he tumbled headfirst into the flames. It was over in seconds, and the doll dropped to the floor. With one eye closed, Cassey shuffled away awkwardly on stiff porcelain legs. She had to get back to the old ones in the warehouse. The Darkness must soon descend.

CHAPTER 30

Sally loved her new surroundings. No more of the drab mental institution walls and innocuous smells. Her room in the half-way house had a door with a lock and key, which she controlled instead of being forcibly locked in. The single bed, table, and two chairs plus a wardrobe for her few clothes were to her a palace. She was free, with no recollection of the doll.

After a few weeks, she began to venture outside the confines of the small garden, exploring surrounding streets. Every day, she wandered farther and farther. It was an exciting new adventure.

The one thing clouding her new life was the fact that she had not had a period for several weeks. After two months, she suspected the worst and visited a doctor. To her horror, he confirmed her fear. She was pregnant.

The walk home from the doctor was both the worst and best experience. So engrossed was she in the unwanted news, she bumped into a man walking in the same direction who had stopped to light a cigarette.

Sally made to walk on, mumbling an apology, but the man could clearly see she was upset.

'Sorry, miss, can I help in any way?'

Sally stopped, put both hands to her face and burst into tears.

Arthur didn't know what to say or do. He had been walking along without a care in the world when suddenly a maiden in distress stepped into his path. A rather attractive maiden, he couldn't help thinking.

'There, there, now. Whatever it is can't be that bad,' he said.

'It's worse than bad,' cried Sally.

Arthur put a comforting arm around her shoulders,

'There's a café around the corner. Why don't we have a cuppa, and you can tell me all about it.'

Seated at a table in the small café, Sally's crying gave way to measured sobs, gradually lessening as the welcome cup of tea arrived.

'Now then, what's the trouble?' Arthur asked.

Sally couldn't stop herself. She had no one else to turn to.

'They said I was attacked by a man and now I'm pregnant,' she blurted, 'no man will ever look at me now.'

'Who are they?' He asked.

'People where I was staying,' she replied, her memory still very hazy.

Arthur wondered where she had been staying but refrained from voicing his thoughts.

'No man will ever look at me now,' she repeated.

Arthur fell into the innocently baited trap.

'Of course, they will. I think you are very attractive.'

Sally looked up into his eyes,

'Do you, really?'

'Yes, I do,' he replied, springing the trap on himself neatly. But in any case, she was attractive, and he had no one else.

Arthur Dennis was a victim himself. Like so many others, he was a casualty of the Second World War. He had survived the retreat from Dunkirk, a miracle in itself, then the D-day landings. While his fellow troopers fell around him, he had managed to cross the beach. From there it had been a hard slog, gaining territory inch by inch from the defending German army.

He made it all the way to the border before falling. A sniper's shot had taken him through the groin.

A field hospital patched him up and before long he was headed home to England. The war was over for Arthur. Doctors told him that whilst he was generally in good physical shape, he would never be able to father a child.

Now, here in front of him sat this fair maiden in distress. He had never bothered with women. He would never be able to have a family.

Sally was pregnant and desperate. Maybe she would find in him an attractive enough proposition.

She sat opposite, drying her eyes,

'Do you really find me attractive?' she repeated.

Arthur nodded,

'Yes, I do.'

He smiled as the irony of his short statement hit him, the words he would be expected to repeat at the altar.

He reached over and took her hand.

'Would it be okay if I took you out sometime?'

'Oh, yes,' she answered.

'Tomorrow evening?' Arthur said, deciding to take the plunge.

They spent the rest of the day in the café. After several cups of tea and a hot lunch, they parted company. Arthur leaned forward and gave her a peck on the cheek. Sally held his hand as she kissed him full on the lips.

'I can't believe you are real,' she said.

Arthur wondered when he should tell her of his infirmity. Would she still consider him *real*? He decided to wait.

Sally arrived home to her lonely room and sat on her bed, smiling like a Cheshire cat. What a wonderful day, she thought.

The following day, Sally sat at her table impatiently waiting for the clock's minute hand to traverse the dial to 12. It would then be 6 o'clock. Why did it move so slowly?

The knock on the outside door startled her. She had been waiting all day for Arthur to call as promised, and now that he might actually be at the door, her feet refused to obey.

A tap at her door was followed by a low muffled voice.

'It's somebody for you.'

Almost tripping downstairs in her haste, she opened the door to Arthur's smiling face. Her Arthur.

They spent their second date at the local cinema, the afternoon in the café, now considered their first. Arthur led her into the back row, where they spent the entire show kissing like a pair of wayward teenagers.

Arthur applied for a special licence, considering Sally's condition, they thought it best to bring proceedings forward to avoid any gossip.

Father Bertrand Clough performed the ceremony. His instinct told him the marriage was a rushed, job and he guessed the reason. He had presided over many such marriages where the bride's gown covered the evidence of a premarital indiscretion.

Nevertheless, bride and groom left the church indescribably happy. Both had scars that were now neatly covered.

Arthur had told Sally of his war injuries before asking for her hand in marriage, and the fact they would never have children of their own.

'I don't care,' she said, patting her tummy, 'we have this little one, and you'll be the daddy.'

He never asked who the father was or the surrounding circumstances, and Sally never volunteered the information, deciding it was for the best. She had no memory of the incident except what she had been told, and she considered the baby in her tummy a gift from God.

Six months later, their daughter, Rose, arrived without any fanfare.

'She's a premmy baby,' became her stock answer to inquisitive neighbours, who merely smiled knowingly. They would never know that Arthur wasn't the father.

Rose was a pretty baby and slept soundly. Through the day that was; the nights were a different matter. Sally and Arthur took it in turn to sit beside her cot in an attempt to lull her to sleep. In the end, they gave up and left her to scream the night away, much to the ire of neighbours who complained bitterly over their loss of sleep. Arthur and Sally began to earn the reputation of being bad parents but challenged any complainants to do better.

One such kindly woman offered to keep the baby with her for a few nights. Arthur handed her the baby during the day, looking angelic as she lay asleep in the woman's arms. But that night, Rose put on her usual display. Betty Slipper was not used to such dramas. Her own children had been easy to live with both day and night.

She leaned over Rose, lying in the cot she had used for her own youngsters.

'Hush now, baby, you are keeping everyone awake.'

Rose looked up blearily into Betty's face, a strange smile illuminating the features normally angelic but now changing into something darker.

Betty withdrew, feeling fear for the first time since the war. That child is not normal, she told herself, as the screaming recommenced.

The following morning at 6 o'clock, she was at Arthur and Sally's door.

'Here, take her. I can't do anything with her either. I feel sorry for you. She's not normal. You should have her looked at.'

Sally accepted her bundle of joy, now firmly asleep, wondering why she should have her *looked at.* Arthur sighed as Sally plonked the child on his lap. Thank God for work, he thought. I wonder if I could get a night shift.

He didn't and continued to suffer from lack of sleep. Both he and Sally's nerves began to suffer, and they appeared to be ageing quickly. Rose continued her sleepless nights for three years, when she suddenly changed. Nights became peaceful at last, and her grateful parents slept deeply.

It soon became noticeable that Rose's stages of childhood development were far more advanced than those of other children, and she began to spurn her parents' company. This didn't disturb Sally and Arthur too much. After all, it was quite something to be the parents of a gifted child in their neighbourhood.

The only thing they found difficult to cope with were Rose's growing temper tantrums. Neighbours laughed and said it was a normal part of childhood, but Sally wasn't quite so sure. Both she and Arthur possessed mild temperaments.

On one occasion a woman down the street had poked fun at Rose, telling her that if the wind changed, she would keep her sour look for the rest of her life. It was a common saying and meant in fun, but Rose stared at the woman, pure venom in her eyes.

'Don't look at me like that, miss!' The neighbour exclaimed.

'Like what?' answered Rose.

'Like the rude little thing that you are, you're no better than you ought to be!' the woman spat back.

'Shut up, or it'll be the worse for you,' said Rose, staring into the woman's eyes.

The neighbour couldn't help herself,

'You are the spawn of the devil.'

Rose's face broke into a grin.

'Yes,' she replied, turning to walk away.

The woman stood stock still, looking at the child's back as Rose walked away; crossing herself in the hope that it might protect her from evil.

Her husband found her two days later slumped on the pavement outside their house. Apparently, she had slipped and fallen off the front step, breaking several bones in her back and her right hip. An ambulance conveyed her to the closest hospital, where she lay in agony for several days before finally giving up the struggle to cling to life. Her husband leaned over the bed to catch her final whispered words,

'She's evil.'

Her husband sat down on a chair next to the bed, asking,

'Who's evil?'

But it was too late, his wife had already passed away.

Funerals were not uncommon in the East End. Mary Bennet was laid to rest with a minimum of fuss and expense. Her husband, Alfred, followed the hearse in a car.

Rose stood silently as the small cortege passed, meeting Alfred's eyes with an icy stare. He shivered, and it wasn't from the cold.

CHAPTER 31

Rose

1961

Alfred met his fate in an alleyway close to home. He had chosen to walk the long way home from the pub, having consumed more pints of beer than usual. His wife had died only four weeks before, and he managed to drown his sorrows practically every evening. Staggering into the alley, he slid against the wall, cursing as his arm grazed against the coarse bricks.

His body was found the following morning lying in a congealing pool of blood.

Police were in attendance and paled as the dead man's head was lifted to reveal a jagged cut to his throat almost from ear to ear. Whatever the weapon, it had left a crude incision, as if it had sawed through flesh and gristle.

Having no known enemies and a complete lack of motive, police were puzzled. It appeared to have been a violent spontaneous murder by person or persons unknown.

Door to door enquiries led nowhere and the police, although leaving the case open, had nothing to go on. Once more, a funeral cortege passed slowly down the road as Arthur, Sally, and Rose looked on.

'The place is going to the dogs,' murmured Arthur.

'There used to be a time when this sort of thing happened

once in a blue moon,' agreed Sally, 'now it seems to be a daily occurrence.'

Rose remained silent, a vacant look in her eyes. She was tired. It had been a sleepless night.

Arthur and Sally were not to know that the child had inherited a dark evil spirit from her father. It was the dominant side of her nature, effectively crushing any of Sally's inherited kindness.

During that first meeting with the old couple in the disused warehouse, Rose had not picked Cassey. Rather, it had been the other way around. The doll recognised a kindred spirit, and it had been easy for her to draw the attention of the girl. Sarah Plunkett had been waiting for the right child with the qualities that Cassey demanded, and Rose fitted the bill exactly.

'You can have that one if you would like, but you must promise to love and care for her in every way,' Sarah had urged.

Rose drew the doll even closer and promised she would always cherish it.

Cassey's influence on Rose increased daily until the child became ever more controlled. There was already something different about the child that neighbours were aware of, but of which her parents were blissfully ignorant. Cassey merely exploited it. Rose already had a dark spirit. Somebody in her lineage had been tinged with evil, a quality that Cassey recognised immediately and could put to good use. She knew the Darkness was not far off and that she had only a short time to enjoy herself among these useless humans.

The girl had been easy to bend to her will, but the parents would need to be dealt with in order to give her the freedom she craved.

Cassey had perfected the art of hypnotising them, sending them off into a deep sleep. When Arthur and Sally looked into her open eye, they became mesmerised. The one open eye appeared to pulse, shining brighter, then dimmer until they were unable to look away. Later, they would have no memory of what had happened. Waking in the morning still sitting in their chairs in the kitchen, they would laugh at the fact that they had been so tired they had both dropped off to sleep where they sat.

Rose would look on as they fell under the doll's influence before carrying Cassey upstairs, where she herself would fall into a deep sleep.

It became a nightly ritual. Cassey had her freedom, and having no need of sleep, wandered far and wide, wishing only that her unstable porcelain legs were more mobile.

She had to come up with a new plan. Her legs were far too limiting, so she decided Rose would be her method of transport, ensuring the girl took her everywhere, despite her appearance. With her broken eye and tufts of missing hair, Cassey looked frightening to other children.

The nasty little brat of a boy had been the first. How dare he ridicule her appearance! She transmitted her anger into Rose who, holding her by the legs, swung her towards the boy's head, felling him with her porcelain body. The blow connected with his head with the force of a ten-pound hammer, shattering his skull with ease. Nobody would dream that a young girl and her doll would be capable of such destruction. But Cassey, with the spirit of Lilith, exuded pure evil and the strength of a demon.

After the boy had been dealt with, the local Catholic priest came calling. Cassey had struggled to maintain a straight face, her body still wet from Rose's bathing to wash the boy's blood away. Father Clough asked the girl where she had found her new doll.

Later, as the priest walked away, she had stood in Rose's arms, staring after him, thinking that he might have to be dealt with. Religious zealots were always the hardest to control.

Several days later, Father Clough once again called on Rose's parents. He was intrigued by the girl. Her attachment to the doll was, he thought, a little unusual for a nine-year-old. Most young girls, by that age, had relegated their dolls to the bedroom, becoming mere decoration. This opinion had also been expressed by the girl's schoolteachers who found it most odd that when they attempted to separate the pair, Rose had kicked up such a fuss they were forced to relent.

Father Clough sat in the small kitchen as Sally poured him a cup of tea.

'Why are we blessed with your visit today?' she asked.

'Just doing my rounds,' he answered. 'Is Rose here?'

'In her room, she spends most of the time up there. I can't seem to get her outside,' said Sally, afraid the priest might frown at her lack of mothering ability.

A movement in the corner of his eye made him look up sharply.

'Hello, Rose.'

'Hello, Father,' answered Rose.

The doll was tucked under one arm as usual, its bottom resting on her hip.

'How is Cassey this fine morning?' the priest asked, smiling blandly towards the doll.

'It's a doll. How do you expect it to be?' Rose snapped.

'Rose don't be so rude,' said Sally, wondering from where this new and wholly unwelcome attitude had emerged.

Rose shrugged her shoulders and turning on her heel disappeared back upstairs, leaving both her mother and Father Clough nonplussed.

'I'm so sorry, Father. I don't know what's got into her these days. She is always with that doll, and it worries me.'

'Let me go up and talk to her,' said the priest. 'Maybe she will open up to me.'

Father Clough began to climb the stairs but stopped when Rose appeared at the top.

'Don't come any further, Cassey says no!' she exclaimed.

The priest faltered. Something about Rose's voice made him feel uneasy.

'Very well, I won't come any further, but you really must not be so unkind to your mother,' he said, trying to assume a kindly nature although suddenly feeling afraid. He sensed an evil spirit had entered the house, and it was, in fact, looking down at him.

Hurriedly making his exit, Father Clough made his way back to the sanctity and safety of his church. He knelt at the altar in supplication, hands together, appealing to his Lord for help. A dark cloud passed over the sun and he felt chilled as a darkness surrounded him, his church no longer feeling so safe.

The following week, Rose went back to school, Cassey still firmly tucked under her arm, and daring anyone to mock her. The look in her eyes warned of dire consequences should they even hint at derision.

Teachers fared no better, preferring to leave the girl to her own devices. A wave of fear had swept through the school.

One cloudy afternoon, the school lights suddenly went out. Pupils and teachers alike wandered around classrooms, laughing nervously in the dimness. Rose, however, made her way down a corridor towards a large grey box, the door of which hung open with the janitor poking around inside.

'Must be a fuse,' he mumbled, removing each porcelain fuse holder to check that the little piece of wire was intact.

Rose reached forward; her finger poised to touch the bare contacts.

'Don't do that, girl. You will electrocute yourself,' said the janitor, putting his hand over her wrist.

He was not in time to stop Rose touching an empty fuse holder.

She didn't make a sound, but the janitor's surprised scream rent the air as the powerful current coursed through their bodies.

Rose, unable to stop herself from grasping the contact, allowed the current to course through both herself and the janitor until someone turned off the master switch. They fell to the floor, pupils screaming in fright as teachers ran to their aid. Both appeared to be smoking, and there was an acrid smell of burnt flesh pervading the corridor.

The janitor and Rose both appeared to be dead.

The school was closed immediately, and the children sent home. The police arrived followed by an ambulance to ferry both victims to the hospital, even though they appeared to have no signs of life.

They lay side by side in the ambulance, Rose still clutching Cassey, her burnt hand incongruous against the pasty white pallor of the rest of her body. The janitor appeared to be peacefully asleep, although the lack of a pulse signified different.

At the hospital, both bodies were conveyed to the emergency department, where both were declared dead by electrocution. A nurse attempted to pry Cassey loose from Rose's lifeless hand, but to no avail. The girl clutched her doll tightly in death as she had in life.

Considering the unusual scenario, they had been presented with, the nursing staff decided to leave the doll with the child, and both bodies were wheeled down to the mortuary where they would be prepared for autopsy.

They made a sorry sight, laid out side by side on adjacent white slabs, awaiting the probing scalpel of the pathologist.

The janitor's examination was carried out first. His body, cut from under the chin to his pubic bone, revealed organs that no longer functioned. After each part had been examined and weighed, it was replaced inside the now empty cavity. A sack stitch pulled the flesh together, and once again the body resembled that of a human being, apart from the livid scar which gave the late janitor the appearance of Frankenstein's monster. A white sheet now adorned the corpse with a neat white ruff around the throat to disguise the pathologist's handiwork.

Giving instructions for the body to be conveyed to the cooler, the pathologist moved over to the frail body of the little girl, still clutching her doll. He hated this part. Cutting open an adult was one thing, but it never sat easy with him to invade callously the innocent body of a child with his scalpel. It felt like a violation, such a horrific end to a young life.

In all his years of pathology, what happened next shocked him to the core. As he made the first incision, the doll crashed to the floor, and the girl's eyes sprung wide open. Blood spurted from the wound, which is never expected from a corpse, and the pathologist fell back in shock, spattered in blood, his scalpel clattering to the tiled floor next to the doll.

The pathologist's assistant fell to his knees, hands in prayer position, his face deathly white. A strangled scream escaped his lips as the apparently dead girl sat bolt upright on the slab.

The small body appeared to survey the situation, devoid of any emotion, controlled and calculating within.

She found it difficult to maintain a straight face, wanting to burst out laughing but managed to contain her composure.

'Where is the doll?' she asked.

The Dennis household was in an uproar. It had been a place of great sadness just moments before the police had arrived to inform them their precious little girl had not in fact died but had instead been the victim of a mysterious episode in which she had appeared to be deceased.

The officer omitted details regarding the autopsy and the pathologist's scalpel wound. However, Sally and Arthur were over the moon that their one and only child was still alive.

They hurried to the hospital and were shown to Rose's ward where she was sitting up in bed, devouring a plate of ice cream. Arthur and Sally were speechless.

Her burnt hand had been skilfully bandaged, and there was a neat dressing on her chest, but apart from that, Rose looked to be in good shape considering her recent experience.

Sally dared to ask.

'Where is Cassey?'

'Under the bed,' said Rose, 'it's only a stupid doll.'

CHAPTER 32

Rose arrived home to a chorus of well wishes from neighbours. The authorities had insisted she remain in hospital under observation for a week but released her when she appeared to be in perfect health. Even the burnt hand appeared to be healing well and it was doubted whether there would even be a scar from her recent ordeal.

She, along with her parents and most of the school, attended the janitor's funeral. It was a sad occasion. He left a widow and five young children. Arthur and Sally hugged Rose to them. They had been so blessed.

A handful of dirt rattled on the coffin as the janitor's widow made her last communication with her dead husband. Others followed, including Sally and Arthur. Rose stood at the graveside waiting her turn. She cast her token goodbye into the grave. There was a loud rap as a stone struck the coffin. All eyes turned to her; the looks of condemnation clear on sad faces. She mouthed the word, *sorry,* as the stone clattered on the coffin. The smile on her face as she turned from the grave could best be described as enigmatic, like the model in the famous painting, *The Mona Lisa.*

People crammed into the small, terraced house, where the traditional wake was in full swing. The bereaved wife felt duty bound to put on a good spread for the mourners. Pint bottles of beer fitted snugly into the hands of men, while their wives delicately sipped tea. Rose sat in a corner with a glass of lemonade and a plate of jam tarts, which she commenced devouring in double quick time. Once again, Sally cast her a deprecating look of disapproval.

The following day, it was back to school. Rose passed through the school gates, satchel in one hand, Cassey in the other. At first, other children were curious about how she had survived the accident and asked how it felt to be declared dead.

'Did you see Jesus?' was a popular question.

'I don't know, what does he look like?' Came her devilish reply.

Her classmates soon tired when she was less than forthcoming and returned to the old jibes about her doll. Cassey was certainly looking the worse for wear. Rose had not bothered to care for her since the accident, and her sparse clothing had become grubby.

John Bird was and had been since the beginning of term, the school bully. Every school had one, it seemed to be de rigueur in all schools.

He was feared and avoided by boys and girls alike. If you were unlucky to encounter him when alone, it meant being on the end of a hard punch to the midriff. It had become his favourite punishment, leaving no marks but at the same time causing excruciating pain.

It was inevitable that their paths would cross, and it was between classes when Rose rounded a corner, bumping into Bird.

The impact caused her to drop the doll, and he brutishly kicked it across the path.

'Ugly thing makes a better football than a doll,' he said, laughing at Rose's emotionless face.

'You shouldn't have done that,' said Rose.

He should have noticed the look in her eyes but was too oafish and arrogant.

As Rose went to retrieve the doll, he let fly with a fist aimed straight at her midriff. Usually, the victim would have doubled up in agony. However, Rose stood rock firm. The boy's fist seemed to meet a wall of steel and he howled in pain, looking at his hand, which was already beginning to swell.

He never saw Rose's fist approaching at great speed, but

he certainly felt the impact on his cheek. The blow cracked the bone, taking part of his eye socket with it.

A teacher found John unconscious and bleeding. An ambulance ferried him to the hospital, where doctors attempted to patch him up. He would, they said, require surgery, and there was no guarantee he would regain the sight of his eye.

A loud knock announced the arrival of police at Arthur's door. He answered, surprised at the presence of three police officers.

'We need to speak to your daughter,' said one, 'an injured boy in hospital has reported being beaten by her at school.'

Arthur laughed,

'My daughter isn't exactly a fighter. Who is she supposed to have beaten?'

'A lad by the name of John Bird,' said the officer, which evoked more laughter from Arthur.

'You must be joking. Have you seen the size of that boy? He's twice the height of Rose and three times her weight?'

The police officers looked a little abashed,

'May we speak to her?'

Arthur showed them through to the kitchen where Rose stood, guessing the reason for their visit.

'Show them your hands,' said Arthur.

Rose did as she was bid, holding out both small hands.

'Now make a fist,' commanded her father.

Again, she obeyed and curled both hands into a fist. The officers looked at her unmarked puny little fists, their body language acknowledging the error of the accusation.

'The boy's lying,' remarked one officer, 'how could she possibly have inflicted that amount of damage with a single punch?'

'One punch, you say?' said Arthur.

'That's what the hospital report says. One punch collapsed half the boy's face and damaged an eye.'

Arthur dropped the smile.

'That's terrible, but my daughter is obviously not to

199

blame. You've seen for yourselves, it's simply not possible.'

The police officers tramped along the hallway and out through the front door. By this time, they had a large audience of neighbours watching events unfold.

Arthur closed the door solidly without offering an explanation.

'Nosy sods,' his only comment to nobody in particular.

In the kitchen, he confronted Rose,

'Well, what happened?'

'He hit me first,' she replied.

'How many times did you hit him back?'

'Only once,' she snapped, an impish grin touching the side of her mouth.

Arthur looked at Sally.

'We'll say no more about it. As far as we are concerned, you never touched him.'

'Thank you, Daddy,' Rose lisped, turning away, and disappearing upstairs.

Sally cocked her head to one side, barely catching Rose's words as she entered her bedroom.

'Everything is all right, he won't touch us again.'

CHAPTER 33

Cassey

1962

School became easier after that. The bully was no more. When he eventually returned to class, John Bird was a different person. The damaged eye could not be saved and was permanently blind. Subdued and nervous of everyone around him, he constantly, and fearfully, avoided his nemesis, Rose Dennis. Surely there must have been others in the attack. Maybe all his victims had banded together in an act of revenge. He became wary of every girl and boy he had previously attacked, which meant most of the students.

Arthur and Sally worried for their daughter. Ever since the electrocution accident, she had somehow changed. They began to question her every action, talking quietly to one another at the kitchen table after Rose was asleep.

In bed, Rose lay with Cassey, listening to every word Arthur and Sally were saying. They had no idea she could hear them, but then, she was different.

'I don't want to go to the priest,' said Rose.

'No arguments, my girl. You'll do as we say. Father Clough suggests you attend him every Sunday after Mass. You need to learn the holy sacraments. You are privileged to be a loyal member of the one true faith.'

Sunday arrived and, as usual, Rose trudged behind her parents to church. Like most children, she viewed Mass an ordeal rather than a blessing. Other children walking behind their parents sniggered at each other in recognition of their mutual dislike of Sunday church.

Standing in groups along the street were other children, not of the faith, who viewed their Sunday mornings as an opportunity for a day of play before the gruelling school week ahead.

Rude signs between the different children crossed and recrossed the road, but it was light-hearted.

Mass lumbered painfully on, the seemingly endless diatribe of conjecture lightly tripping off the priest's lips as it did every week. His flock hearing but not hearing as the priest droned through his oft repeated sermon. He was aware that very few listened with any attention and those that did dismissed it as soon as the pub opened its welcoming doors. Father Clough licked his lips, the vision of the first foaming pint of beer flitting across his own fertile imagination.

But his first pint would have to wait. Rose was due in the church office. He was to teach her the holy sacraments. Maybe it would help the girl. In his opinion, she needed some help and guidance. He hoped she had left that doll at home. The sight of it made him uneasy.

Rose tapped lightly at the door. Visions of the tiny fist crept into his mind, aware of the damage it may have inflicted on that hapless boy, John Bird.

Father Clough began his lecture, Rose staring at him with cold, challenging eyes.

'Rose, my child, you really must pay attention. The sacraments are the basis of our faith. Without them, there is no Catholicism.'

'Do you believe in God?' Rose suddenly asked.

Father Clough spluttered,

'Well, of course I believe in God.

'Why, *of course*?' asked Rose.

'Because I have absolute faith that God exists and the Roman Catholic church is his instrument here on earth,' said Father Clough. He had never encountered an argument of this nature before, especially from one so young.

Rose tilted her head to one side.

'So, what about all the other religions?'

Father Clough was on more comfortable ground now.

'They are all trying to come to the Father in Heaven, but we know the only way is through the Catholic church. It is the original and only true faith.'

It was his turn to ask a question, and he did so before she could find another avenue to confuse the issue.

'Rose, do you believe in God?'

She smiled a heavenly smile, the smile of the innocent.

'Yes, Father, I believe in God.'

The priest returned her smile. At least she believed, he was more than halfway there.

'But God is no longer here. He left a long time ago,' she added.

Father Clough was puzzled. Why would she say that?

'Explain what you mean,' he asked condescendingly.

Rose had neatly turned the tables and adopted the role of teacher, standing while speaking to the seated priest as if he was the student.

'God gave up after Adam and his new wife broke the rules.'

'What do you mean by his new wife? Eve was Adam's only wife, made from his own rib,' said the priest.

Rose smiled. She knew she had touched on a subject that Father Clough would rather not discuss, The Old Testament.

'Father, you know very well that Adam's actual wife was Lilith. After she left, Eve was made by God to be second in place to man. A servant or slave was the intention, an instrument for breeding future humankind, but she ended up controlling Adam with her superior intellect.'

Father Clough sat, bemused. How did this child know about Lilith? Adam's first wife was rarely, if ever, mentioned. Better she be forgotten. He wondered again at the words being spoken by this young girl. How could she know?

Rose continued in the face of the priest's reluctance to offer any comment.

'After Adam tasted the forbidden fruit, God gave up and left. He went elsewhere to create his perfect specimen, leaving the failed humans to fend for themselves.'

'No, no, that cannot be right,' cried Father Clough, finding his voice at last, 'God is with us always, he is all around us, even inside us, guiding us on the path of righteousness.'

Rose showed her most enigmatic smile.

'Not doing very well, is he?'

The priest was taken aback by her heretical words,

'But that is a human failing and cannot be attributed to God.'

'It cannot be attributed to God because he is not there, or here, or anywhere,' Rose fired back. 'God left thousands of years ago. He gave up. We were a failed experiment. Only your own ego insists he is here.'

At that point, Father Clough also gave up, showing Rose the way out without comment. What could he say? The child was both unteachable and unreachable. Her tender years belied the dramatic aspersions. Where had she found this version of *truth*, who was she?

At home, Arthur and Sally were waiting expectantly.

'How did it go, dear?' Sally asked.

'He doesn't know much, does he?' Rose answered.

She was horrified at her daughter's reaction to the priest. The church and its teachings had been drummed into Sally as a child and to even consider otherwise was unthinkable.

'Father Clough knows more than you, child. You will go to class with him every Sunday from now on.'

'I don't think he wants me there,' said Rose. 'He didn't even say goodbye.'

The following Sunday came around all too fast, both for Rose and Father Clough. Seated once more in his office, Rose stared blankly at the kindly priest.

'What will we talk about this week?' she asked.

'Our Lord Jesus,' replied the priest, once again feeling on

safer ground. The Old Testament had not gone well. He would try the New.

'What about Him?' Rose asked with a straight face.

'He is part of the Holy Trinity, the Father, the Son, and the Holy Ghost,' incanted Father Clough.

Rose giggled, 'That's silly, he can't be all three.'

'But he is,' insisted the priest, unused to being questioned about such things, and certainly not by one so young. What he said was usually accepted as the truth.

'God had a son here on earth and accepted his sacrifice on the cross for our sins,' insisted the priest, smiling into Rose's face, waiting for her reply, which he anticipated would be contrary to his assertion.

Rose laughed out loud rather vulgarly.

'God could not have had a son on earth because he wasn't here. It was all a fraud perpetuated by men seeking power, and obviously it worked.'

The priest could take no more of this blatant blasphemy.

'Leave now, child. There is, I'm afraid, an evil presence in your mind. I cannot teach you something which you so strongly reject. You are still so young. What do you know of life?'

The low rumble of laughter coming from Rose's mouth startled the priest, a tremor of fear passed through his body.

Without saying another word, he pointed at the door and Rose walked out, swishing her skirt as she swept by.

Father Clough retired to his desk and from a drawer produced a large bottle of Irish whisky. It was sometime later that his head finally connected to the desktop, where he fell into a deep drunken slumber.

So deep was his sleep that he didn't hear the clanging of the fire engine bell as it swept to a halt in front of the church, his church. He was still fast asleep as the first whisps of smoke entered his office from beneath the door.

Firemen worked frantically, trying to control the rapidly spreading blaze and searching for anybody who might have been inside the church. When they opened the office door, it created a massive back blast, killing Father Clough and two firemen instantly.

It did not take long for the news to reach the faithful.

'The good Father is in Heaven with God now,' Sally sobbed.

'No, he isn't,' whispered Rose.

'What did you say?' Said Arthur.

'Nothing,' replied Rose, hiding her hands behind her back. She had scrubbed and scrubbed, but still the smell of paraffin lingered.

Retreating upstairs to her bedroom, Rose closed the door and climbed into bed. The doll remained propped up in the chair where she had left her.

Lilith had temporarily left the doll to enter Rose's mind, taking her over to deal with the meddling priest. When Rose spoke, it was Lilith saying the words. Now, she spoke aloud to the empty room,

'Sad people, the Darkness is coming and still they persist in believing God will save them.'

She walked over to the chair and, taking hold of the doll, shook it playfully, watching in amusement as one eye opened and closed rapidly while the other stayed shut.

CHAPTER 34

Rose passed another birthday and at the tender age of ten, had become noticeably more belligerent. Sally and Arthur no longer corrected or confronted their daughter, not since the change had come over her. Now they tip-toed around, afraid they might get *that* stare, the look they had come to fear.

It was time to pay the old couple a visit, and Rose walked out the front door into the street. She no longer had to creep out surreptitiously; she made the rules now.

The old ones were at their usual stations. The man still writing, walls and ceilings covered in his scrawl; time and again he had written over what was already there until only he could decipher their meaning, while his wife sat in the corner of her room knitting the everlasting scarf.

Sarah welcomed the girl into the room. Rose realising that the same record was playing, and it was coming to an end. In a well-practised movement, the old lady swiftly reset the record and it began its monotonous dirge once again. It would drive any sane person mad, Rose thought, and looking at the woman, decided insanity had set in many years before.

'Mind the dolls, dear. There are a few more this time,' said Sarah.

Rose picked her way across the room, mindful of the broken dolls, stopping to stroke Albert, the stuffed cat.

'He's looking well,' said Rose, without a trace of sarcasm.

Sarah nodded,

'He doesn't change much, just a little dustier.'

'How is Mr Plunkett?' Rose asked.

'Still writing, he's getting a little desperate to finish. *The Darkness* isn't far off now.'

Rose's ears pricked up.

'When, when will it be here?'

'Patience, dearie, it'll come when it's ready, then we can all rest,' said Sarah.

Rose's lips set in a thin line and the old lady recognised the change in her.

'How is Cassey?' she asked.

'She's all right.' Rose replied.

'Not been up to any mischief?'

'No.'

'Powerful men are gathering, jostling for control. The same old story except that now their destructive power has no limits,' said Sarah.

Rose smiled,

'Good, I've waited a long time for that to happen.'

She turned to leave and as she made her way back across the room, she accidentally kicked one of the newly broken dolls. Instead of apologising, she laughed,

'Fucking dolls, I hate them!' she exclaimed rudely.

Sarah cringed inside. She recognised what was happening to Rose. All over the world, the network was reporting that *the Darkness* was about to descend.

Arriving home, the sight of a young man confronted Rose, dressed in black with a white collar, and she assumed this was another man of the cloth.

'Rose, come in and meet our new priest,' said Sally.

'In a minute,' said Rose, hurtling upstairs.

She slammed the bedroom door closed and sank onto her bed beside the doll. Picking it up, she watched as the doll's eyes flicked up and down rapidly for a few seconds, connecting with her.

Gently laying the doll on her bed, Rose opened the door

and ambled slowly downstairs. The new priest sat at the kitchen table with the obligatory cup of tea gently steaming in his right hand.

'There you are, Rose, this is Father Mahoney.'

'Hello,' said Rose, shyly.

'Hello to you,' replied young Father Mahoney. 'I'm new to all this so perhaps you will be able to help me. This is my first appointment since leaving the seminary.'

Rose approached the seated priest and leaned against his shoulder.

'I'll try to help,' she said innocently.

Sally was delighted in the change of attitude. Rose seemed to be back to her old self.

Upstairs on the bed, Cassey smiled. It was never a nice smile, more of a cruel grimace. She could hear every word from downstairs, could see everything through Rose's eyes. Their connection was so much stronger now. She thought the new priest would be fun.

Father Patrick Mahoney, having finished his chore of visiting the faithful, returned to the church and the small ground-floor flat that was to be his home for the foreseeable future.

From the smoking ruins, the burnt-out church had been reconstructed, the surrounding flats having been left untouched by the blaze. The work had been carried out in a very short time; many said miraculously quickly, but the Catholic Church has limitless wealth and money can always move mountains.

Father Mahoney gazed lovingly on the newly appointed interior. It had only ever been a tiny church, but the new altar, glittering with shiny gold leaf, caused him to fall to his knees in supplication. Surely, he was blessed.

However, his flat was altogether different. It was old and dingy; the paint peeling through age and use. A bad smell welcomed him inside and he recognised the stench of urine. The first thing that caught his eye was the overturned collection box lying on the floor. Lifting it up, he noticed the lid open, and the coins deposited by worshippers missing.

The police attended, and an officer smiled knowingly.

'Same as last time, Father. In fact, it's the same every time. We can't catch the bugger, but we know it's the same thief. He pisses everywhere before making off with the spoils.'

'Been going on for some time then?' ventured the priest.

'Yes,' agreed the constable, 'your predecessor, Father Clough, had quite a few break-ins. The collection box seems to be a magnet, always the same target.'

'He hasn't broken in by the looks of things. Maybe I should have the lock changed?'

'Good idea, although I think Father Clough had it changed before. It never seemed to deter this fellow.'

It was midnight before the priest finally finished scrubbing the urine affected areas and retired to bed. He had only just closed his eyes when he was jolted awake by a low rumbling noise. It sounded like something heavy moving, but he knew he was nowhere near an underground railway. Relaxing back into a deep sleep, he began to dream.

He was standing in the church next door. It was dark, and the altar was illuminated by two large candles, one on either side. He was alone except for a solitary figure standing before the altar. She should be kneeling, he thought, out of respect.

In his dream, he called out to the figure, and a young girl turned around to face him,

'You should kneel before the altar in supplication to God,' he said.

'I kneel to no one,' replied the diminutive figure.

It was the little girl he had spoken to earlier that day, Rose.

She finished talking and a smile lit up her face. Father Mahoney thought the smile to be so angelic his heart skipped a beat. A soft light ringed her head. It seemed she might be an angel.

As she faded from view, he attempted to shout out to her,

but no words came out of his mouth. He wanted her to stay, had never before seen an angel; he had heard many claim to have witnessed the miracle, but never himself. Now he had, and he believed, oh, how he believed.

Slowly coming out of his dream, he found the pillow wet with tears, his own.

The priest lay on his back, staring at the ceiling, wondering if this was a vision or merely a dream. He fervently hoped it was a vision.

The return of the rumbling instantly shattered his revelry. Much louder this time, his previous rapture changed to fear. What could it be?

Frank Double sat at the kitchen table, counting the spoils of his latest adventure into the flat below. He lived directly above the priest and smiled at the thought that nobody had suspected it was him who constantly broke in. He was a heavy drinker and needed to fund the habit, the same obsession that had brought his previous occupation of locksmith to an end.

The days of success had all but disappeared into forgotten memories. He and wife, Doris, had married many years before. Two children had followed, a boy and girl. They were the ideal family, lacking for nothing. Frank had purchased a modest home, and they seemed to be set for life.

The rot had set in one night at the local. He had always been a half-pint man at best, usually one or two, then home to a delicious tea with Doris and the kids. However, on this occasion, a young man was celebrating his twenty-first birthday and bought drinks for everyone. Frank contemplated the foaming pint glass sitting in front with apprehension. He had already supped his usual two small glasses of beer and this big one would make it a total of four small glasses, well beyond his usual limit. Not wanting to offend the young man's generosity, he gulped it down.

To his horror, the group next to him applauded. Apparently, it was quite something to down a whole pint of beer in one go.

'Get him another. That one barely touched the sides,' quipped an onlooker.

Before he could say no, another pint appeared. With the encouragement of the audience, he once again knocked it back.

This time, the cheers resounded throughout the bar. Frank felt a little funny. Not nasty funny, but hilarious funny. From then on, pint after pint magically appeared and he downed them all.

10 o'clock came, and the landlord called time.

'Last orders, ain't you got no homes to go to?' The familiar cry rang out, echoed throughout the hundreds of pubs in the land at precisely the same time.

Frank had no memory of getting home. He fell through the door as Doris opened it, wringing her hands.

'Where have you been? I've been so worried, I thought you must have had an accident.'

Frank looked at her through bleary eyes.

'I've had the best time, it was wonderful.'

Doris had already fixed her eagle eye on Frank's neck and collar, where smudged traces of bright red lipstick were clearly evident.

'Who have you been with?' Doris demanded, eyes flashing with indignity.

'Nobody special,' slurred Frank, who in all honesty had no idea. He vaguely remembered a woman cuddling up to him, but guessed she was as drunk as himself.

Doris stormed upstairs yelling over her shoulder,

'Your dinner is in the bin and your children are in bed. What they are going to think, I have no idea!'

Frank lay on the floor, giggling stupidly. He fell asleep as urine saturated his trousers, blissfully unaware.

Morning found him cleaned and tidy, sitting at the kitchen table sipping a cup of tea.

'I'm surprised you haven't got a hangover,' said Doris.

He attempted a conciliatory smile,

'Sorry about last night, love. It got out of hand at the pub, and no, I feel fine.'

Two nights later, sitting in the same pub at the same table enjoying his usual half pint of beer, Frank felt a hand on his shoulder, along with a strangely familiar perfume.

'Hello, Frank. I've been thinking about you a lot since the other night.'

Frank looked up into the heavily made-up face of a middle-aged woman. Bleached blonde hair showing dark roots circled a chubby face wreathed in smoke from the cigarette held in one hand.

'Have you forgotten me already?' she laughed.

An onlooker shouted across the room,

'Who could forget you, Stephanie? We all remember, don't we boys.'

'Fuck off, you lot, I'm talking to my man here,' shouted Stephanie, much to the amusement of the others,

'Buy me a drink, Frank. Don't take any notice of that bunch.'

Frank didn't know what to do. He had no memory of this woman apart from the smell of her cheap perfume.

The man who had shouted came over, patting Frank on the back,

'You gave her a good seeing to the other night, put on a good show around the back of the pub after closing. Had her against the wall you did, spectacular, allow me to buy the drinks.'

The landlord arrived carrying two drinks. A pint of beer for Frank and a brandy and babycham for Stephanie, he obviously knew her tipple.

'Great show the other night, Frank. I'm almost tempted to go there myself, most of the others have.'

Stephanie chuckled,

'I always aim to please.'

Frank downed the pint, not knowing what else to do. The worst part was that he had no memory of what had supposedly taken place behind the pub that night.

A cold shiver ran down his spine. If Doris ever found out it would be the end of their marriage.

He numbly reached for the other pint, which had mysteriously replaced the last, downing it without thinking.

Pint after pint followed until the landlord approached him to settle his tab.

'What tab?' Frank slurred.

'The tab I set up for you earlier, you have been very generous. Must be great to have your own business,' said the landlord, presenting a piece of paper listed with the drinks Frank had supposedly agreed to.

Stephanie sat opposite, swaying gently from side to side as if she was following an unseen tune. Mascara from heavily made-up eyes had run down her cheeks and her hair hung lank on her shoulders.

'Pay the man and let's go,' she said.

Frank pulled out his wallet and placed it on the table, indicating with a sweep of a hand that the landlord should help himself.

Frank, together with his now empty wallet, staggered out of the pub arm in arm with Stephanie, serenaded by numerous catcalls from the others.

'Give her one for me,' one shouted after them.

Stephanie lived in a mean little flatlet not far away. It had one bedroom, and a small kitchenette in the corner of what passed for a living room.

Frank sprawled on the bed as Stephanie roughly pulled off his clothes, then she joined him, naked.

The following morning, Frank woke to the unwelcome sight of Stephanie lying on her back and snoring loudly. He looked in disgust at her more than ample naked body, capped off by her face smeared with makeup. He guessed she was at least fifteen years his senior, fifteen hard years.

Without waking her, he made his way out of the flat and headed home. Doris was waiting at the door, her arms folded and tapping one foot,

'Don't say a word, Frank Double. I know where you have been, the entire street knows. You've been with that tart up the road.'

Frank hung his head.

'I'm sorry, Doris, I don't know what got into me.'

'You had better go to work, it's late,' her only comment.

Frank didn't argue and walked off to his little shop.

When he was out of sight, Doris slammed the door and walked upstairs. She cried as she packed the childrens' clothes along with her own, filling two suitcases.

An hour later, a car pulled up outside and tooted its horn. Doris herded the confused children out to the car, her father squeezing suitcases into the trunk as they climbed into the rear. Her mother leaned over and held her hand.

'I told you he would come to no good,' she said, exactly what Doris didn't want to hear.

Frank came home that evening clutching the biggest bunch of flowers he could find. He had rehearsed exactly what he would say. No more drinking, and he would never go into another pub for the rest of his life. He loved Doris and the children; they were his life.

The coldness in their house was like the lid coming down on his coffin, shutting out the light and all hope for the future. He guessed her parents had collected them, and knowing how much they disapproved, and disliked him, he accepted he would never see his wife and children again. Frank was quite simply a quitter. He would not fight for his family, nor would he get into an unwinnable argument with her parents. He simply gave up.

Drinking became his solace, and the endless procession of empty beer bottles on the kitchen table bore testimony to his despair. Each morning, he counted them before throwing them away, intent on adding at least one extra each time.

The business suffered and his skill as a locksmith waned as the drinking increased. Regular clientele moved their business elsewhere as his unreliability increased.

The shop was the next to go. After three months of unpaid rent, the landlord kicked him out, keeping his equipment in lieu of the money he owed.

Frank spent the next few months sitting in the cold house, slowly drinking himself into oblivion. That came to an end when he found pinned to the front door a large notice. The council wanted their arrears, and the bank wanted the house. Frank was left with nothing but debt.

With very few options available to him, he rented the small flat above the priest in a false name, living as inconspicuously as possible. Only leaving the flat to steal enough money for beer and meagre food. Beer always came first and if it meant more beer, he would manage on food scraps gleaned from refuse bins behind shops.

The priest's flat below became a regular source of small change. The old priest left the collection box in the same place, and he could easily pick the door lock.

It was like manna from heaven, and even though he was never rushed, his nerves usually got the better of him. As he walked around the flat looking for any loose change, he couldn't stop the urge to urinate and consequently left his victims with a pungent smell after his departure. He became nonchalant about it, but to the police, it became his *trademark*.

To Frank, it was a mystery as to why he was never interviewed by the police. However, he was pleased to see the new priest was doing okay. His collection was proof of that.

CHAPTER 35

Where was that horrible smell coming from? Father Mahoney looked everywhere around his tiny flat, both inside and out. The smell was getting worse. He had first noticed the awful smell three days earlier. At first it smelt like a dead mouse, but it must have been huge because it increased in intensity daily.

Finally, he could stand it no longer and once again called the police. To them, the smell was familiar, the smell of a corpse.

After a brief reconnoitre of the surrounding area, the police began knocking at neighbouring doors.

As before, visits to the flat above yielded no answer. On previous investigations, records showed the flat to be unoccupied. However, on this occasion, an officer stooped to peer through the letterbox, and the smell from the flat knocked him back on his heels. They had found the source.

A forced entry revealed the gory truth. Strapped to the kitchen table lay the remains of Frank Double. He had been skinned. Large strips of withered epidermis lay around the base of the table. Even Frank's face had been peeled. Only the section around the tape binding his mouth had been left untouched. Scattered on the floor were several collection boxes, all empty. It was later established they belonged to all the local churches, regardless of denomination.

Father Mahoney insisted on attending to perform the last rites. He had no idea of the religious beliefs of the victim but insisted he needed preparation for entry into the Kingdom of Heaven.

Inspector Nobes stood to one side as the priest entered the

room.

'I understand your good intentions, Father, but you will need a strong stomach for what you are about to see.'

Father Mahoney's face turned deathly white as he began the mercifully brief incantation for the departed soul. The smell was sickening, but nothing compared to the vision of a human body devoid of large sections of skin.

Somewhere at the back of his mind, the collection boxes struck a chord. He would consider that later, once away from the horrific scene.

Frank Double, or the remainder thereof, was removed and after a forensic team had finished, the cleaners moved in.

Still, the smell persisted, and Father Mahoney wondered if it would ever completely disappear.

The matter of the collection boxes continued to bother him, and he sat for hours in the local reference library, poring over articles relating to thefts from the church.

Nothing gelled until he came upon a book relating to the history of the church in early Norman times. Apparently, in the 12th and 13th centuries, theft from the church carried very harsh penalties. It was for the bishop to choose the sentence for an offender, ranging from a severe beating to hanging. The worst offenders could be publicly flayed alive.

He read on, horrified at the very thought that his own order and faith could conduct such unchristian acts.

Father Mahoney visited Inspector Nobes at the police station to impart what he had learned.

'I cannot believe this is happening today in these so-called enlightened times,' said the young priest.

'Looks like a *crazy* to me,' answered the inspector, 'let's hope it's a one off or we could be looking at the beginnings of a serial killer.'

The authorities tried to keep a lid on the story, but soon the newspapers were full of it. They vied with each other to present the shocking details in the most horrific manner. The case was compared to *Jack the Ripper*, the notorious 19th century serial killer who disfigured his female victims with a knife. All occurred in the same area of Whitechapel, and the murderer never discovered.

Frank Double had finished every bottle of beer bought with the collection money from that daft young prat downstairs. He needed more, always needed more. He knew that alcoholism had finally trapped him, knew he would end up lying under a bridge somewhere with the rest of the helpless homeless drunks, sipping methylated spirits as an alcohol substitute.

He felt the trickle of urine down his leg and stared idly at his trouser leg as the dark stain became rapidly bigger. Too drunk to care, he allowed the pool of yellow water to spread over the floor, laughing insanely while he emptied his bladder.

He had not heard the door open. The blow to his head felled him instantly, and he sprawled ingloriously into his own mess.

Waking up, the first sensation he felt was one of sheer panic. Something was covering his mouth, and he struggled to breathe through his nose. He couldn't object verbally; no sound could escape his mouth.

Frank realised he was tied down onto his own tabletop, so tightly that he felt his circulation falter. Looking up he saw a dark shadow flit over but couldn't recognise it. He certainly felt the pain as something sharp made a neat slice down one cheek. Another joined the first, parallel to the first. The pain of that was nothing compared to the pain of his flesh being torn along the strip. He looked up to watch his skin disappearing upwards as it was drawn away from his cheek. Every one of the thousands of tiny nerve endings screamed in agony as they were ripped away. Frank couldn't scream, couldn't make any sound other than a stifled groan. At last, it was over. His cheek hurt like hell, but the pain had lessened. Then the blade appeared again and sliced the other cheek. He passed out then, but a glass of cold water thrown into his face brought him round to face more pain. And so, it continued. The entire day he lay on the table as inch by painful inch, the skin was flayed from his body. He fainted one last time and lay still.

When Frank finally came too, it was straight into a living hell. His body was exposed without its covering of skin, and he immediately felt cold. He had never felt so cold. Shivering didn't help, merely exacerbated the pain from still active nerve endings.

He lay like that all night and the whole of the next day, fervently wishing that death would come to end his suffering. As he lapsed into unconsciousness for the last time, his final thought was that he would never again steal from a church.

CHAPTER 36

Arthur Dennis passed the newspaper to Sally,
'Look at that, seems the *Ripper* has returned.'
Sally skimmed through the front-page story, skipping over the goriest details.

'It must be a copycat killing. The *Ripper* would be over a hundred years old by now.'

'You daft mare, of course it's not the actual ripper,' rasped Arthur, 'I'm off to the pub.'

Sally sighed as her husband left the room. He had been to the pub a little too often lately, returning home well after closing time. Even Rose had noticed, constantly asking where Daddy was.

Arthur jovially walked into his local pub, feeling the cares of the day disappear into the smoky interior of his favourite haunt. Putting up one finger to the landlord, indicating his usual pint of beer, he made his way over to a corner table.

'Hello, Stephanie,' he said to the blonde already at the table.

'Hello handsome,' she chirped, waving her empty glass at him.

Sally cleared the kitchen table and began washing up as Rose, unseen, slipped out the front door. With Cassey tucked under her arm, she made her way down the street. Two turns later, she was outside the *Broken Crown*, her father's favourite pub.

Standing on tippy toe, she peered through a grimy window into the smoke hazed room. There was her father, sitting at a table, head back, roaring with laughter. She had never witnessed him behaving that way at home. He barely managed a smile when he was with them.

Feeling Cassey moving in her arms, Rose held her up to the window so they could both peer into the room.

A shout went up,

'Hey, Arthur, your daughter wants you,' someone yelled.

'And her ugly friend,' another quipped, bringing laughter from the rest of the customers.

Arthur glanced over at the window to see his daughter and ugly doll staring at him. The doll had both its eyes open, which unnerved him. Normally one was permanently shut.

Springing up, he quickly made his way to the door,

'Bugger off home, Rose,' he said quietly, but menacingly.

'Who's she?' Rose demanded, pointing towards Stephanie.

'Never you mind, just a friend, that's all,' said her father, trying to cover his guilt with anger.

'She's not as nice as mum,' persisted Rose.

'Bugger off or you'll feel the weight of my hand,' said Arthur, angry now that his daughter had stumbled upon his little secret.

Rose turned towards home, carrying Cassey in her arms, the doll's eyes looking back over her shoulder.

Arthur shuddered as he caught the stare. The doll's eyes seemed brighter somehow, like they were illuminated from within.

Walking back to his table, he placed a hand on the blonde's shoulder.

'Shall we?'

'If you want to,' she replied, scraping her chair back from the table.

They left the pub together with the knowing smirks and ribald comments of the others following them outside. None of which deterred Arthur, Stephanie could give him more pleasure than Sally had for the last couple of years, and he needed pleasuring. The atmosphere indoors was getting him down. Sally with her dour attitude and Rose with that bloody, ugly doll. He felt like a complete outsider, so he might as well act like one.

As soon as they set foot inside her flat, he was on her like a wild animal. She objected at first, but as he tore off her clothes accepted the inevitable graciously. He was more generous than most, and Stephanie was high maintenance.

The blokes at the pub had wanted to enjoy her ample charms for the price of a drink, but eventually even they tired of her.

Arthur had always been the untouchable one. The archetypical faithful married husband and father, until she noticed the change. He would sit with her at the pub, lamenting how his life had turned to shit lately. Especially his precocious daughter and that ugly doll she insisted on carting everywhere.

'She's not even my daughter,' he whined on one occasion. 'Sally was pregnant when we met. I have no idea who the real father is. She won't tell me. Must have been some kind of nutcase because the girl isn't quite right in the head.'

It had taken Stephanie some time to breach his defences, but once inside she made short work of seducing him. It was all too easy once he had a few drinks.

Laying side by side on her bed after a hectic session of lovemaking, she wondered if she could lure him away from his wife and kid. Stephanie always put her own considerations first, and she needed a permanent man in her life. The years were passing quicker than she would like and mother nature was taking a toll on her hitherto good looks. Her face was drooping, like the rest of her body. Saggy boobs hung down to meet an ever-expanding tummy.

Arthur lay quietly, thinking the exact opposite. What did he find even vaguely attractive in the woman beside him? She was well past her prime and in the light of day her face evidenced the passing years with deep lines. He realised she was merely a vent for his suppressed anger. Life with Sally had not turned out as he had hoped, especially with her child being so strange. Like many men, his staying power was limited, and he was looking for a way out. Maybe he wanted Sally to find out; in that way, it would be her making the decision to divorce, not his.

The sound of crying greeted him as he walked into the kitchen. Sally sat at the table sobbing, Rose beside her with Cassey on her lap. All three stared at him, Sally with red-rimmed eyes, Rose staring unblinking, her dark eyes almost black, and Cassie, both bright hazel eyes fixed on his face.

Arthur sat at the table, not knowing what to say. Obviously, his regular trysts with Stephanie were secret no more. He shuddered inwardly as he realised the doll's eyes had followed him as he sat down.

'I need to talk to your mother, Rose. Why don't you take your doll upstairs for a while?'

'Why should I?' Rose answered rudely.

'Please, Rose,' Arthur begged.

Sally stopped crying,

'Whatever you have to say, you can say it in front of Rose. She knows everything. She saw you with that woman.'

Arthur spent the next hour apologising and promising that it would never happen again. His thoughts of being free had disappeared as soon as reality set in. He didn't want to be alone in the world, reduced to sleeping with tarts like Stephanie, and paying for the pleasure.

At the end of his long speech, Sally sniffed,

'We'll see,' was all she said. 'Rose needs a father she can be proud of, not some ageing reprobate!'

Three days later, Sally was startled by a loud knock at the front door. She opened it to two excited neighbours, their eyes sparkling with excitement.

'What on earth has happened?' Sally asked.

Freda was first to speak,

'They found a body this morning. It's that bloody tart from the pub, Stephanie.'

'Shouldn't speak evil of the dead,' remonstrated Ivy.

'Well, anyway, she's dead,' said Freda.

'How?' Sally asked.

'They say her throat was cut from ear to ear,' said Ivy, beginning to enjoy the gory details; anything to lift the perpetual boredom of being a housewife.

Sally went quiet,

'Do they know who did it?'

'Probably one of her boyfriends,' said Freda, casting a sly look at Ivy, well knowing that Sally's husband had recently had the honour of being one of those *boyfriends.*

Sally sat down heavily at the table.

'Shall I put the kettle on for a cuppa?' Ivy suggested, feeling a little guilty, realising that Sally was more than shattered by the news. Arthur may well have done away with her.

'No, I have to go out for a while,' said Sally, her face a deathly white.

Her gossiping neighbours left in a hurry, having achieved their aim. Nothing like being the bearers of bad news to stir up a little interest in their lives.

Sally summoned Rose, and they left the house, hand in hand.

'Where is your doll?' Sally asked.

'Oh, she's tired and didn't want to come,' Rose replied.

Mother and daughter met Arthur several streets away as he walked home from work.

Arthur saw them approaching and wondered if he was going to get the order to leave. It had been several days since the conversation in the kitchen, and he thought things had maybe worked themselves out.

'Have you heard the news?' Sally asked.

'What news?' said Arthur, relieved that at least it wasn't an order to leave the house and never return.

'That blonde woman friend of yours from the pub, Stephanie, she's been murdered,' said Sally.

Rose met his eyes with a stare,

'Had her throat cut,' she said unemotionally.

Arthur's face blanched; his mouth so dry he couldn't speak.

'What's the matter, cat got your tongue?' Rose said cheekily.

'Now then, Rose, don't be rude,' said Sally.

But Rose wasn't to be denied,

'Did you see her last night?'

'No, I did not!' Arthur exclaimed through dry lips.

'Just checking,' Rose smirked.

Arthur, Sally, and Rose made their way home, the accusing stares of neighbours following them.

At the front door, they almost collided with Father Mahoney.

'I suppose you have heard the dreadful news?'

'Yes, Father, we have,' said Sally.

'Two horrible murders in one week, the newspapers are hinting that it might be the return of *The Ripper.*'

After her husband's rudeness the previous evening, Sally kept silent, but not Rose, who seemed to enjoy the sombre mood.

'He must be ancient by now.'

Father Mahoney managed a smile for the sake of the young girl. After all, what would she know of such things at her tender age.

'Well, I had better be off,' said the priest. 'I have to attend the mortuary to give the victim the last rites.'

Rose put her head to one side.

'She won't be able to hear you, she's dead.'

Father Patrick thought that an odd comment from one so young but merely smiled.

'God will hear me and accept that poor soul to His side where she can rest in everlasting peace.'

'He cannot hear you. He's not here anymore. He left a long time ago.'

Father Patrick was not ready for that comment and quickly excused himself, pretending he hadn't heard.

'Rose, whatever has got into you?' Sally hissed.

'May I go up and play with Cassey?' Rose answered.

Sally dismissed her with a wave, and Rose raced upstairs.

Arthur and his wife exchanged puzzled glances, he not being able to resist, said, 'Well, she's your daughter.'

'And what's that supposed to mean?' Sally said huffily.

Arthur realised his mistake, but having taken the first step, was obliged to finish.

'Who was the father? You never did tell me. Maybe he's strange too.'

Sally cast her eyes to the ground. She knew only too well that the father had been more than a little strange. In fact, he was a rapist, lunatic, and a murderer. Over the years, parts of her past had filtered back, but she could hardly tell Arthur.

They sat at the kitchen table, both silent, the food in front of them untouched. Their marriage was well and truly on the rocks, and both came to the same conclusion inwardly, neither wanting to bring up the '*D*' word. There would be absolute finality once *that* word was used.

Rose had joined them at the table, cheerfully eating. Cassey on her lap with her blank stare set off by the one open eye. Arthur glanced over at her and noticed the eye seemed to be brighter this evening. Strange how it seemed to follow him as he moved, it was like one of those famous paintings he had seen at a gallery once; the eyes appearing to follow the observer around the room.

The young priest was not prepared for the sight of Stephanie's mutilated body. He turned ashen as the mortuary assistant swept aside the sheet to reveal what remained.

She lay on a white porcelain table, her body already displaying the usual *post-mortem staining*. Normally, when dead, a person's blood sinks to its natural uniform level, leaving a defining line indicating the level of blood. In her case, the level was decidedly low. Much of her blood remained in the alley where she was found. It had dried at the scene, leaving a large stain on the ground around her head.

Father Mahoney eased forward to look at the monstrous wound in her neck. Whoever had wielded the cutting instrument had done so without much finesse. The gash was wide and ragged, as if something had sawed across her throat.'

Another figure joined them, the pathologist,

'Looks like whoever did this used a saw. I've never seen that before. Knives, yes, but not a bloody saw,' he said, shaking his head from side to side. 'It must have been horrifying for the poor woman.'

The priest was lost for words, but the pathologist spurred him on.

'Well, get on with it man, I haven't got all day.'

The Father began the prayer for the pastoral care of an already deceased person while the pathologist stood to one side, scalpel at the ready.

The moment the priest finished, he stepped forward and made an incision from the gash in her throat down to her pubic bone.

The priest's pallor turned even paler as he made a hurried excuse and bolted for the door. The pathologist smiled as the sounds of the Father's vomiting echoed through the room.

Stephanie's funeral was a sombre affair befitting any funeral. There was no big crowd, merely a few of the regulars from the *Broken Crown*, most of whom had known her in the biblical sense.

Father Patrick conducted the funeral using the standard service. The by now meaningless words meant nothing to the mourners, especially the part pertaining to everlasting life. No one believed that anymore.

A few handfuls of dirt were cast into the grave, whereupon the small gathering dispersed; a notable absentee being Arthur, Sally would never have tolerated that.

There was, however, one strange witness to Stephanie's final farewell, Rose. She stood opposite the priest, Cassey in her arms, as he read out the words from a well-thumbed prayer book.

She elected to walk beside the priest as they left the graveside, the sounds of shovels filling in the hole behind them.

'Where will she go, Father?' Rose asked, 'Heaven or Hell?'

Father Mahoney glanced down at this strange child and her battered doll, confused as to why she was not accompanied by her parents.

'Her soul will rest in Purgatory until God decides,' he said, giving the traditional answer.

'What's that?' The girl asked, looking up at him with her dark eyes.

The priest rapidly explained the meaning of Purgatory as the cemetery gates loomed. The graveyard was some distance from his church, which, being surrounded by buildings, had no graveyard.

'Perhaps someone will be able to give you a lift,' he said as the few spartan mourners walked through the gates. 'You should not be out by yourself so far from home.'

'I'll walk, Cassey and I like to walk, don't we Cassey?' Rose said.

Father Mahoney stumbled as the doll's eye flicked open of its own accord, transfixing him now with two staring hazel eyes. He was unable to break their hold over him.

What was it about this child? He wondered. She appeared at times to be just an ordinary little girl, but then at others mature beyond her years, especially when commenting on religion. He was often confronted with arguments about the differing Gospel accounts of Christ's life by the faithful, but never by such a flagrant dismissal of God Almighty. Especially by one so young and innocent. And the doll, what was the story there?

CHAPTER 37

The daily newspapers quickly caught on to the two Whitechapel murders. Their gruesome nature and the location in which they occurred led to comparisons to the old Victorian *Jack the Ripper* case.

It knocked the current top story of the Cuban *Missile Crisis* off the front page. The public were at first aghast at the news of a direct confrontation between the United States and communist Russia, but the to-ing and fro-ing of political rants by both sides saw interest rise and fall daily.

The American President, John Kennedy, had issued an ultimatum to the leader of the Russian Communist Party, Nikita Khrushchev. If Russia went ahead with installing nuclear-tipped missiles in Cuba, within easy reach of the United States, they faced the very real risk of all-out nuclear war. Russia, on the other hand, felt threatened by America's newly installed missiles in neighbouring Turkey, Moscow being within easy striking distance. Both sides had heavy bombers constantly in the skies carrying nuclear weapons. Missile silos were primed and ready, and the oceans hid submarines that played a cat-and-mouse game with each other, both sides armed with nuclear tipped torpedoes.

Alarm bells were ringing around the world, the only hope that both sides respected the acronym MAD, *Mutually Assured Destruction.*

Rose sat with Sarah in the upstairs room of the warehouse, the ever-clacking sound of knitting needles unwavering.

'Everyone is talking about Cuba. This could be the beginning of the Darkness,' Rose said.

'Lionel says it's really bad, he's writing even faster,' said Sarah.

Sarah paused, something that rarely occurred whilst knitting. However, she recognised the girl was not her usual self. She seemed far too mature for a girl of ten.

'Where's Cassey?' She asked.

'At home in bed,' snapped Rose, 'she's beginning to fall apart.'

'Why don't you bring her back then?' Sarah suggested, 'you can pick another doll in her place.'

Rose allowed the glimmer of a smile to spread over her face, covering the unusually hard countenance.

'No, I'll keep her a bit longer. She has her uses.'

Sarah looked down at her knitting. This was not Rose. The situation was getting out of hand, and for the first time in years, she felt genuine fear.

During the following week, the so-called *Cuban Missile Crisis* once again dominated the front pages. Apparently, the Russians had agreed to remove their missiles, and the world rapidly settled back into complacency.

The *Whitechapel Murders* returned to headline the front pages in all the London newspapers.

Arthur threw the paper onto the kitchen table.

'I wonder who will be next?'

Sally replied rather more forcibly than she had intended.

'For God's sake, stop being so morbid, especially in front of Rose.'

Arthur threw a glance at Rose, sitting quietly at the table pretending to feed the doll a biscuit.

'Do you have to? It's a bloody doll, Rose, it doesn't eat biscuits. Surely you should have grown out of this bloody obsession by now.'

'Cassey is hungry,' lisped Rose in a new, annoying habit

she had developed.

Arthur grabbed the biscuit from her and threw it across the room.

'Just bloody stop it and grow up!'

Rose slowly raised her eyes towards him in a frown.

'Don't make Cassey angry.'

The lisp had disappeared. Her voice now had a hard edge to it.

Arthur tried to stare her down but was the first to blink. When his eyes refocussed, he noticed the doll's eyes were both open, glaring at him, leaving him unsure who he had been in fact talking to, Rose or the doll.

Scraping back the chair noisily, he left the table.

'I'm going to the pub!' He exclaimed loudly.

Sally sighed wistfully.

'That's your father all over. The first sign of conflict and he's off to the *Broken Crown*. He's changed a lot since we first met.'

She left the table herself and didn't hear the whispered comment from the doll.

'He's not your real father.'

A few days later, while Arthur was at work, a knock came at the front door. Rose ambled along the hallway to answer it. She didn't seem to have much energy lately.

'Hello, Rose, is your mummy in?'

It was the *Tally Man,* calling to collect the weekly payment for a new dress Sally had bought on a whim some time ago, hoping to renew Arthur's flagging interest in her. Arthur hadn't even noticed.

Sidney Butler door knocked the area weekly with a suitcase full of bits and pieces, plus a colourful catalogue featuring clothing which might interest the ladies.

Sally appeared at the door behind Rose,

'Come in, Sid, we need to talk.'

Rose took the opportunity to slip outside. She needed a break from the stuffy interior.

'I'll have to owe you for this week, Sid. Arthur has left me short.'

'Spending it at the pub, I suppose,' said Sid, smiling.

Sally blushed,

'He seems to prefer the pub to his home these days.'

Arthur had continued his nightly visits to the pub after Stephanie's murder, and Sally wondered if he had already replaced her with another tart. She had attempted to win him back but couldn't stir any interest. Arthur merely became angrier and more difficult to live with.

'I hate to mention it, but you're already three weeks behind,' said Sid, fixing his eyes on her.

Sally wrung her hands, looking down at the floor.

'I'll try to get some money for you next week,' she said meekly.

Sid Butler had been a *Tally Man* all his working life, starting at the tender age of fifteen. He had been quick to see an opportunity and rapidly built up the business. He was a slick salesman with a way with the ladies, and never failed to capitalise on his good looks, inherited from a father he could barely remember. Mr Butler senior had been killed in the war when only a young man himself, the victim of a German U boat. Sid had been ten years old when the telegram arrived to convey the tragic news. His mother had fallen apart, and he found himself at the head of their small family.

Marriage was out of the question for him; he considered it to be a trap. All his friends had married early, fathering babies either just after the wedding or, more often than not, just before. None of them appeared to be happy, and he was determined to avoid that pitfall.

Instead, he concentrated on older married women, not too old, but old enough to fall for his youthful charms.

He had built up a regular *clientele* among the ladies. All were married, so there was no risk of them wanting a permanent relationship, just a bit of fun.

Sally was not on his list of possibilities. She was not really his type, but he now saw an opportunity and couldn't resist the challenge.

'How about we come to an arrangement?' Sid said.

'What sort of arrangement?' Sally asked, not liking the glint in the younger man's eye.

'Well, you owe me a fair bit now and I can't see that husband of yours coming through with the money. I bet he doesn't even know about the dress, does he?'

Sally stared at the kitchen floor.

'He didn't even notice when I wore it for him, and he won't like me being in debt to you either.'

Sid saw his opportunity and slipped an arm around her waist, his hand resting on her breast. Suddenly, it seemed as if he had completely surrounded her, and she felt trapped.

'Come on, Sal, just a quickie.'

'Rose might walk in,' Sally gasped.

'No, I saw her going out the front door. There's just the two of us,' said Sid, fondling her breast while working his other hand underneath her dress.

Sally felt herself being pushed forward over the table, Sid's dexterous fingers pulling down her underwear.

She prayed fervently to God that Rose wouldn't suddenly appear at the door and witness her mother being defiled.

Sid stepped back quickly and adjusted his clothing while Sally did the same. He was breathing heavily when he spoke.

'So, that takes care of this week, same time next week then?'

'I thought that would clear my debt,' she stammered.

'It does, one week at a time,' he laughed. So, that's three left and then we are up to date. That is, if you have money for me next week. Otherwise, I'll add that one as well. Maybe we should make it twice a week? Pay it off a lot faster that way.'

Sally realised she had fallen into the oldest trap in the book. There was no way out for her. She had to do as he said. Arthur would kill her if he ever found out.

The following week, Sid rapped at the door, and Sally opened it, beckoning him inside.

'Your money or your life,' Sid quipped, using the old highwayman's holdup shout.

'Arthur's spending even more time at the pub. I don't have any money,' said Sally. She had worried all week about how she would get out of this situation, but no solution had presented itself. She had considered making sure Rose would always be there but couldn't keep her out of school forever, besides, as time went on the debt would rise.

Not wanting to soil her marital bed with any signs of illicit lovemaking, Sally led Sid upstairs to Rose's bedroom. Cassey occupied her usual place against the pillows, and she gently moved the doll down to the floor.

'You have to be quick,' she said.

'Don't worry, the neighbours will think I'm having a cuppa; now get those clothes off.'

Naked, Sally lay on Rose's single bed, watching Sid undress. Even through her fear of being caught, she had to admit he had a beautiful youthful body.

This time, she allowed herself to enjoy his skilful lovemaking, realising that the same act with her husband, which nowadays was rare, had become very disappointing. Arthur always reeked of stale beer and cigarettes.

Afterwards, they dressed and returned downstairs, Sally ensuring Cassey was replaced just as her daughter had left her.

Week followed week, but Sid now called more often. He always crept in by the back door, making sure that neighbours didn't see him. The sessions became longer as Sally found more and more pleasure in his visits. Sid surprised himself in that he didn't bother so much with his other ladies anymore. Sally held some sort of unique attraction for him and each time he visited seemed better than the last. He began to bring gifts in the form of clothes and even posh shoes, which she carefully hid at the back of her wardrobe.

The tally debt was soon forgotten as their trysts became more intense. Arthur was oblivious and pleased that his wife no longer chided him for spending every evening at the pub.

It soured one day as Sid removed his clothes prior to joining her.

'We should throw that ugly bloody doll under the bed; I've seen it watching us a couple of times.'

Sally laughed,

'She's not ugly, Sid, she is Rose's pride and joy. Besides, it's only a doll, she can't tell on us.'

They both giggled like naughty teenagers as Sid fondled her breasts.

Fully concentrating on the task, he was unaware of Cassey's face, contorted in sheer hatred.

CHAPTER 38

'**B**loody hell!' exclaimed Arthur, 'have you seen the papers?'

'No, why?' asked Sally.

'That bloody ponce, Sid Butler, has been murdered, about bloody time, too. I bet it's a jealous husband. He's shagged just about every woman in the neighbourhood.'

Sally's face turned ashen, and she quickly excused herself from the table. Arthur would surely notice her reaction to the news.

Inspector Woods from Scotland Yard had been summoned to attend the scene of the latest Whitechapel murder. He specialised in homicide and his commander was under fire from those above to solve what was becoming a three-ring circus. The media were having a field day and accusing the police of not having a clue, one particular daily unkindly referring to them as *The Keystone Cops*.

He stood by the body, looking down at the remains of Sid. It wasn't very pretty, and the large pool of blood suggested he had been killed after losing most of the life-sustaining substance.

The inspector lowered himself on his haunches to examine the body, carefully avoiding the congealed blood. It was clear that Sid had initially been attacked from behind. Both heels had been deeply slashed, which would have seen him come crashing to the ground. The killer had then drawn a sharp instrument from behind the knees down to meet the ankle wounds. It was obviously sadistic and designed to render him defenceless in the most painful of ways.

However, the most horrifying injury was to his groin. Someone or something had physically torn his genitals completely off. They lay in a bloody mess beside him, causing one of the younger police officers to vomit.

Finally, Sid's throat had been hacked open. It looked as if it had been cut with the same instrument used on Stephanie.

This was certainly shaping up to be the work of a serial killer, but the inspector believed the newspapers were wrong in suggesting it was a return to the days of the infamous *Jack the Ripper*, whose victims had been women of low class, and mostly prostitutes. The current victim had nothing in common with the ongoing cases.

In the morgue, three men stood beside Sid's body. It lay on the same white slab as Stephanie had occupied. Present were the pathologist, Inspector Woods, and Father Mahoney. All three glanced at the sight where Sid's genitals had been formerly located and shared a mutual internal shudder. It was every man's nightmare, the most delicate part of the male anatomy.

'I have no idea who or what could have done this,' began the pathologist. 'Human skin is actually very tough and elastic, it's almost impossible to do what has obviously been done to the victim without some kind of machine. His genitals were literally ripped off in one fell swoop.'

'Then what are you suggesting?' Inspector Woods asked.

'I'm not suggesting anything,' said the pathologist, 'merely that whoever did this used some kind of device or had superhuman strength.'

Father Mahoney heaved a sigh,

'You mean maybe supernatural?'

'I didn't say that Father,' said the pathologist, 'I don't believe in all that hocus pocus, begging your pardon.'

The autopsy proceeded, whereupon the priest, remembering his discomfort on the last occasion, made his exit.

Inspector Woods remained, unflinchingly, having spent a good part of his career watching the human body being dismembered in similar surroundings. He had become inured to both the sight and smell of autopsies.

The results of the procedure came as no surprise, death from an excessive loss of blood. The toxicity report showed he had consumed a fair amount of beer, but that was nothing unusual.

Motive was the real problem for Inspector Woods. The victims were unconnected.

Later, the inspector met with the priest and explained the autopsy results.

'Did you know the young man? Apparently, he was a door-to-door salesman.'

Father Mahoney shrugged his shoulders.

'He seemed a nice enough fellow, always had a ready smile and was very dapper. I imagine the ladies would have liked him.'

'Maybe a jealous husband caught him giving his wife something more than a little credit,' said the inspector. 'That would be motive enough for some.'

Father Mahoney didn't answer. The seminary hadn't prepared him for that sort of thing.

Inspector Woods had nothing to work with, no clue to who may be committing these horrendous murders, so did what any good detective would do; he made his way to the pub, the *Broken Crown*.

Sitting at a table in the corner of the main bar, and listening to the other patrons' chatter, he realised they were talking about Stephanie. One man in particular had a loud voice, and his comments rose above the general hubbub.

'That Stephanie was a right one, not many in here haven't enjoyed the pleasure of her company.'

This comment was met with raucous laughter from the others; a few looked at the floor guiltily and the inspector guessed they were the married ones.

He moved towards the group at the bar.

'Anybody in particular?' he asked.

A silence fell over the room. They could all sense the man speaking was a copper.

'Who was her latest man friend?' Inspector Woods asked.

Nobody spoke. A few nervously shuffled their feet.

'You maybe?' The inspector said, poking a finger into a man's chest.

'No, not me. Arthur was her latest,' he replied, looking down at the floor as the others glared.

'Arthur who?' asked the inspector.

It was too late to retract, and the man mumbled his name.

'Arthur Dennis.'

'Thanks,' said the inspector and walked away, much to the relief of both the patrons and the landlord. Coppers were bad for business in the East End. He would return to ask about Sidney Butler later.

Sally's face dropped as she answered the door. Even she could sense the man was a policeman.

'Yes, what do you want?' she asked, not meaning to sound so harsh.

'Is your husband at home?' Inspector Woods asked.

'No, he's at work,' said Sally, softening her tone; no need to get the copper offside.

'So, where does he work?' the inspector persisted.

Sally told him and began to close the door.

Inspector Woods turned to walk away, but on impulse did a complete circle.

'Did you know the Tally Man, Sid Butler?' He asked, carefully watching for her reaction.

'Yes, everybody did around here,' Sally replied, quietly.

He caught her look and continued to stare directly into her eyes.

'Some more than others, maybe?'

Sally dropped her eyes to the ground, unable to match the police officer's stare.

'I don't know what you mean,' she stammered.

He had touched a nerve and took a gamble.

'How long have you been showing him a few favours? Until the debts are paid off?'

Sally's face crumpled and tears trickled down her face.

'You had better come in,' she said, opening the door wide.

They sat in the kitchen facing each other; the detective remaining silent, waiting for her to open up, and as he expected, she did just that.

Within the first minute, she garbled her story as if she were in the confessional.

'I didn't know what else to do,' she began. 'I owed him for a few things, and he was pressing me to pay, but my husband has been spending a lot of time at the pub. Arthur spends most of his wage there, which leaves precious little for anything else.'

'So, Mr Butler helped *you out*, as they say,' said the inspector, 'what about your husband. Did he know?'

'God, no, if he found out, he would have killed him,' said Sally, wishing she could take back the words.

The inspector allowed the silence to thicken before speaking again. Sally sat wringing her hands with a handkerchief, her face becoming mottled as the import of what she had just said sank in.

'So,' said the inspector, 'what a to do, your husband is drinking away all he earns while the Tally Man is sorting you out.'

'Don't be so crude!' Sally exclaimed, getting angry.

'Now, now, no need to get touchy,' replied the inspector. 'I'm just saying it's odd that he ends up dead.'

Sally dissolved into tears, head in hands.

'I'll leave it there, for now,' said the inspector, 'but I'll be back after I've had a word with your husband.'

Sally stopped crying, alarm showing in her face.

'Please don't say anything to Arthur about me and Sid,' she begged.

'I'll do my best,' he replied, 'but I've got more than one murder on my hands.'

Closing the door behind the police officer, Sally sagged against it,

'What's wrong, Mummy?' A voice called from upstairs.

Sally looked up into Rose's face.

'Everything!'

Rose was torn between her two identities. Cassey was enjoying the chaos, while she hated to see her mother upset and crying.

Both had heard the interview downstairs, Cassey revelling in the mother's pain, and Rose glaring at the doll, hating both Cassey and the policeman. Her dual characters were now constantly at odds with each other, sharing one body. Cassey had successfully guided and coerced Rose's inherited evilness to the point where her good side had almost been eliminated.

Arthur walked out of the works gate, his mind elsewhere when a voice rang out,

'A word, Mr Dennis, if you don't mind.'

The inspector walked beside Arthur, who recognised him for a copper right away. The ingrained mistrust of the police, a feature of every East Ender, coming to the fore.

'What can I do for you?' Arthur asked bluntly.

'Stephanie Fairly, you were pretty friendly with her, I hear,' said the inspector cheerfully.

'I sort of knew her,' said Arthur guardedly.

Inspector Woods laughed and winked.

'You were *sort* of shagging her regularly, I heard.'

Arthur couldn't deny what was blatantly common knowledge amongst the *Broken Crown's* patrons.

'So, what? I wasn't the only one.'

'But you were the last before she went and got herself killed, weren't you?' the inspector said, his cheerful demeanour gone to be replaced by an accusing stare, 'anything you'd like to tell me about that?'

'It wasn't me, if that's what you mean,' said Arthur, becoming afraid, not liking where this conversation was going.

Inspector Woods abruptly changed tack.

'Sid Butler, the Tally Man, did you know him?'

Arthur chose his words carefully,

'Sure, everyone knew Sid. He was a greasy young bastard. You couldn't trust him. He wasn't shy about putting it on the ladies if you know what I mean.'

'No, I don't know, how about you tell me?' said the inspector.

'Why should I talk to you, let me see your warrant card!' said Arthur. He wanted to make sure this bloke was a real copper and not one of those scumbag private detectives. They were usually retired coppers, but they all smelled the same.

The card read: *Detective Inspector Charles Woods, Metropolitan Police.*

Arthur gave it a cursory glance; he was too busy trying to think things through to pay it much attention.

'Sid was a slimy sod who delighted in taking advantage of ladies who owed him money,' said Arthur.

'You mean, he demanded sexual favours instead of payment,' the inspector suggested.

'Yes,' replied Arthur, 'he wasn't too choosey by all accounts, he'd shag anything that moved.'

'So, an angry husband might have wanted to sort him out?' suggested the inspector.

'I reckon so, wouldn't you be angry if you found out your missus was being used by that sod?'

Just for a moment, the image of his own sweet wife passed across the police officer's mind. He dismissed it immediately but acknowledged to himself that he agreed in principle with Arthur's statement.

'Did your wife ever buy anything from him?' said the inspector, watching for any reaction.

'Not bloody likely. She knows better. I wouldn't allow it,' said Arthur.

Charles nodded; his vast experience of human behaviour told him that Arthur was telling the truth. He knew nothing about his wife's little escapade with the notorious Sid and considered it would be both pointless and unfair to reveal it now.

He had spent the day chasing leads that led nowhere. Neither Arthur nor Sally was capable of such gruesome acts. They were merely players in a complicated game of life and love.

Sally, visibly rattled, was in the kitchen attempting to put together the evening meal when Rose, holding Cassey, walked in.

'Who was that man, and why were you crying?'

Sally tried to make light of it,

'I wasn't crying, and he was a police officer asking about recent events.'

'The murders, you mean?' Rose said glibly.

Sally looked up at her young daughter, attempting to shield one so young from anything as gruesome as murder.

'Yes, but I couldn't help him, so no need to worry yourself about it.'

'What about that man who was killed. Did you know him?' Rose asked, not to be put off.

'Well, yes, I knew of him. Everybody did, but I have no idea what happened to him,' said Sally.

'Cassey said she knew him, saw him quite a few times,' said Rose. The doll's one closed eye slowly opened to join the other, both staring at Sally. The mixing bowl crashed to the floor, shattering, and spilling the contents.

Leaving her mother to stand looking vacantly at the mess, Rose, with Cassey, ascended the stairs to her bedroom.

CHAPTER 39

Nikita Khrushchev was a proud man. As the First Secretary of the Communist Party of the Soviet Union, he had risen to be a leader over many others by clever politics and naked ambition. Any that stood in his way were quickly brushed aside, disappearing into the background, or simply disappearing altogether.

Currently engaged in a diplomatic row with the United States, Khrushchev was fast losing patience with the new upstart President. John Kennedy had taken the dangerous step of installing missiles in Turkey, which he regarded as being far too close for comfort. In retaliation, Khrushchev successfully negotiated with President Castro to install soviet missiles in Cuba, on America's doorstep. These actions demonstrated to the new president that the Soviet Union was not to be toyed with.

'The bloody *Reds* are at it again,' voiced Arthur as he read the front page. A new and bigger threat had pushed the Whitechapel murders off the front page.

'What does that mean for us?' Sally asked.

'Bugger all, I suppose, as usual. We never get a say in anything. Those at the top dish out the orders and we obey,' murmured Arthur while he read the lead story.

'Will we have to join if they go to war?' she asked.

Arthur grimaced,

'That silly sod Macmillan will throw his hat into the ring,

nothing surer.'

'But why?' Sally asked.

'Because we always do what our American Lords tell us,' Arthur replied bitterly, 'unless it's the other way around and then they drag their heels. They didn't help us in the last lot until 1941 and only then because the Japs attacked Pearl Harbour.'

Sally shook her head as if it was above her understanding.

'I suppose Prime Minister Macmillan will do what's right,' she said.

'What's right for the toffs!' Arthur exclaimed, his labour party roots coming quickly to the surface.

Silence reigned for some minutes as Arthur continued to pore over the newspaper. He raised the paper, so it covered his face as he read, causing Sally to stare, what was he up to now, she thought.

'Did a copper call asking questions?' Arthur's voice came from behind the paper.

Sally, caught unawares, stammered a reply,

'Yes, he wanted to know about the Tally Man.'

'What did you tell him?' again, from behind the paper.

'Nothing. What did you expect me to say?'

Rose, standing behind the partly open door, listened to her parent's conversation.

'The slimy sod got what he deserved if you ask me,' said Arthur maliciously.

Sally's reticence turned to anger.

'Just like that bloody tart from the pub.'

Arthur, hiding behind the paper, felt a pang of remorse. His attempt to elicit from his wife a confirmation that she might have been having it off with Sid had backfired. He had no proof, merely a suspicion fuelled by good old-fashioned jealousy. However, he himself was guilty of sleeping with *the tart from the pub*. The hole he had dug was becoming deeper with each word, so throwing down the paper, he rose to leave with the usual parting shot.

'I'm off to the pub, don't wait up.'

Sally was glad to see him leave, but inwardly she shook with guilt.

Rose approached and slid a skinny arm around her mother.

'Don't worry, Mummy, I won't say anything.'

Sally's head shot up,

'What are you talking about?'

'You and that man, Sid Butler.'

'Nothing happened between us,' said Sally.

Rose put her head to one side as she replied,

'That's not true, Cassey saw you on my bed.'

Sally reacted harshly, alarmed at her daughter's knowing smirk,

'But how could Cassey know anything. It's a doll for Christ's sake?'

'Cassey is my friend. She tells me everything,' said Rose, turning to leave.

Sally glared at her departing back, hoping she wouldn't say anything to Arthur.

Sitting in his usual spot at the pub, Arthur nursed a mood so black that other patrons avoided him. On the one hand, he felt enormous guilt about Stephanie, and on the other, a growing suspicion that his wife had entertained that sleazy swine, Sid Butler. Things were beginning to fall into place. Where had his wife got the money for the new clothes she had tried to hide at the back of the wardrobe? He hadn't thought about it at the time.

Absorbed with his own troubles, he didn't notice the inspector until he sat down beside him.

'Hello again,' said Inspector Woods.

Arthur merely stared at him.

'Had anymore thoughts on those two that were murdered?' the inspector persisted.

Arthur became flustered as if the police officer was privy to his sordid activities.

'No,' he said, 'why should I?'

The inspector lounged back in his chair nonchalantly,

'Well, you were probably the last to see her alive, and you didn't like Sid Butler, did you?'

Arthur got up and quickly strode off, slamming the pub door behind him.

'My, my, he seems a little on edge,' said the inspector loudly. The other patrons turned away, attempting to make small talk, aware that each one of them may be a suspect in the murders for the same reason as Arthur.

Sally jumped in her chair as the front door crashed open. She had her hand to her mouth as Arthur stormed in.

'That bloody nosy copper came into the pub asking questions again; why can't he look for the killer instead of bothering me?'

Sally recovered herself sufficiently to answer.

'I suppose everyone who knew Stephanie as well as you did will be of interest.'

The barbed retort didn't go unnoticed.

'I suppose he'll be back here to ask about you and the bloody Tally Man in that case,' Arthur fired back.

An icy silence fell over the room, neither wanting to speak lest they incriminate themselves to each other.

Arthur resumed his position at the table and buried his head in the paper while Sally pretended to read an old magazine.

Inspector Woods spent the rest of the evening buying drinks for the other men in the bar. His expense account would look a little extravagant at the end of the month, but he needed a lead in this baffling case. Realising that neither Arthur Dennis nor his wife had anything to do with murder had not stopped him from needling the pair. A casual comment, however obscure, might just lead to something positive.

The landlord called time, and the bar began to empty. The inspector stayed until the last drinker left in order to have a private word with the landlord, hoping that he might be able to shed some light on this most mysterious of cases.

The landlord was very unhelpful, displaying an all too obvious dislike for the police in general and the inspector in particular. Disappointed by the lack of useful information, the Inspector made his way outside. The cold night air made him realise he may have had one too many. Exchanging the comfortable warm fug of the pub for the icy blast of an easterly wind made his head spin uncomfortably, and his feet seemed to have a mind of their own. He realised he was giggling like a drunken teenager and managed to keep silent as he weaved a path away from the pub towards the tube station. It was quite a walk, but he decided it might help him sober up.

By the time he was halfway to the tube station, the chill wind had done its job. He shivered uncontrollably, figuring the alcohol was contributing to his discomfit.

A mist had crept over the land from the nearby River Thames, and it reminded him of old photos of the area when smog had been a constant source of irritation. New regulations were helping to douse coal fires and lessen the effects, but to-night his vision of the road ahead was getting worse by the minute. Nobody else was abroad, and he suddenly felt lonely and vulnerable.

A childish voice came at him out of the mist.

'Help me please, I'm lost.'

The call of duty imbued in the inspector came to the fore and he turned back towards the voice.

'Where are you?' he called.

'I'm here, in the alley, beside you,' came the sweet reply.

Inspector Woods guessed it was a young girl who shouldn't be out at this time of night.

He looked around, turning in a complete circle, until he noticed an alleyway on the same side of the road.

Venturing down the narrow alley, he followed the plain-tive sound.

'Where are you? I still can't see you?' He shouted.

'Here, I'm here, please help me.'

The mist was so thick in the alley the inspector could

barely see a hand in front of his face. He found the owner of the voice by stumbling against her.

'Sorry, my dear,' he said, 'but I can barely see you down there.'

Deciding to assume the role of knight in shining armour, he knelt beside the girl, feeling the warmth of her young breath on his cheek.

'You're safe now. I'm a police officer. I'll take care of you and get you home,' he said warmly.

He was so close to her now that recognition was possible.

'Why, you are that young Dennis girl, Rose isn't it?'

The answer came in a different voice.

'My name is Cassey.'

The inspector had no time to react. The thin screwdriver entered his ear, driving its full length through his brain.

Confused, Rose stood back from the crumpled figure of Inspector Woods.

'Cassey, what have you done?' she cried.

A loud harsh voice erupted from the doll.

'Carry me back home, quickly, before they notice we are missing.'

Scared, Rose scooped up the doll and ran home.

'Faster,' urged the doll, laughing uncontrollably.

Entering silently through the back door, she avoided the statue like figures of her parents at the kitchen table as she tiptoed upstairs.

Safe in her bedroom, Rose changed into her nightdress, barely managing to scramble under the covers, eyes shut, still, and seemingly sound asleep as the door opened.

'Are you awake?' asked Sally.

With only silence for an answer, she shook her head and closed the door, certain she had heard noises.

CHAPTER 40

'Jesus!' Arthur exclaimed. Once again, the *Cuban Missile Crisis* had been relegated to page two in the evening paper. The banner headline read; *POLICE OFFICER MURDERED IN WHITECHAPEL*. The article went on to suggest that a multiple murderer was at large. Other newspapers were quick to jump on the bandwagon. There was nothing more likely to sell newspapers than insinuating to the public that a serial killer was on the loose.

'It was that bloody nosy copper that kept bothering us,' said Arthur. 'At least he won't be back.'

'There will be others though,' said Sally. 'I wonder why the killer picked on him? The police hate it when one of their own is killed. The place will be crawling with coppers now.'

The couple resumed their uneasy relationship, exchanging only a few words to break the almost impenetrable silence that had built up around them since Inspector Woods had instilled in them a mutual mistrust of each other.

Rose appeared, heading for the door.

'Where are you going?' asked her mother.

'Out,' said Rose rudely.

Arthur looked up from the newspaper.

'Don't be so bloody rude to your mother!'

Rose turned back and walked up to the table. With one smooth movement, she upended the table with a crash, sending condiments cascading over the floor. Shocked, Arthur and Sally remained seated, the table now wrecked lay forlornly in a corner of the room.

They looked at each other in horror. From where had the

ten-year-old girl summoned up the strength to do that?

Rose turned on her heel and walked out, her parents lost for words. The door slammed behind her with such force that the house literally shook.

'I'm off to the pub,' announced Arthur.

'No, you bloody are not,' shouted Sally. 'You're not leaving me alone with her.'

'She's your sodding daughter, not mine. I want nothing to do with her. I don't know her anymore!' Arthur shouted.

'You have to help me with her. I can't cope on my own,' pleaded Sally. 'Her father was a madman from the asylum.'

She had blurted out the statement without thinking.

The recent traumas had released her past, like a switch had been turned on. Her memories were painfully clear. She remembered in detail what had happened at the Mental Hospital.

'Asylum, what bloody asylum?' shouted Arthur now thoroughly alarmed. Who had he married?

'I was put there by mistake,' cried Sally. I wasn't mad.

'Not bloody much,' shouted Arthur. The volume in their small house had reached a pitch where the immediate neighbours were privy to every word spoken.

'I married a nutter,' Arthur screamed, 'who had a child to another nutter. I'm going to the pub.'

He stood up, kicking the broken condiments across the floor as he made his way out, slamming the door as Rose had done only minutes before.

Sally began to cry; her world had finally come crashing down around her. Another memory now found its way to the forefront of her mind. The doll, Rose's doll, Cassey, had once been her own. She clearly recalled how it had once dominated her life and how it now dominated her daughter's.

Racing upstairs, she entered Rose's bedroom. Cassey was lying on the bed, both eyes closed. Picking up the doll, Sally cradled it in her arms. She stopped herself, aware that she was slipping back into her old ways, when she had considered the doll to be her only friend.

Pulling herself together, she walked back downstairs, clasping the doll tightly to her chest. The eyes were still shut, and she shushed the doll once again as if it were a real baby. Sally forced herself to concentrate. It's only a toy, *not real, not real*, she chanted.

Walking aimlessly outside, still holding Cassey, Sally made her way to a group of local children. They had made a fire in a disused metal drum and were standing toasting their hands. The evening chill had set in, and the gleeful childrens' faces shone in the reflection of the flames.

Sally approached them, and recognising her as a neighbour, they parted to allow her into the circle around the drum.

A little girl spoke as she recognised Rose's doll.

'Have you bought Cassey out to get warm?'

Sally didn't answer. Inside she was battling with herself, knowing what she had to do, but doubting her willpower to carry it out.

As the children looked on in shocked silence, she threw the doll into the heart of the fire.

A scream shattered the quiet street! Sally stared in disbelief at the drum. Cassey was screaming and her eyes were wide open. Sally froze in panic as she recognised her daughter's eyes. They were pleading with her.

Her anguished cries tore at Sally's heart as she reached into the flames to retrieve the doll.

Children ran in every direction, screaming and crying. Neighbours spilled out onto the street, comforting their little ones as Sally stood holding the charred doll with her burning hands.

An ambulance roared into the street, swiftly followed by a police car with siren blaring.

Despite the excruciating pain, Sally held on to the charred doll, which could not be prised from her blistering hands.

'My daughter, my daughter is inside the doll,' she sobbed.

A neighbour had rushed off to fetch Arthur from the *Broken Crown*, and he arrived just in time to see the ambulance driver climb aboard.

'Hospital, mate, her hands are a mess, but she won't let go of that bloody doll.'

Arthur was left in the middle of the road, staring at the disappearing ambulance. That bloody doll was evil and had a lot to answer for.

Sally spent the night under sedation in casualty. Nursing staff gently removed the doll to work on her hands, attempting to avoid scaring, but were not hopeful. The doll now lay in a box next to her bed, strings connecting limbs and eyes had disintegrated with the intense heat, and the porcelain body blackened.

The following morning, doctors shook their heads as, now awake, Sally pleaded for the doll to be placed next to her, crying out her daughter's name.

'What have I done to my darling girl? Rose, speak to me.'

A kindly nurse retrieved the doll from its box and placed it next to her. Sally cooed at it as if it was real, but the blackened body was empty. There was no trace of her daughter. Rose had been burnt to a cinder.

Arthur didn't visit. He preferred to play victim. Sally had married him under false pretences. He had no idea she was fresh out of the looney bin when they met, and he had stupidly allowed himself to be pulled in by her pathos.

Sitting alone in the house, he waited for Rose's arrival. Not sure what he could do with *her* daughter, he decided to contact the authorities in the morning. Arthur Dennis would not bring up the spawn of two mental patients,

'Who knows what she is capable of?' he said aloud.

He need not have worried. Rose would not be home that night, or any other night. She had perished in the flames. Looking out of the doll's eyes as heat from the childrens' fire penetrated the porcelain body, she had screamed at her mother to save her. But it was too late. Her life snuffed out in the fiery inferno.

In her hospital bed, Sally cradled the charred remains of the doll.

'My darling little Rose, Mummy is so sorry, please don't be angry with me, I will never leave you again.'

Sally's obsession with the doll did not improve, and doctors agreed that she needed far more help than they could provide. It was determined that as soon as her burnt hands permitted, she should be transferred to an appropriate facility. An asylum.

After dealing with the nosy policeman, Rose and Cassey had returned home. Slipping into bed, Rose feigned sleep as her mother opened her door.

When Sally returned to bed, Rose held Cassey away from her frowning,

'Why did you do that to the inspector? He was nice.'

The doll's face creased into a smirk.

'No such thing as nice, all humans are horrible.'

'What about me, aren't I nice?'

The doll stared at her,

'No human is nice, including you.'

Rose was shocked. Her beloved doll had turned against her. For a moment she felt actual fear, but the doll's one eye had become brighter, shining in her face,

'Sleep, Rose, go to sleep,' cooed the doll.

She couldn't resist the compelling look in the doll's eye as it became even brighter. Sleep took over, and she began to dream. In her dream, the doll grew and grew until it was her size. The doll then drew closer until their faces touched.

In the morning, Rose awoke to daylight shining through the window. She liked to sleep with the curtains open. Somehow it seemed less threatening than a completely darkened room.

Opening her eyes fully, she tried to stretch but found that her arms and legs would not obey. Lying on her back, seemingly unable to move, she was shocked to see herself looking down at her.

'Who are you?' she managed to say through small rosebud lips.

The figure hovering over her laughed.

'I am you and you are me. The doll was far too limiting. Your body is far better for my purposes.'

The figure held a small hand mirror overhead, and she could stare up at her face. But it was no longer the reflection of her face, it was that of the doll's face, and she was looking from within.

Cassey sat on the bed, gently stroking the little porcelain face. Rose stared up at her in disbelief.

'This can't be happening. I must be dreaming,' she managed to say.

'No, you're not dreaming, Rose. See how you like it in there.' Cassey taunted.

A hand appeared over the doll's face and a voice began to chant a quiet dirge. Rose began to feel very sleepy and although trying to keep her eyes open, felt her resistance fading. Both porcelain eyelids clicked shut over her eyes. She was asleep.

Rose slept until she was dragged from her induced sleep by a dramatic increase in the surrounding temperature. The porcelain eyelids snapped opened, and she found herself looking up into the face of her mother. The roaring flames terrified her, and she screamed, pleading with her mother to save her. She smelled burning, then nothing:

For Rose the Darkness had come.

CHAPTER 41

October 27Th, 1962

The Darkness

Father Mahoney woke up early. He enjoyed a leisurely breakfast before walking the few steps to open his church. In times long past, the doors would never have been locked. The church was a place of sanctuary and was always available to those seeking help. However, modern society had little respect for that, and an open door was merely an invitation to thieves and vandals. Churches were now secured at night, many having complex security systems to deter would be criminals.

The door creaked open, making the noises befitting its age. It had survived the fire and now stood sentinel to a resplendent new interior.

Father Mahoney dipped one hand in the water at the entrance, making the sign of the cross on his forehead, before walking down the aisle where he would perform the genuflect in front of the altar.

Halfway along, a small figure stepped out to greet him,

'Hello,' said the figure.

'It's Rose, isn't it?' He replied with a smile, 'what brings you to church so early?'

The thought struck him that the little girl was already inside, but he had only just unlocked the doors.

'I have more right to be here than you,' she said.

Puzzled, the priest asked why she thought that to be the case.

'Because you have no power, and I do,' she answered.

'But I have the power invested in me by God,' said Father Mahoney, condescendingly, comfortable that his faith would hold against any obstacles in the House of God.

'Can you do this?' the girl shouted.

The young priest was stunned into silence as objects began to move around him. A circular force swept around his feet like a mini tornado, picking up objects and smashing them against walls. His face turned chalk white as he realised the girl had summoned dark powers into this holiest of places. The new leadlight windows began to shake as the vortex created by the wind pulled them inwards. With a rush of air, they shattered, raining broken shards of glass down onto the pair standing in the aisle. The girl appeared impervious, but Father Mahoney was cut down like a flower beneath a scythe. He lay prostrate in the aisle facing the altar, arms outstretched in the shape of the cross, his life's blood draining from hundreds of small cuts.

The wind ceased as suddenly as it had begun. The girl stooped beside Father Mahoney, who turned his face towards her, eyes full of questions but unable to voice them.

'I am not Rose,' said the girl in a deep stentorian voice.

'I am Lilith.'

Father Mahoney's life ended there in his own church. His last thought, that God had deserted him in his time of need.

Lilith left the wrecked church, making for the old couple in the warehouse. As she walked, the sky appeared to darken around her, and a chill wind followed, making passers-by curse at the English weather. Her hatred towards humankind made her chuckle at their discomfit. How she wished she could make it worse. She had tried for so many thousands of years to bring about the end to God's quest for perfect creation. It was her against ever-growing humankind. The dream of a perfect race of people created in God's own image had faded long ago. Humans were very far from perfect; Lilith had hoped they would destroy themselves over time. They were certainly arrogant and vain enough. She had tried to assist their demise by fuelling countless conflicts and wars throughout the ages, but it had never been enough.

In their respective capitols, deep down in the supposed safety of underground bunkers, John Kennedy and Nikita Khrushchev sat in conference with their generals. On the one hand, Kennedy had issued a firm ultimatum while on the other Khrushchev faced his commanders red-faced. He couldn't back down, it would mean the end for him.

Weakness was not tolerated in the new Russia. His generals urged a first strike, but Khrushchev hesitated. A full-scale nuclear war could well result in the end of the world. If both sides exploded their complete arsenal of devices, a nuclear winter might result, meaning that all plant life and animals, including humanity, would perish.

Kennedy sat, stoically confident that his bluff would work, equally unwilling to start a conflagration that neither side could win, waiting for the Russian reaction to his ultimatum. Already his aircraft, loaded with nuclear bombs, circled high in the sky. They would remain in position until told to attack or stand down. Airborne fuel tankers refuelled them in mid-flight. Missiles sat on their launch pads deep underground in obscure desert areas, all aimed at Russia, waiting for the codes that would send them on their way.

In Russia, the process was duplicated. Identical weaponry facing off over two men's opposing willpowers. Two men out of billions who held the fate of the world in their hands. Both had already sent the codes, it only remained for either or both to push one button.

Both sides were on the brink, neither wanting to be first but fearful of being second.

In the Atlantic Ocean, deep underwater, a Soviet submarine was en route to Cuba. The captain and officers had been briefed on the state of a possible conflict between the two superpowers and were understandably on edge. They had spotted a large United States fleet and remained on station, observing their movements. The captain chose an aircraft carrier as a likely target should things escalate.

Warnings rang throughout the boat as their sonar station detected an American destroyer steaming directly toward them.

Aboard the destroyer, the captain received orders to deploy small explosive charges to be fired over the side into the water to indicate to the submerged vessel that unless they surfaced and showed themselves, they would be depth charged for real.

Inside the submarine, the exploding charges felt like they were being attacked. Had war already started? Strict radio silence prevented them from communicating with their base; they had to rely on their own judgement.

Equipped with nuclear tipped torpedoes, their target, the aircraft carrier, would be vaporised in an instant. For this reason, a strict protocol had to be followed. The captain and his two senior ranking officers had to be in complete accord before the devastating weapon could be fired.

As the barrage continued from above, it appeared certain that they were under attack. The expected war had already begun. The submarine captain nodded his assent to the other two officers. The first immediately followed the captain. It only remained for the third man to give his agreement. He hesitated, realising the enormous responsibility that now lay on his shoulders. The fate of the world rested squarely on his shoulders. Were they in fact already at war, or would he be the first to fire a nuclear weapon that would start World War Three?

A flurry of explosions in the surrounding water decided him!

Lilith walked with purpose towards the warehouse, still scheming.

The old couple had finished their labours. Sarah had completed knitting the scarf for the last time. Lionel had completed his task of writing a complete history of the world, penning the final two words boldly and legibly.

"The End."

Together, they stood framed in the window, hand in hand, watching as the girl approached.

Lilith stopped; her attention drawn to the sky above. She raised her arms lovingly and smiled as a flash of light, a thousand times brighter than the sun, lit the sky:

The Darkness Had Come.

For other great titles from this author go to

www.raymondmhall.com

ADDENDUM:

Lilith

Lilith is a demonic figure in Judaic mythology, supposedly the primordial she-demon and alternatively first wife of Adam. She is presumed to be mentioned in Biblical Hebrew in the Book of Isaiah, and later in Late Antiquity in Mandaean Gnosticism mythology and Jewish mythology sources from 500 CE onwards. Lilith appears in historiolas in various concepts and localities that give partial descriptions of her. She is mentioned in the Babylonian Talmud, in the Book of Adam and Eve as Adam's first wife, and in the Zohar Leviticus 19a as "a hot fiery female who first cohabited with man". Lilith perhaps originated from an earlier class of female demons in the Ancient Mesopotamian religion, found in cuneiform texts of Sumer, Assyria, and Babylonia. Lilith continues to serve as source material in modern Western culture, literature, occultism, fantasy, and horror. **Wikipedia**

Printed in Great Britain
by Amazon

75580316R00149